PRAISE FOR
WALTER WAGER

"A good storyteller with the infallible formula."
—*New York Times Book Review*

"Walter Wager grips your attention . . . what distinguishes him from other thriller-spinners is the deliberately cool, suave tone he maintains throughout."
—*John Barkham Reviews*

"Walter Wager is a better-~~~ money bet when it comes ~~~ out bestselling thrillers . . ."
—*Variety*

ALSO BY WALTER WAGER

DESIGNATED HITTER
WALTER WAGER

TOR

A TOM DOHERTY ASSOCIATES BOOK

Copyright © 1982 by Walter Wager

Reprinted by arrangement with Arbor House

A TOR Book

Published by:

Tom Doherty Associates,
8-10 W. 36th St.,
New York City, N.Y. 10018

First printing, January 1984

ISBN: 0-812-51025-9

Can. Ed. 812-510267-7

Printed in the United States of America

Distributed by:

Pinnacle Books
1430 Broadway
New York, New York 10018

*This novel is cheerfully dedicated to
sage and civilized Perry Knowlton,
yachtsman . . . Princetonian . . .
connoisseur of cigars, brandy etc
. . . and literary agent of distinction.*

W. W.

CHAPTER ONE

The big deer was dead. Even as a bloodied corpse lashed to a baby blue station wagon, the horned animal seemed regal. Dr. Alan Sarett, a chubby man whose red down vest made him appear even puffier, looked much less patrician. The glow on his moon face was smug and naked triumph.

"That's a *ten*-point buck!" he exulted as he pointed his rifle at the creature he'd slain.

The four other hunters studied the ample antlers that crowned the stag like the helmet of some barbarian prince, and they nodded in admiring assent.

"Ten pointer on the *first* day of the season!" the Boston dentist celebrated. It had been a long drive through the Vermont mountains to Latham Falls, a tiring journey into the chill blackness of a late November night. Now he stood in front of the little village's only grocery, weary and red eyed and proud of his accomplishment. It was 9:40 on a clear crisp morning, and the cramped and unromantic world bounded by lost fillings and whining children lay far behind. It had all been worth it.

7

At that moment a lean tanned man carrying a large paper bag emerged from the store. His brown parka and gray corduroy pants contrasted sharply with the bright-colored costumes of the hunters. There was something of the outdoors about him, and *something* more. Whatever it was, Sarett could not resist the impulse to share his success with the strong-faced stranger.

"One shot at eighty yards," the dentist announced, and patted his "custom deluxe" Remington 742 affectionately. The man with the bag of groceries did not reply. He stood staring at the weapon, shaking in small uncontrolled tremors.

"What's the matter, fella?" Sarett asked in the considerate tone that he used with nervous patients. He tried to establish eye contact. That always worked . . . but not this time. The shuddering man saw nothing but the rifle.

"Afraid of guns? Don't let this baby bother you," the dentist urged. "It's perfectly safe in the hands of anyone who knows how to use it."

The man with the bag did not speak. With a visible effort he forced himself to walk to a Jeep Scout parked a dozen yards away. The lanky owner of the grocery hurried after him with a carton of canned goods, which he placed on the back seat. It was not easy for the man with the twitching hands to insert the ignition key, but he finally did and the Jeep rolled away.

"Is he an alcoholic?" a hunter wondered.

The store owner shook his head.

"Could be a brain tumor," Sarett speculated earnestly. "How long has he had these tremors?"

"Can't say," the merchant answered carefully. He was not going to reveal that Ted Colby had those shakes when he arrived in Latham Falls almost two years ago. Vermonters did not volunteer that sort of information, and they certainly didn't ask prying questions like these nosy out-of-state hunters. In this part of New England, people still respected their neighbors' privacy.

The Jeep was three miles from the grocery before the man at the wheel felt his panic begin to subside. He had been stupid to react that way to some fat oaf with a shiny new .30-06. He reminded himself that there were only thirteen more days in the state's hunting season, and then the outsiders and the sound of gunfire would be gone for a dozen months. Would the sickness be gone by then? The doctors had said that it would *probably* fade, but what the hell did they know?

The muscular man, who called himself Ted Colby, glanced at the rearview mirror again. There was very little traffic and almost no chance of a police car on this unimportant two-lane blacktop, but looking back at frequent intervals was an old habit. He did it again a mile later, and when he slowed for the turnoff onto the gravel side road, he scanned the woods on both sides. He had been trained to do that too.

He loved these forests. Cool and dense with green nature in the summer, they also had a stark splendor when the trees were naked as they were now. There were people who came to this part of New England from distant cities to enjoy the fiery golden wonders of the autumn foliage, but hardly any of them ever reached this area. That was a blessing, he thought, and then he automatically eye-swept the nearby slopes again.

Something glinted—up there at the crest. The sun hit it through the leafless trees, and the man in the Jeep computed instantly. Whatever it was, it hadn't been there yesterday. Metal? No campers or teenage lovers came here. A gun? If so, whoever held it had a clean shot at the front of the cabin. That was where Colby would park the Jeep to unload his groceries. He'd be a perfect target.

Was it a sniper, or was it paranoia? He stopped the vehicle, dropped into an infantryman's low combat crouch and started to circle up the hill. He moved slowly and carefully, watching where he tread to minimize the noise. The fact that he didn't have a weapon himself did not dismay Colby. Now he paused behind the thick trunk of a century-old tree, and he looked at his empty hands. They weren't shaking any more. Neither was the rest of his body.

He crawled the next sixty yards—inch by inch. Perfect. Not a sound. It had all come back when he needed it. Maybe it had never gone. His breathing was even, and his mind was cool and clear. It was like some field exercise. Now he could see what glinted. It was a rifle with a scope, cradled against the shoulder of a gray-clad marksman sprawled flat twenty-five or thirty yards away. The gun was aimed at the cabin.

Situation estimate: ambush. The sniper would not be alone. Plan of attack: disable this marksman first, and use his weapon to take out his partner or partners. Standard field procedure: improvise a weapon to neutralize the sniper silently and instantly.

Colby took off his right shoe and sock. Then he used his car key to scratch loose some earth, which he packed into the cloth cylinder. It was only dirt, with no stunning power—not yet. He carefully urinated on the sock, and now it was a small but effective bludgeon. He'd taught this trick to Army Special Forces recruits at Fort Bragg a decade earlier—the mud club. He hadn't expected to use it in the peaceful mountains of Vermont.

Moving on his belly, he advanced warily towards the man who waited to kill him. The son of a bitch was wearing a duck-bill cap with the peak turned to the back, and there was a brown container on the ground beside him. Canteen in khaki cloth so he wouldn't get thirsty. All the goddamn comforts of home. It took Colby seven minutes to cover the thirty yards.

Then he was upon the sniper. One blow to the back of the head smashed the marksman into unconsciousness, but Colby wasn't taking any chances. He hit him again, wrenched the rifle from his numb hands and rolled him over. Caucasian, early thirties and lucky to be alive. Colby used the sniper's belt to tie his hands behind his back, and then he took off the man's wool socks to jam them into his mouth as a gag. He *might* choke, but he *surely* wouldn't scream a warning to the others.

Colby set out to find them. He wriggled to the far side of the hilltop and looked down. Where were the bastards? How many? A full twenty seconds passed before he spotted the Ford van 150 yards away on the rutted road loggers had used years earlier. He could barely make it out through the skeletal trees. It was the men—not their vehicle—that he had to pinpoint. He crawled down the slope until he was only 70 yards from the van, raised the gun to his shoulder and peered professionally through the four-power scope. He adjusted the focus, grunted softly and began to search for the driver.

There he was, right in the cross hairs. One squeeze of the trigger would splatter bits of his large head across the interior of the windshield. This was the lookout and wheelman, waiting in the van to drive the marksman away as soon as the job was done. There might be another rifle or submachine gun on the front seat beside him, and he was probably carrying an automatic pistol too. Shooting him with the sniper gun would be easy but unthinkable. If there were others, they would hear. They might fight or flee. Neither suited Colby's objectives. Both necessity and principle required that he take them *all*. He always had.

The minutes passed slowly, and in a while the driver yawned. It wasn't that he was bored. Waiting patiently in stuffy vehicles, rebreathing stale air and flexing leg muscles to avoid cramps were part of the wheelman's trade. He wasn't bored at all, but rather a bit puzzled as to why this hit was taking so long. He looked down toward the highway, and then turned his head to glance up the hill where Jean was lying on the ground in firing position. Jean was an excellent marksman. He wouldn't miss.

Nothing but trees. No sign or sound of human life. The driver yawned again, and then he heard some sort of noise. He drew the .38 from his shoulder holster, swung open the door and slid out of the van. Colby rolled out from under the vehicle, uncoiled like a steel spring and hit him in the throat with the butt of the sniper weapon. The wheelman dropped his automatic to clutch his throat in agony. He didn't scream. He couldn't. Choking gasps escaped from his lips, until Colby jammed the muzzle of the rifle into his stomach. The driver doubled up, and as he collapsed, Colby slammed the butt up under his chin in a metallic uppercut.

Colby heard something break. It was probably the wheelman's jaw, but there was no time for medical research. He took the unconscious foe's handgun, and set out to stalk the others. He searched the area for more than half an hour before he was convinced that there were none, and mounted the hill to drag down the limp body of the shooter. He dumped the sniper on the ground beside the wheelman, and recomputed.

Situation estimate: area temporarily secure. Enemy strike unit disabled, but whoever had sent these two would dispatch others. There was but one man in a distant metropolis who knew of Colby's cabin here. He was a complicated and powerful executive who had ordered other executions in the past—a clever, stubborn man with a devious mind. Logically, there was no obvious reason why he'd want to kill Colby now. However, if he had done this, there was a perfectly simple and realistic solution. Colby would get him first.

CHAPTER TWO

Sinbad was missing in Poland.

Another Cuban freighter riding low in the water with a heavy load of Sov munitions was 130 miles off Guatemala.

The president was still annoyed about the failure of Tall Turkey, and Howard Barringer knew that there was a distinct possibility that the National Security Council would veto Mixmaster at its weekly meeting tomorrow.

It had been raining when Barringer drove out of the basement garage of the Kennedy Center—carefully. As Deputy Director of Operations for the Central Intelligence Agency, he did everything carefully. No lover of ballet, he had prudently bought two $100 tickets for tonight's performance because it was a benefit to raise funds for the pet charity of the man who ran the agency—the DCI himself. The purchase was tax deductible, and wouldn't hurt his chances for promotion one bit when Fitzgerald retired next year.

Now Barringer was thirty-five minutes and fourteen miles from the Washington cultural complex, and it was still raining as he guided the sedan through the wet streets of the gracious suburb. He had lived here, in Chevy Chase, for a dozen years. He had a three-bedroom house on a manicured green acre, a good reputation in the so-called intelligence community and an attractive, responsible wife who was deeply concerned about the future of the performing arts in America. She sat beside him on the front seat of the car, pleased that she'd worn the blue gown and the pearls and proud of how well her husband looked in his tuxedo.

"Nureyev *was* wonderful, wasn't he?" she said.

"Never saw him better," Barringer replied effortlessly. He'd barely noticed the dancing because his mind had been busy with Sinbad, the Cuban freighter and other problems—as it was now while his wife continued to analyze and discuss the performance. He dropped in an occasional all-purpose remark that gave the appearance of participation, but he was actually thinking about Charlie. Why hadn't Charlie answered the two telegrams, he brooded as he saw his house ahead.

"It's raining like mad, hon," he pointed out, "so I'd better drop you right at the door and then put the car in the garage."

His wife lifted her skirts and gracefully swung out of the car. Barringer drove on to the garage, took the electronic gadget from the glove compartment and pressed the button that would open the garage door. The portal did not move. He tried again. Nothing. *Of course* the damn thing would go on the blink on a lousy night like this, sending him out to be drenched.

And she'd taken the umbrella with her. Barringer shrugged, drew in a deep breath and sprinted out of the car to raise the garage door manually. He unlocked it swiftly, pushed hard to roll the barrier up onto the overhead rails. He took two steps inside, stopped. There was a van in his garage, and he didn't own a van.

Suddenly there was a cold metal thing in his left ear.

"Freeze," someone he couldn't see ordered. The harsh whisper seemed familiar, but Barringer wasn't sure.

"Charlie?" he tested.

If it was Charlie Dunn, the metal thing would be lethal.

"I'm closing the door. Move and you're dead."

That sounded like Charlie Dunn all right. The man rolled down the door, dragged/pushed Barringer three steps to the wall switch and turned on the lights. The CIA executive noticed that the van bore Canadian license plates from the Province of Quebec, and wondered whether he dared try to turn his head. If it was Dunn behind him, that would be a serious mistake.

"That you, Charlie?" he asked again.

"Sure, and the thing in your ear is a Smith and Wesson .38 Special. That wasn't a nice thing you did."

"Could you take it out of my ear—please?" Barringer said politely.

"I ought to shove it right through your head and out the other side, you bastard."

It was definitely Dunn.

"Charlie, what's this all about?"

"I came all the way from Vermont to find out. Why did you send those guys?"

"Send *who*? All I sent you was a couple of telegrams. Didn't you get them?"

"I got 'em, and I got your goddamn hit men too."

Barringer started to shake his head in denial, but stopped and winced as the gun dug deeper into his ear.

"Not mine," he vowed.

"They're not very good, Howard. They really stink," Dunn declared scornfully, and swept open the rear doors of the van. Dunn had spoken literally. There were two naked men in the vehicle, gagged and tied up with lengths of nylon fishing line that held them spread-eagled. Loops on the same cord circled their throats so that any effort to move would choke them, and the foul odors of urine and excrement made it clear that they'd been denied access to a lavatory for some time. They *stank*.

"Total strangers," the CIA executive said without much hope that Dunn would believe him.

"Then I'll introduce them. The one on the left is the wheelman. That's his piece in your ear. According to his papers, his name is Pierre Dubois and he works for a Toyota dealer in Quebec."

"Charlie, that thing in my ear hurts—and I can't hear you too well."

Dunn ignored the interruption.

"I'll talk louder. He's supposed to be a salesman. Pretty old-fashioned cover story, I'd say. I'd say it sucks. What would *you* say, Howard?"

"Agree with you hundred percent, Charlie. It's trite. Can we discuss the telegrams now? It's sort of urgent."

"The *other* creep has papers that say he's Louis Courville from Montreal. He's the son of a bitch who was up on the hill near my cabin with a long gun, a nice sniper piece—complete with a goddamn scope. Louis the Shooter was waiting for me to come home so he could blow me away. What do you think he does for a living?"

"I don't care."

"He's supposed to be a marriage counselor. Somebody's got a sense of humor. Don't you think that's funny, Howard?"

Barringer could see the terror in the captives' eyes, and the way the driver's jaw hung, it was probably broken. The lips of both men were parched and cracked, suggesting that they were suffering from acute dehydration. No telling how long it had been since they last ate or drank anything—or how soon they would die. Charles Dunn had been the best assassin the Agency ever had. He knew all the tricks. He had all the moves. He was fast and he was both shrewd and intelligent. Those who tried to kill him did not live long. At least, that had been the pattern when Dunn retired with the shakes two and a half years ago to a quiet life in Vermont and with a new identity.

"Not funny at all," Barringer replied frankly.

"Hell, you never had much of a sense of humor. How's your memory, Howard? These creeps coming back to you?"

"No."

"Then you don't give a shit what I do with them?"

"I don't care if you mail them to your favorite charity," Barringer answered irritably.

"I'm not a charitable person," Dunn said as he closed the van doors, "so I think I'll gas them."

He began to walk Barringer toward the front of the vehicle.

"I'll simply turn on the motor," he explained, "and you and I can talk about the telegrams out in your car while the carbon monoxide does them in. No blood or anything. That all right with you, Howard?"

The Deputy Director of Operations almost stumbled with fear.

"You could blow up the house!" he protested.

"It's insured, isn't it?"

Dunn was serious. Destroying people and cars and buildings had been his profession. One more house wouldn't mean a thing to him.

"Charlie, my *wife's* in there."

Thunder crashed twice outside in melodramatic menace. Dunn paused to consider.

"She got a raincoat?"

"For God's sake, Charlie!"

"After we turn on the motor and close the garage door, she can sit in the car with us. We can drive down the block so we'll all be safe if it does blow. Hell, I've got nothing against your wife, Howard. *She* didn't send two creeps to hit me."

"Don't be crazy," Barringer pleaded.

"I never even met your wife. You probably shielded her from nasty people like me, right? I'll bet she has no idea of all the odd types and weird deals you've been involved with. She raises money for Egyptian orphans and still plays one helluva game of tennis. A civilized lady of high principle, much too smart to ask any questions about your work."

Thunder boomed again.

"She's gonna be all shook up to find two stiffs in the garage. How are you going to explain *that*, Howard?"

More thunder in a salvo, and then a female voice called from the intercom speaker on the wall.

"Howard, you left the car lights on again— You hear me?"

Barringer squirmed.

"You better answer her. Wouldn't want your wife to worry."

The two men were almost at the intercom when the womanly voice sounded again.

"What *are* you doing, Howard? It's midnight. Whatever it is can wait till morning. Stop fussing and come to bed."

"She's afraid of the lightning. Always was," the CIA executive explained protectively. Then he flicked the switch to assure her that everything was all right and that he'd join her in the house in a few minutes. He turned off the intercom and sighed as Dunn nudged him back toward the front of the van. He realized that this was his last chance.

"I think I know who sent those two," he announced.

"I'm *sure* you do. That's why I'm here."

Dunn stopped a scant yard from the left front door of the vehicle, and announced that he would listen.

"You got two minutes, Howard. Two, *max*, and no bullshit."

"When you got sick two and a half years ago, Charlie—"

"When I had a goddamn *nervous breakdown*," Dunn corrected harshly.

"Sure. As soon as the doctors told us that you might not be available—perhaps for a long time—for these terminations—"

"*Executions*. I was the fucking lord high executioner for what people tell me is the greatest democracy in the world."

"You were number one, Charlie," he agreed.

"Number one with a bullet. Like that? I got it from a girl in the record business."

"It's great. Now when you were—when you had the breakdown, you trained two men to take over. Victor Spalding and Ken Perry, remember?"

"I'm interested in *these* two men in the van, and nobody else."

"I'm getting to that, Charlie. About fifteen months ago, Spalding disappeared. He went free-lance, for a lot of money. He's out there killing people—important people—for cash. Some of these targets are people we'd rather have alive. There are governments that think he's still working for us. It is extremely embarrassing and disturbing. He has to be stopped."

"As the deli waiters say, it's not my table, Howard. Send Perry after him."

"We did. Spalding killed him. Four days ago, we decided to get in touch with you to find out whether you were over the shakes and available for a sixty-day contract—top pay—to solve this problem."

"To blow him away, Howard. To cut his throat or burn him up or shoot him in the head. To kill him dead—like in those insecticide ads. Been a while since I did that kind of work," Dunn reflected.

For a moment Barringer considered whether this might be the right time to ask him to take the gun from his ear. Not quite. He decided to wait. You had to be extremely careful and cautious with Charlie Dunn. It was a simple fact that Dunn had been the most dangerous man Howard Barringer had met in twenty-one years of covert-operations service at the Agency. On the basis of tonight's performance and the two men in the van, he might still claim that title.

"You can do it," Barringer encouraged.

The .38 was no longer gouging his ear.

"I want you to hear this and see this. Turn around, Howard."

Dunn looked bronzed, healthy and alert. Definitely lean and mean. The expression on his handsome face was a mixture of confidence and hostility. There was no resemblance to the thin, pale, burned-out case who'd been pensioned off as totally unfit for duty.

"No more shakes, Howard. Not since the second I spotted that sniper gun. One moment I was trembling Ted Colby, and the next good old Charlie Dunn. No, bad old Charlie Dunn."

"Congratulations."

Dunn waved the .38 angrily.

"That was a very sick thing to say, Howard. You're a lot sicker than I ever was. I could take Spalding for you, but I won't. I'm out of all that. As I said, it's not my table."

The deputy director rubbed his sore ear, and wondered how to tell him. This might be one of those unusual situations where the direct approach would be most productive.

"Charlie, I think it *is* your table. I'm afraid—"

"Your two minutes are up."

"Charlie, I give you my word. We didn't send those two."

Dunn pointed the gun directly at Barringer's navel.

"Your word's worth shit. You lie before you brush your fucking teeth in the morning."

"It had to be Spalding. He or the people he's working for must have found out that we meant to hire you to stop him, so they decided to hit you first. Think about it. You trained him. You know him better than anybody else does."

Dunn stood silent for several seconds before he nodded.

"Victor would do that," he admitted.

"So it is your problem, Charlie."

"Yours too. You've been penetrated, Mr. Barringer. There's a leak in your super-secret, world-famous organization. Maybe right in the Ops division itself. It'll be your ass, Howard."

Dunn was right. It had to be faced. The nightmare thing that the Agency had always dreaded was a reality. There was a mole—an enemy agent or traitor—somewhere in the huge building at Langley. It would be a major security flap. The Counterintelligence people had been obsessed with this threat for twenty-five years. Now the paranoids would be vindicated, triumphant and ruthless.

"It's a very serious matter," Barringer admitted, "that I'll discuss with the head of Counterintelligence first thing in the morning."

"He'll go ape," Dunn predicted cheerfully, "and so will the director."

"Let's examine the whole situation in perspective. Let's look at the big picture," Barringer advised in his best executive tone. "This incident with *those* two in the van was disturbing to you, but it may prove to be a blessing. They could be our first lead to the mole. Did you—uh—speak to them?"

The .38 was still pointed at his stomach.

Dunn was taking no chances.

"First thing I did was to hogtie these pigs in the back of the van, Howard, and the second was to clear out of the area in case these creeps had friends. When I was one hundred ten miles from Latham Falls, I made a couple of phone calls. The Toyota dealer in Quebec who is supposed to employ our wheelman here doesn't exist, and there's no number—office or home—for the Shooter in the Montreal directory. I asked the boys about that, but neither of them said much. Maybe your troops can do better."

"They'll be thoroughly interrogated. That weapon bothers me. It suggests that you may not wholly trust me, Charlie. If you wish to be present while we question them—"

Dunn gestured scornfully with the pistol.

"Are you crazy?" he said. "If I show my face anywhere near the interrogation, your mole could whistle up six more hit men. Those bastards probably have pictures of me. You've made me a walking target, Howard."

Another cannonade of thunder gave the CIA executive a few moments to compose a dignified reply.

"Let me assure you, Charlie, that your personal safety—"

"I don't have any," Dunn declared and glanced at his stainless steel wristwatch. "The creeps in the van should have phoned in hours ago, so their buddies must realize that something went wrong. They're probably looking for me now."

"We'll find them first. The men in the van will talk," Barringer pledged.

"Try tenderness. They didn't respond to abuse at all."

His large brown eyes were moving, blinking. Barringer could almost see him thinking.

"You need a safe house," he suggested.

"Not one of yours. No, I need cash. Give me your wallet."

The deputy director shook his head incredulously. Then he took another look at the gun, and slowly drew the wallet from the inner breast pocket of his tuxedo jacket.

"I don't believe this," he announced.

"You're lucky I don't take your goddamn watch too. Now peel out those bills—nice and easy. Any sudden movement could ruin your career."

Barringer extracted the currency, and glared.

"Good. Put the money on the fender, and lay your car keys on top of it."

"I *really* don't believe this," the CIA official said as he obeyed.

"All you've got to believe is that I've killed people, and I'd blow you away just like the others. Get in the back of the van."

Barringer complied with the order, and immediately coughed and choked as he struggled to cope with the stench. Then the man from Latham Falls slammed the doors shut, leaving Barringer in the darkness and the fear. At any moment, Dunn might start the motor to gas all three of them, or perhaps he'd set the garage ablaze. He was capable of anything.

What was he doing out there? The CIA executive heard a noise that he could not identify. His stomach convulsed, and he began to sweat.

He was drenched with perspiration by the time his irate and worried wife opened the van door. Though she was a modern and progressive woman, Aline Barringer was shocked to discover her husband in a reeking van with two nude men who were bound and gagged.

"Who—who are these people?"

"I don't know," Barringer answered truthfully as he climbed down. Breathing hard, he found a handkerchief in his pocket and mopped his brow. In twenty-three years of marriage she had never seen this desperate look on his face before.

"What is this, Howard?"

"It isn't. You never saw these men, and you never saw the van either," he told her.

"What?"

"It never happened, so you won't ever mention it to anyone—not *anyone*. Is that clear, Aline?"

She nodded numbly.

"Not a word. Not on the phone to your best friend, not in a letter to your mother, not even in your sleep. Not one word, Aline—even to me."

"That bad?" she asked.

"Worse," he answered and slammed the doors of the van. "All I can tell you is that it's Agency business and that I never expected it to happen—certainly not here."

She pointed at the vehicle.

"You do *that*, Howard?"

She seemed relieved when he assured her that his job was to sit behind a desk and make policy, and offered no objection when he told her that he had to go out.

"Our car is gone," she thought aloud.

"I'll take the van."

Half a minute later, she watched her husband back the vehicle out of the garage into the rain. Thunder crashed and a scythe of lightning made her recoil, diverting her attention from the receding taillights. For a moment she wondered where her husband was going, and when he'd be back. When she looked down the tree-lined street again, the van was gone.

CHAPTER THREE

"NDC," the night-duty controller at CIA headquarters said into the phone.

"This is Howard Barringer. I've got a package."

"One moment, please."

They'd be running back the tape in the communications bunker buried under the huge building at Langley. The NDC would punch up half a dozen buttons to check whether the voice prints matched, and he wouldn't come back on the line until that security procedure was completed. Barringer waited patiently in the roadside phone booth, watching the sheets of rain and wondering whether his wife would be able to sleep tonight.

"Yes, Mr. Barringer."

"This is a *priority* shipment. The contents of the package are highly *perishable*."

"Will the package require *refrigeration*?" the night-duty controller asked cautiously.

"Absolutely, and *special handling*."

"Hang on a sec."

Now they were running a computer scan to fix the phone number and precise location from which he was calling.

"Sorry to hang you up, Mr. Barringer. You want us to pick it up, or can you bring it to the warehouse in Silver Spring?"

"I'm on my way," he announced. He hung up, stared at the number on the phone and got back in the van. He drove carefully through the downpour. This was no night for a traffic accident or a run-in with some zealous police out to run up their monthly arrest score. The number of vehicles on the road was as low as the visibility, but it still took forty minutes to reach the large building that housed Ajax Freight Incorporated. He stopped the van in front of the big door, ran through the rain and rang the night bell. There was a rumbling sound as the heavy portal slid open some twenty seconds later.

He faced a single large chamber, at least a hundred feet deep and forty feet wide and thirty feet high. There was a pick-up truck marked Ajax, several heaps of crates and smaller packages and two men in gray coveralls.

"Help you, mister?" one sang out in accents that were pure Virginia.

"Got a package for refrigeration and transshipment. My name's Barringer."

"Yeah, they called you was coming. Drive your van in, Mr. Barringer."

Aware that he was being scanned on concealed TV cameras and covered by hidden gunners, the Deputy Director of Operations walked back to the van and guided it into the warehouse. He was about to climb from behind the wheel when the same man in coveralls walked over with a clipboard.

"Hate to fret you, Mr. Barringer, but we need your account number for our book-keeping," he apologized. Barringer had been born on September 4, 1931. 9-4-31. His "account" number was those digits reversed.

"One-three-four-nine," he articulated clearly.

"That's fine. Open her up, Ho-say," the warehouseman ordered with a friendly grin as he flashed a thumbs-up salute to some unseen associate. The whole back wall of the chamber parted, revealing a large inner room painted in a glaring white. The warehouseman pointed his index finger, and Barringer drove the van ahead into the secret rear room. It was very brightly lit. He turned off the motor and wearily descended from the van.

"Jest one more little bitty thing, Mr. Barringer," the Virginian said as the door to the hidden chamber closed. The CIA executive recited the number of the telephone on which he'd called forty minutes earlier, completing the security process. Then he rubbed his eyes.

"Right ahn. Them lights botherin' you, suh? Turn 'em down a bit, Ho-say."

The glare subsided as the lights dimmed. Now Barringer could see the men on the catwalks overhead. They were in coveralls too, pointing M-16 rifles at him.

"Nothin' personal, Mr. Barringer. Rules of the house. Where's the package?"

Barringer gestured toward the van, and the cheery warehouseman swung open its rear doors seconds later. He looked at the two naked captives, then at Barringer in his tuxedo.

"Musta been one helluva party."

In tones of frigid rage, Barringer told him

that there had been no party and that he had not done *that*. Those men were to be *processed* immediately by a medical team and then *transferred* to the interrogation unit.

"These here are *hostiles*, suh?"

"Hostile and dangerous. They kill people, I'm told," the deputy director replied. He found himself shivering, and he noticed for the first time how chilly it was in this secret place.

"Any names go with these packages, Mr. Barringer?"

Repeating the names that Dunn had mentioned would be both unwise and unnecessary. Where the hell was Dunn, anyway?

"Laurel and Hardy," Barringer improvised, "and would you tell those men up there to stop aiming their weapons at me?"

"Crissake, boys! Point those pieces somewhere else!"

The guards hesitated, but finally complied.

"We'll have Laurel and Hardy out of your van in two minutes, suh, and you can be on your way.

"It's not my van, and it's *hot*. Their friends may be looking for it. I want a lab crew to go over that vehicle millimeter by millimeter, and I expect a report on my desk by four o'clock this afternoon. You want to write that down?"

The warehouseman grinned.

"Won't have to, suh. Got it on tape. Now lemme fix up yore transport. Mind riding in a pickup, Mr. Barringer?"

"Whatever's fastest. Why is it so damn cold in here?"

"Don't know. They don't let us in *there*."

So there was another secret chamber hidden somewhere, perhaps in a concealed basement. There might be five more rooms, but Barringer knew better than to ask. The Virginian signalled to a TV camera high on a catwalk, and the wall opened again to let Barringer and the Virginian exit to the outer storage room.

"Nice to meet you, suh," the Virginian said politely, and jerked his thumb toward the small truck. The other man in coveralls slid in behind the wheel, waiting silently for the deputy director to join him. He didn't say a word when Barringer gave the address in Chevy Chase. He didn't talk at all during the drive. By the time they reached the house, Barringer wondered whether the man might be a mute. The rain was slowing down at last as the pickup halted thirty yards from Barringer's home.

"Thanks for the lift, José," he said.

"I'm not José."

Aware that it didn't matter, the CIA executive got out of the pickup and walked wearily to his door. He heard the sound of the motor receding, and he suddenly felt one hundred years old. The truck was gone and Dunn was gone and there was a mole—perhaps in his own office. Even with three large balloons of Remy Martin Cognac, it was nearly 4:00 A.M. before Barringer finally slid off into the temporary refuge of sleep. He slept badly.

CHAPTER FOUR

"Who else have you told about this?"

"Only the Director of Operations," Barringer answered.

The gray-haired man who faced him across the desk was wearing a blue suit, white shirt and muted foulard tie—as he did every working day. He worked a seven-day week, fifty-two weeks per year. He had not taken a vacation in four years. Some people said that he was obsessive, while others held that Martin McGhee took his responsibilities as chief of CIA Counterintelligence very seriously. Even if his taste in clothes was limited and his human-relations talents even more modest, everyone—with the exception of a few who thought he might be paranoid—agreed that he did his vital job well.

"When?" McGhee asked in that odd flat voice.

Barringer looked up at the clock that was the sole adornment on any of the walls. There wasn't even an airline calendar, nothing that might give any clue to the interests or preferences of the Counterintelligence executive.

McGhee *wanted* to be a blank, an enigma so that no one could try to engage or influence him.

"It's ten-twenty," Barringer replied. "I spoke to Mr. Fanelli twenty-five minutes ago. That would be five minutes to ten."

"And what did he say?"

"That this was an extremely serious matter . . . that I should bring it to your attention as soon as possible . . . and let you know that our division is prepared to cooperate fully with your investigation. I've brought this list of our people who were either involved in the decision to approach Dunn or who might have access to that information," Barringer said, and put the file on McGhee's desk.

"Whose people?"

"Operations personnel. There are eleven names, including secretaries and clerks."

"I see," the Counterintelligence chief acknowledged noncommittally.

"The list is handwritten. I didn't want anyone but you and me and Fanelli to know that such a list exists."

The man in the blue suit nodded—about half an inch—and intertwined his stubby fingers.

"Of course, the mole could be outside the Operations division," Barringer observed.

"If there is a mole. It could be that this alleged attempt on Dunn's life has its roots in some of the missions he carried out during his years of active duty. Active and *violent* duty, I understand."

"That was his job. We trained him for it, and he did it well."

The fingers separated for a moment, then meshed again.

"How many people did he terminate?"

"None of your business," Barringer answered. "Those missions had nothing to do with your unit. And what the hell did that 'alleged attempt' mean?"

"We've only got Dunn's word. We don't know what happened in Vermont, or why. Your man had a breakdown. Perhaps he still has problems."

"He has problems with our internal security, Mr. McGhee," Barringer challenged. The counterespionage chief was much too experienced a bureaucrat to be lured into a confrontation. This wasn't the time for it. That would come when he had the facts and tapes and other proof that would assure his victory.

"You could be right, but let's begin by bringing him in to see our doctors," McGhee suggested.

Barringer stood up abruptly.

"I don't think we can bring in Charlie Dunn," he said bluntly. "We probably won't even be able to find him. Dunn operated successfully for more than a dozen years in the worst police states on earth, in the most rigidly organized dictatorships with all kinds of security forces and passes and checkpoints. He beat them all, and you think we can pick him up in a wide-open democracy? He could be in the hills of South Dakota by now, or on one of the smaller Hawaiian islands or somewhere in the Caribbean. Maybe Alaska. He must know thirty-one places where he can cross into Canada without formalities."

"I'm not that familiar with Mr. Dunn, but I'll take your word for this," McGhee replied benignly.

"If you'd rather, check with the Sovs and the Chinese and the East Germans and three Arab governments and four fancy terrorist outfits. Talk to the Cubans in Angola. They'll give him references. While we're on that subject, I'll give him one myself. When I saw him, he appeared completely recovered. The shakes were gone, and the total control was back. He's strong, alert and armed."

"Perhaps the breakdown was a fake?"

The Deputy Director for Operations shook his head.

"You stay away from Dunn, McGhee."

"Are you giving me orders?"

"That's just advice. If you go after him, he'll *destroy* your people. I give you my word. You'll be responsible—*personally* responsible—for the casualties, and you'll blow an important operation. We've got to stop Spalding."

The fingers parted—about an inch.

"Dunn's your only chance?"

"Our *best* chance. Do what you do best. Find the mole. Leave Charlie Dunn to us."

Something unpleasant shone from McGhee's large gray eyes.

"How will you find him?" he asked.

"He'll find us—when he's ready. I've got to get back to Ops now. There should be some word from Montreal any minute."

The estimate was optimistic. The telex from the CIA liaison officer did not reach Barringer's desk until 2:40 that afternoon. He was reading it for the third time when his secretary announced that his wife was on the phone. A man had called to say that their car was parked at the Hilton on Connecticut Avenue.

"Did he say who he was?"

"You can pick it up at any time. Isn't that a relief?"

"It certainly is. Did he mention his name, hon?"

"Good lord, Howard, does it matter? Let's see . . . Yes, it was Stoltz . . . or something like that."

"Thanks," he replied and hung up quickly before she could ask any more questions. With Dunn involved, everything mattered. Charlie Dunn was the most *economical* agent Barringer had ever known. No waste motion, no frills at all. The deputy director closed his eyes for a moment to consider the various pseudonyms that Dunn had used. No, Stoltz was not among them. It was probably the name of some Hilton employee who had found the stolen car there parked illegally.

When the CIA executive entered his home at a quarter after seven that evening, everything appeared to be normal. His wife was wearing the neatly flowered robe that he'd bought her at the charming little boutique in Barbados, and the pitcher of bone-dry Beefeater martinis stood beside Waterford glasses still frosted from the refrigerator. She talked about her day and the letter from their daughter in Hawaii, but made no direct reference to the traumatic events of the previous night. It wasn't until he'd nearly finished the first cocktail that she asked the question.

"Car okay?"

"Sure."

He did not tell her that when he reached the hotel, he had been informed that there was nobody named Stoltz on the payroll of the Hilton. He couldn't. The Agency rules were quite specific on this subject. She had no "need to know." After last night, she probably didn't want to either. He refilled their glasses, and half listened to her report on the Crusade Against Hunger luncheon as he thought about the late-afternoon message that placed Victor Spalding in Tangier. Where the hell was Dunn?

By the middle of the next afternoon, Howard Barringer had an awful headache—his worst since the Bay of Pigs debacle. The Nervous Nellies at the State Department were fussing about the political risks in stopping that damn Cuban freighter, and the report on the interrogation of Laurel and Hardy was hardly encouraging. If that were not enough, the deputy director faced the possibility that Dunn was not going to make contact but would simply keep running. He was rummaging through a desk drawer for the aspirin bottle when his secretary rapped on the door and entered.

"Priority signal from Bangkok," she said and put the sealed green envelope on his desk. Then she glanced down at the telephone-message slip in her hand.

"And there was a call about your concert tickets for Friday night," she announced. "Mr. Brodney phoned while you were in with the director. You're to pick them up at the Kennedy Center box office at six tonight."

"Brodney?"

"Yes. Sorry I forget to tell you sooner," she apologized.

"It's all right."

Now he remembered. When she left the office, he threw the switch that locked the door and then walked to the vault built into the far wall of his office. He dialed the combination swiftly, swung open the heavy metal portal.

"Stoltz and Brodney. Willi Stoltz and Peter Josef Brodney," he recited as he bent over the computer display terminal. He'd read the file a dozen times in the past fortnight, but somehow he had forgotten the names. This terminal was linked directly to the CIA's master memory bank and fact file, a monster machine protected by elaborate security procedures. Only a tiny fragment of the Agency staff had access to this multimillion-dollar device, and still fewer employees had the secret code numbers that made everything—including the most highly classified material—available. Barringer tapped out the three sets of numbers, waited for several seconds until his clearance was approved and then hit the keys to spell out the names.

The computer snarled and then stuttered, and finally photos of the two men appeared on the screen. The deputy director grunted, and tapped in a request for "current status and location." The machine hummed briefly before it answered. The reply for both men was identical.

"Terminated . . . Excalibur." Excalibur had been the code name for Charles Jefferson Dunn, and these had been the first two enemy agents whom he'd been assigned to kill. Dunn was sending Howard Barringer a message in his usual oblique and wary way. He had something to say—at the Kennedy Center box office—in ninety-seven minutes. The headache began to recede, and Howard Barringer was smiling by the time his car slowed in the heavy traffic of downtown Washington. He had no idea that he was being followed.

CHAPTER FIVE

Overlooking the Potomac River and within rifle range of the Watergate hotel-apartment-office complex, the Kennedy Center for the Performing Arts has everything going for it in terms of contemporary realities. Not only is this huge rectangular building named for a martyred chief of state and built of white Carrara marble, but it also has federal funds and a first-class garage in the basement.

Barringer drove down the ramp into the large chamber, parked his car and started for the elevator to the lobby floor where the ticket offices clustered. He did not look back, for he had never worked as a field agent and such security procedures were things he only read about in training manuals. He was a head-quarters executive who *directed* layers of supervisors who ran *missions* and *teams*. It was hardly surprising that he didn't notice the gray sedan that halted thirty yards from his car, or the man in the tan raincoat who emerged from the sedan to follow him.

Barringer liked the mirrored grand foyer on the ground floor, even though some architectural critics had scorned it as too large and beyond human scale. Perhaps it was the eighteen Orrefors crystal chandeliers glittering overhead that pleased him. He did not look up to enjoy them today. Staring straight ahead, he strode directly to the box-office window to collect his tickets.

"That will be thirty-six dollars, please," the young black woman behind the glass announced pleasantly.

Only Dunn would stick him for thirty-six dollars to make contact. The CIA executive paid, mechanically thanked the box-office clerk for the tickets and walked away to examine them. Barringer ground his teeth when he discovered orchestra seats for a concert by five of Bombay's most brilliant sitar players. It was Charlie Dunn all right. The ex-assassin was among those who knew how intensely Barringer loathed Indian music. The deputy director tried to look casual as he let his eyes sweep the marble hall. Dunn was nowhere in sight.

Barringer glanced into the envelope again. There was no note inside, and when he ran the tips of two fingers over the envelope itself, he felt no microdot. Perhaps there was no message at all. Maybe Dunn would get in touch with him at the damn sitar concert. It was difficult to be certain about anything when dealing with Charlie Dunn. He never did anything the same way twice, and no one ever knew where he was. He might be here now, watching and mocking from some hidden observation post or cunning disguise.

Barringer was wrong. The man who had

been Excalibur was not looking at him. Behind a pillar in the basement garage, Dunn was studying the balding chauffeur in the gray sedan. Dunn had watched the car arrive, seen the tracker in the tan raincoat follow Barringer upstairs and made his plan of attack. It was time now, for Barringer and the agent trailing him might descend at any moment.

The man behind the wheel glanced around the garage, saw nothing disturbing and adjusted the shoulder holster that was chafing his left armpit. Crouching behind a Volvo nine yards away, Dunn pulled up the right leg of his trousers to tear loose the ice pick taped above his ankle. He twisted and tugged the cork from the needle tip, then circled toward the sedan.

Barringer emerged from the elevator three minutes later. He was halfway to his car when the man in the tan raincoat stepped into sight. The CIA executive entered his vehicle, slid the key into the ignition and suddenly decided to check the tickets again. He reached into his jacket for the envelope.

"Start the car, Howie."

Barringer froze, glanced into the rearview mirror and saw nothing.

"It's me," Dunn assured. "I'm in the back, and I can rip you open in five seconds if you get cute."

Barringer's head began to turn.

"Look straight ahead, idiot. They're watching you—the creeps in the gray Dodge. Start the goddamn car—*now*."

Barringer twisted the key, and put his vehicle into gear. His throat was dry, his stomach knotted. He had thought that he'd left the fear and personal danger back at the freight warehouse with the two hit men and their van, but it was all back again. To make things even grimmer, Dunn probably thought that Barringer had brought the men in the Dodge to trap him.

"Fifteenth and M—Northwest," Dunn ordered.

That was half a block from the offices of the Washington Post.

"You're right," Dunn announced as if he'd read Barringer's mind. "I want to buy a paper."

He was probably lying, but Barringer didn't care. He'd reestablished contact with Dunn, and that was all that mattered. Now they were outdoors, heading west. The gray Dodge was three cars back.

"I brought some cash, Charlie. Two thousand in twenties and fifties. It was all I could put my hands on right away—without anyone noticing."

"You mean *McGhee*."

It was a statement, not a question.

"He wanted to talk to you, Charlie, But I—"

"He wanted to *listen* to you. He put a bug in your car, Howard."

Barringer blinked in shock. The traffic light turned red, and he stepped hard on the brake.

"Nice little transmitter under the dash. Don't worry. I disconnected it. I didn't *break* it. Destroying federal property is a crime," Dunn mocked.

"Those men in the Dodge?"

"Ask your friend McGhee. He doesn't trust you, Howard. What do you think of *that*?"

Barringer shook his head, and realized that he should have expected something such as this. McGhee was compulsive and tenacious. He had almost unlimited manpower. There was no telling how far he'd go to seize Dunn. Barringer's office and home phones were almost surely wired. There might already be agents watching the house in Chevy Chase, or even following his wife. First the incident in their garage and now *this*, the deputy director thought. The wall he'd put up so many years ago to shield her was crumbling.

"There's probably some misunderstanding," Barringer said ambiguously.

"I understand it perfectly. He's trying to hunt me down, and I don't like it. I don't like it *a lot*."

"I'll tell him," Barringer promised. "Now about those two in the van. They don't know much. They're professionals, free-lance hit men who do jobs for a Corsican heroin mob in Montreal. Somebody gave them a picture of you, five thousand dollars and the location of your cabin. Five thousand more coming when the job was done. They didn't even know your name."

The light turned green, and the traffic flowed again.

"RCMP is checking out the Corsicans now," Barringer continued.

"Don't hold your breath. How's the Dodge?"

It took Barringer several seconds to find the car in his rearview mirror.

"Still following us," he reported.

"Not for long. I carved some holes in a back tire while you were upstairs."

That should teach McGhee a lesson.

"Good," Barringer ratified righteously.

"Not very. There'll be other cars. Mobile surveillance teams run in packs. Don't you know *anything* about field procedures?"

"I didn't come to be insulted. I'm here to help you."

"Did you bring me a gun, Howard?"

The CIA executive coughed as he strained to phrase his reply.

"Not ready to help *that* much, huh?" Dunn challenged. "No gun till I say I'll play, right? I don't think I like you, Howard."

"You never did," Barringer snapped, and shook his head again. Dunn had always been as blunt and difficult as he was brilliant. It had never been easy to deal with this man.

"And I was right," Dunn thought aloud. Barringer managed to control his annoyance. He twisted the wheel sharply to avoid a huge Cadillac with diplomatic license plates that was abruptly switching lanes, grunted and looked up at the mirror just as the Dodge pulled to the curb.

"The gray car is gone," he announced, and immediately changed the subject. "Spalding's getting four hundred thousand per hit. He's convinced people he's the best."

There was no answer.

"It's all in the report," Barringer continued. There wasn't much time. The Washington Post was five blocks away.

"You can jam your report."

"Six big hits in fourteen months," the deputy director pressed. "Europe, South America, Middle East, Africa—he's making quite a name

for himself. Two jobs for Libya, one for a
French banking syndicate, one for General
Sorriano and—"

"It won't work, Howard. Spalding doesn't
mean a thing to me. You're the one who code-
named him Cleaver and gave him delusions of
grandeur. To me he was always *garbage.*"

Four blocks.

"You trained Ken Sperry, Charlie. Vic shot
him in the back and pitched him off that
restaurant on the radio tower in West Berlin.
No face left. We couldn't let his wife see the
body before we buried him."

"You're getting desperate, aren't you?" Dunn
accused.

"Absolutely—and you should be too. It's *you*
he's after. You *know* he won't stop till you're
dead, Charlie."

Three blocks.

The son of a bitch was right, Dunn con-
ceded. It was like the day after the Japanese
sneak attack on Pearl Harbor. Having failed
to destroy his foe in the first battle and having lost the element of surprise, Spalding must
realize that he now faced a global war. He
would know that Dunn was as fit and fierce
as ever. The nervous breakdown was over.
The job done on the Canadian hit men was a
message Spalding could not ignore. On full
alert, Charlie Dunn was combat ready and
dangerous again.

"I can handle him, Howard."

"That figures. You trained him too. He's
quite a credit to you," Barringer taunted.

"Trying to make me feel responsible for Spalding won't play either. You guys hired him

and used him for six years before I ever met him. He's your monster, Howard."

Two blocks.

"Okay, let's get to the bottom line," Barringer said grimly. "No guilt trips, no patriotism, no ego. You've got to destroy him before he destroys you. We didn't *plan* it that way, but we don't mind. Is that blunt enough for you?"

"How do I know what you've planned, or why?"

"We've got a common cause here, Charlie—a common enemy. We'd get him ourselves sooner or later, but it'll be sooner if we all work together."

"Later's okay with me. What's *your* rush?"

Barringer hesitated. He could see the Post building a block ahead.

"We have reason to believe . . ." he began carefully, "that his next target . . . may be someone . . . of special importance. *Very* special importance."

"But you can't say who? Fine, I don't trust you guys either. Shove the money under the seat, and get some more. Another fifteen thousand by the day after tomorrow. That's non-negotiable," Dunn said in a voice as hard as granite.

The deputy director recognized the almost palpable hostility. He took the envelope from inside his jacket, and followed the instruction. Dunn pulled the envelope back, opened it.

"What the hell is *this*?" he demanded.

"Microfilm of the report. One hundred eighty-eight pages might be bulky for you. Here's the

Post, Charlie," Barringer said, and stepped down on the brake. The car slowed.

"Forget the Post. See the garage on this side of the street—twenty yards before the Madison? Park there—down below."

Diagonally across Fifteenth Street from the newspaper, the Madison was one of Washington's most fashionable hotels. Barringer knew it and the nearby garage well. When he turned off his car's motor in the basement, he looked to see if any person or vehicle had followed them from the street.

"Nobody came down with us," he reported.

"They're waiting for you upstairs—a whole bunch of them. What the hell am I supposed to do with this microfilm?"

"Study it," Barringer said as he pretended to search for something in the glove compartment. "Get a projector the same way you'll be getting your guns and other gear. You're a pro, Charlie. Covert operations are your specialty. You know how to improvise, how to put your hands on weapons, cars, explosives, poisons—and just about anything else. That's why you're still alive. You've done it in places a lot tighter than D.C., haven't you?"

Dunn crammed the envelope into his pocket before he replied, "What makes you so sure I'm buying?"

"You're in the middle, Charlie. What else *can* you do?"

"I can walk across the street and tell those crusading journalists that a senior CIA official tried to recruit a private U.S. citizen to kill another U.S. citizen. Between the papers and the wire services and all those good-looking

TV reporters, they'll rip your ass from here to Sunday. You'll be famous, Howard—and out of work."

"I don't think you'll do that."

He heard Dunn laugh.

"If the choice is between my survival and your career, you're shit out of luck. You'll have your picture on every front page from here to Tokyo, and you'll be able to repaper your whole damn living room with all those subpoenas from congressional committees. Half the country and three-quarters of the press already thinks the Agency's full of homicidal goons anyway. You'll be *Mr. Murder*, Howie," Dunn predicted sarcastically. "Ministers and rabbis will revile you from coast to coast, and college kids will picket your house."

"That's not funny."

"It wasn't meant to be. Think about it, Mr. Barringer. If you push me too hard, I can take you out—I can destroy your career, your power, your fancy position in the community—in nine minutes flat. You won't go down alone, if that's any consolation. I'll tell them McGhee was in with you."

"Nobody'll believe you!"

"You want to bet? Now you listen to me. I'm sliding a note under to you in a minute. It gives the location of a phone booth. I'll call the day after tomorrow at 6:20 P.M., on the button. I'm not saying it aloud because that bastard McGhee might have another transmitter in your car. Memorize the address, and burn it in the men's john right away."

"What men's john?"

"The one on the ground floor of the Madison.

Then go up to room eight-oh-three. I'll meet you in the corridor outside that door in five minutes."

The man was insufferable.

"Anything else?" Barringer asked bitterly.

"Medical advice for McGhee. Tell him I know where he lives."

"*Jeezus*, Charlie!"

"And I know where *you* live too. No tricks, Howard. That's not a threat. That's a promise."

Barringer slammed shut the glove compartment and swallowed hard before he replied.

"This is—uh—it sounds crazy."

"Why not? It's crazy time, Howard, and you made it. Get out."

Barringer took the slip of paper, put it in his pocket and left the car. He walked up to Fifteenth Street, turned right and managed not to look around as he headed for the entrance to the hotel. One of the Madison's adroit uniformed doormen opened the portal courteously. Barringer strode through the lobby to the men's lavatory, entered a booth and locked the door before he took out the note.

It was ridiculous.

The idea of a CIA deputy director reading a message from an assassin—even a *retired* assassin—in a toilet was gross. He shrugged, memorized the address Dunn had written and set the piece of paper ablaze with his lighter. Then he waited until it was three-quarters consumed before he dropped it into the bowl and flushed it away.

He returned to the lobby, found a pay telephone and dialed 936-1212. The woman had a rather pleasant voice, but her report was depressing. It would rain in the District of Columbia most of tomorrow, starting in the early afternoon. Barringer's attention wandered before the taped weather report ended, but he stayed to the finish as a simple way to pass time until his rendezvous on the eighth floor.

They were probably watching him right now.

It all seemed strange, exciting and awful. So far as he knew, he'd hadn't been under surveillance since that training course more than two decades earlier. He looked at his watch, saw that it was time and took the elevator up to the eighth floor.

Dunn wasn't there. Barringer walked down the corridor uncomfortably and then back to the door marked 803. He checked his watch, wondered and trudged on to the end of the passage once more. Only when it was nine minutes past the rendezvous did Barringer realize that Dunn wasn't coming. He'd probably never meant to. He'd used Barringer as a tactical diversion to escape the watchers.

Barringer returned to the basement garage, opened the door of his car and looked into the back. It was empty. Dunn was gone. Barringer smiled at the thought that McGhee's surveillance team had failed. The Deputy Director of Operations was halfway home before a disturbing thought made him frown and look into his rearview mirror uneasily.

What if the watchers weren't McGhee's at all?

What if they were Spalding's people?

Were they still there—three or four cars back? What should he do? What did *they* mean to do—whoever *they* were—and when?

For several moments he wondered whether this was what Dunn's life had been like for so many years. Whatever it was, Howard Barringer didn't like it.

CHAPTER SIX

The quivering belly dancer had large breasts and even ampler hips, but Adam Whaley was not impressed. He had seen much more talented performers during his four years in Morocco. What's more, he could think of several other kinds of native dances that were more interesting: the *ahouach* of the High Atlas tribes, which only the Chleu women danced; the *tissint* dagger rite, traditionally done by both sexes in garb of indigo blue; the rifle dance of the Ghiatas; the virile *haha* with its rhythmic hand clapping and foot stamping; and the graceful ballet that mimed the reaping in the Larache region came to mind immediately.

But this was Tangier. There was still profit to be mined from the port city's fading reputation as a seamy center of unbridled sin. Owners of local nightclubs such as the Palais des Amoureux were convinced that rolling rumps and bouncing mammaries were what tourists expected here.

If the rippling flesh aroused affluent patrons, the management could provide more personal entertainment in soundproofed private rooms on the next floor. Whaley had watched Victor Spalding ascend the stairs fifty-five minutes earlier with an attractive young man and woman whom the headwaiter brought to his table. For a little while Whaley had wondered exactly what the three might be doing. Then his thoughts drifted from sexual geometry to the question of when Spalding would return to the El Minzah Hotel on the Rue de la Liberté.

It was nearly 1:00 A.M., and Whaley was tired. This was the third day that he'd been one of the agents tracking Spalding. The CIA did not maintain a large force in Tangier. Aside from arms smuggling and an occasional rendezvous of some itinerant terrorist group, there wasn't much activity here. The arrival of a stranger described as cunning and ruthless had promised a welcome break in the routine chores.

But the first sixty-seven hours of surveillance had been utterly uneventful. Spalding had swum and sunned at his hotel, dined at such first-class restaurants as the Hamadi on Rue de la Kasbah and Chez Gagarine on Rue Victor Hugo and visited two expensive brothels. He'd bought a camel-leather belt at the Grand Socco market and a silk shirt at a unisex boutique on Boulevard Mohammed V. He'd gone to the Royal Air Maroc ticket office to reserve a seat on Saturday's flight to Rome, and made two local calls from a phone booth near the Spanish Cultural Center on Rue Pasteur. Spalding had moved around the city with the open manner of a tourist, apparently either unaware of or indifferent to the watchers.

There he was, descending the stairs slowly with that oddly ambiguous smile. It was as much a part of his appearance as his curly blond hair, trim six-foot physique and perfect teeth. Whaley saw him signal to the head-waiter for his bill. The CIA man gulped the last of his Sidi Harazem mineral water, put a fifty-dirham note on the bar and hurried out to his car half a block away. Weary as he was, Whaley took the precaution of checking under the Peugeot's hood before he unlocked the door. There was no booby trap linked to the starter or engine. He opened the door, slid in behind the wheel and inserted the key in the ignition.

Then he waited in the darkness. He wanted to smoke a cigarette, but he couldn't because the glowing tip might betray his presence. He didn't mind that much, for the deprivation would be brief. In seven or eight minutes Spalding would be back at the El Minzah for the night. Curtis, who was watching the hotel, would take over, and Adam Whaley could drive away to smoke and shower and sleep. It had been a long day.

Spalding emerged and immediately entered the nearest of three taxis lined up outside the nightclub. The cab moved off in the direction of the El Minzah, and Whaley followed at a discreet one hundred yards. In the back of the taxi, Spalding took what looked like a flat leather-sheathed cigarette case from the inside pocket of his jacket. It was just as the cab turned left onto the cross street that he opened it and pressed the red switch within the case.

Whaley saw the taxi make the turn. Then he didn't see anything. The radio-controlled bomb clamped under the Peugeot's fuel tank exploded, killing Adam Whaley and turning his car into an instant fireball. Burning chunks of it flew through the air in a wide arc, setting three parked cars ablaze. People were jerked from their sleep by the blast. Some began to shout and scream. Several telephoned the fire department.

Spalding paid off the taxi driver at the hotel a few minutes later, entered the front door and walked through the handsomely furnished lobby. Instead of taking the elevator, he made his way out through the kitchen to the staff exit that led to the street behind the hotel.

At 1:25 A.M. he cut the throat of the CIA operative who was watching the hotel.

At 1:40 he paid his bill and checked out of the El Minzah.

Three and a half hours after that, he stepped from the smuggler's speedboat onto a dock at the Spanish fishing port of Tarifa.

CHAPTER SEVEN

Not Hertz.

Not Avis either, or any other large auto-rental firm.

Dunn needed a smaller company that wasn't linked to a national computer system, a local firm that anyone looking for him might not check right away. McGhee was capable of putting out a false report that Dunn was wanted for arson or armed robbery—mobilizing the entire Washington police force to search for him. That was why Dunn was here in Baltimore.

At 8:05 A.M. he found the Friendly Car Rental Company only four blocks from the railroad terminal. McGhee's people would be monitoring the major credit-card computers too, Dunn calculated as he arranged for the use of a tan Honda for two days. With that in mind, he told the Friendly clerk that he'd left his cards home in Vermont and put down a $300 cash deposit. That did it.

At 9:20 A.M., he drove into the long-term parking lot at Dulles Airport and found a place where the attendant at the gate could not see

him. He got out of the Honda, removed the
license plates from an adjacent green Chevy
and slid them under the seat of his rented
vehicle. Then he drove the Honda out, shaking his head as he paid the attendant.

"Change your mind?" the man in coveralls
asked.

"Women," Dunn replied ambiguously.

The attendant chuckled sympathetically.
Dunn drove south to Bailey's Crossroads, a
Virginia town of some 8,600 people about nine
miles west of Washington. Though many resi-
dents commute to work at federal agencies in
the nearby District of Columbia, there are few
government departments of any kind in this
"bedroom" community. One of these is a
branch of the state's Division of Motor Vehicles.
Dunn entered the DMV office at a quarter to
eleven, and smiled politely at the plump
woman on duty under the sign that read New
Licenses.

"Help you?" she asked.

"Yes, ma'am. Just moved to Virginia, and
I'd like a driver's license—please."

It took twenty-eight minutes. The clerk gave
him a small yellow card with half a dozen
questions to answer. When he had to supply
his Virginia address, he put down 1212 Court-
house Road in Arlington. He didn't know
whether it was still a CIA "safe house." He
didn't care either. Next they took his picture
and handed him a written examination with
a score of simple questions about the basics of
driving and traffic regulations. The clerk
scanned his answers, and then glanced at his
yellow card again.

"That'll be nine dollars, Mr. McGhee."

The man who called himself Martin McGhee paid, thanked the chubby civil servant and returned to the rented car. Dunn hummed as he drove south on Route 29-211 through the rolling hills of Prince William County. Just before noon, he saw the sign he was looking for and turned off to park in front of Glasgow and Son's one-story cinderblock building.

Guns—large and small—by the hundreds. There were row on row of hunting rifles and shotguns, as well as scores of handguns that ranged from .22-caliber target weapons to heavy .44 Magnums. Dunn studied a pair of the 9-millimeter M 1951 Berettas used by the Italian and Israeli armed forces, an 8-millimeter Japanese Nambu 94 and a Brazilian-made .38-caliber Taurus.

"Anything special, sir?" J. F. Glasgow asked.

"You got a French P-15?"

"That's pretty special, sir. *Heavy* firepower."

"I'm a collector," Dunn lied. "Special guns are my thing."

"You're in luck, sir."

The semiautomatic P-15 had two features that Dunn wanted. It threw large 9-millimeter bullets, and a lot of them. Its magazine carried fifteen rounds, twice as many as most handguns.

"You're not from out of state, are you?" Glasgow tested.

Dunn produced his brand-new driver's license. Glasgow nodded and reached under the counter for one of the yellow F 4473s, the form that the Federal Bureau of Alcohol, Tobacco and Firearms requires handgun buyers to complete. The questions raised no problems, for Dunn was neither a drug user, ex-convict, fugitive from justice nor psychiatric patient. He signed, paid $283.50 for the P-15 and four magazines and departed. It took three more gun shops and two and a half hours to find and buy the other P-15 and six more clips.

He started north. Halfway to Washington, he realized that he had time to stop at the store on Eskridge Road in Fairfax. Progressive Apparel was such a graceful name for a shop that specialized in bulletproof clothing. He bought an undershirt and a raincoat, each of Kevlar nylon twenty-two layers thick and backed with thin scales of Lexguard to prevent bruising from the impact of the slugs. The protective undershirt cost him $252, the raincoat $638. He had only $190 of Barringer's cash left.

It was time to call Terry. Shortly after 4:00 P.M., he parked the Honda in a garage on South East Seventeenth Street in a black section of Washington. He'd have to choose his words carefully, he thought as he entered the phone booth. There was always the risk that some police narcotics unit might be tapping the line to monitor a local drug dealer. Dunn dialed, and heard the phone ring six times.

"Yes?"

"Terry?"

"Who's this?"

"Bob Marco," Dunn replied.

"Good to hear from you. How's your sister?"

"In the hospital again."

Sign and countersign. Terry was good at security rituals.

"I thought that was over, Bob."

"So did I."

"High fever?"

"Very," Dunn answered to signal the situation was hot.

He heard Terry grunt in understanding.

"Can I help?"

"I hope so," Dunn said, and they agreed to meet at three the next afternoon at Smitty's. It was one of the safer places in Washington for a rendezvous, as the hordes of tourists who flowed through the Smithsonian Institution's exhibit halls would provide good cover. Dunn looked at his wristwatch as he left the booth. Then he left to meet Howard Barringer.

CHAPTER EIGHT

Barringer winced when he saw the telephone booth. It was directly outside an "adult" bookstore whose windows were crammed with pornographic novels and hardcore video cassettes of "Swedish Nymphos in Action." There was a sign offering "HOT Loops in Private Cubicles" for twenty-five cents, and the tarty-looking woman who lounged against the phone booth looked as if she wouldn't charge much more. She smiled knowingly at the CIA executive, and licked her fire engine red lips in a manner intended to inflame him.

It only added to his irritation. Dunn's choice of this location was an act of deliberate provocation. Barringer scowled at the whore, then circled around her impatiently. He glanced at his wristwatch as he entered the booth.

6:18 P.M.

Dunn would call in two minutes. The prostitute smiled again as she pressed one hefty breast against the glass panel beside Barringer's head. His tension and annoyance grew more acute. How could he talk to Dunn with this *person* hovering six inches away? Unable to find the words, he gestured for her to go away. She shrugged.

"*Fag,*" she said in casual insult and strutted to a new post against the building.

Now Barringer looked up and down the street. On the four-block walk from his car, he'd doubled back twice and frequently paused to check on whether he was being followed. He'd seen nothing suspicious. Despite that, he felt extremely uneasy.

The whore was speaking with a well-dressed man who was carrying an attaché case. He was about forty, Barringer judged, and looked like a lawyer or corporate executive. Could *he* be one of McGhee's men? Was it only coincidence that *she* was at this corner? The phone rang. Barringer grabbed it.

"No names."

"Sure," Barringer agreed.

"When's your wife's birthday?" Dunn tested.

"March ninth."

"Now I'm sure. Here's what you do. Turn left on E Street. Walk two and a half blocks to the Jo-Mar Garage. When you pick up the car there, drive it out the back ramp onto F Street. That way you should lose the chopper."

"What chopper?"

"The one McGhee's had following you, dummy. It's circling about three blocks from you right now."

Barringer's whole body twitched under the impact.

"Listen, I had no idea that—"

"*You* listen," Dunn interrupted. "Drive the car to the long-term parking lot at National

Airport. Dump it there, and meet me at the Pan Am counter. Everything clear?"

"Everything except how I get this car."

He heard Dunn laugh.

"Thought you'd never ask. Reach under the phone."

Barringer obeyed, and found the parking ticket taped there.

"Got it. Anything else?"

"Drive carefully," Dunn said and ended the call. Twelve minutes later as Barringer guided the brown Ford onto the bridge across the Potomac, he wondered what other tricks Dunn had planned. There would be several. That was the way the man worked. He never did what he said he would, never was where he was expected. Even the things he said had a double meaning.

Dunn did not meet him at the Pan American Airways ticket counter in the terminal. Moments after Barringer locked the door of the car in the parking lot, he saw Dunn step out from behind a large station wagon. He was wearing the khaki uniform and overcoat of a sergeant in the U. S. Army. Barringer nodded in admiration for the simplicity of the disguise. No one ever paid attention to noncommissioned officers here. With the Pentagon and other military headquarters less than five miles away, there were thousands of sergeants around all the time.

"You okay, Charlie?"

Dunn's response was to thrust forward his hands in the overcoat pockets. The outline of a pistol in each showed clearly.

"I brought the money you asked for," Barringer announced.

"Let's have it."

The CIA executive unbuttoned his overcoat, reached in slowly and took out three bulging envelopes.

"There's five thousand in each," he said. Dunn looked around carefully before he stepped forward to accept the envelopes. He used his left hand to shove them inside his military tunic. His right still held a 9-millimeter P-15 pistol.

"It's all there, Charlie."

Dunn shook his head.

"You're one hundred eighty-five thousand dollars short, Howard. The down payment is two hundred thousand. The other half when it's finished."

"You want *four hundred thousand dollars*?"

"No, it's four hundred thousand and one. Spalding gets four hundred thousand, and I'm better than he is. You have half a minute to decide."

Now it was Barringer who shook his head.

"You've lost your mind," he said.

"Watch your mouth. It goes to four hundred and fifty in twenty seconds," Dunn announced, and looked at the stainless steel Omega on his right wrist.

"Is that a joke?"

"*Ten* seconds, Howard."

There was no time and no choice.

"It's a deal," Barringer blurted.

Dunn handed him a sheet of lined paper torn from a student's looseleaf notebook. It was covered with a neatly block-printed list of things that Dunn required. Six passports, four United States and two Canadian. One small MAC-11 submachine gun equipped with silencer and ten of the thirty-six-round magazines it took. A pair of R-23 walkie-talkie radios. A bulletproof vest and a U.S. Army sniper rifle with infrared night scope and one hundred bullets. Five pounds of plastic explosive, plus three DX timers.

"No radio-controlled detonators?" Barringer asked bitterly. "That's what he used on one of our people in Tangier yesterday."

"How did he kill the *other* one?"

"Who told you?"

"Cut his throat?"

"How did you know?"

Dunn took out a cigar, bit off the end and lit it.

"Nobody told me, Howard. I know because I know Spalding. He *had* to top me. I *captured* two of his, so he raised the ante by *destroying* two of mine. They're really *yours*, but he doesn't understand that."

"Are you saying this is a *game*?"

Dunn puffed on the Don Diego Corona and nodded.

"To him. Actually, he sees it as a competition. He's got a very sick ego. Maybe it's because his mother abandoned him when he was two days old—I don't know. Check the psychiatric profile your shrinks prepared."

"I read it all—the whole package," Barringer replied. Then he shuddered in the chill wind sweeping across the parking lot. His wife had been right when she'd urged him to wear the damn overcoat.

"Then you should remember he likes to use a surgical scalpel to cut throats. Ear to ear—he's flashy. Carries the thing in a plastic case that looks like a fountain pen."

Barringer opened his mouth, but closed it without speaking.

"You don't have to say it, Howard. I taught him."

"And you'll stop him. Listen, there's somebody I want you to meet. Could be very helpful. We've been thinking about Spalding's next target, and—"

"Is that supposed to be funny?"

"I'm sorry," Barringer apologized. "Next target *for money*. We've put a ton of research into this, worldwide computer scan and four top analysts. There are three names on our list of his likely targets."

"Spalding's the only name on *my* list," Dunn said as he tapped the ash from his cigar.

"Charlie, this person I mentioned—"

"No, thanks. You bring the hundred and eighty-five thousand here Monday at noon. Main terminal, the Eastern shuttle counter. There'll be a phone call for Mr. Lee Strouse. That's you."

Barringer shivered again and shrugged in assent. One had to be patient in dealing with people like Dunn. They would talk about the three names and the woman next time.

"Come on, Howard," Dunn said and pointed his cigar at a nearby Honda. "I'll give you a lift to a cab at the terminal."

"What about the car I drove out?"

"I stole it an hour ago. You could be arrested if the cops stopped you in that Ford. Be bad for your image, Howard."

Barringer was silent as he trudged beside Dunn to the Honda. The dossier said that Dunn was six feet tall, thirty-nine years old and a jazz enthusiast who could shoot a gun or throw a knife accurately with either hand. The file bulged with facts about his family, education, skills and CIA career—but what did it tell about Dunn as a person? As they got into the car, Barringer tried to remember why the man beside him had become an executioner. He couldn't. Who the hell *was* Charles Jefferson Dunn?

"Where do you want me to deliver the hardware, Charlie?" the CIA executive tested warily.

"I'll let you know," Dunn replied, and said nothing more until they saw the line of cabs directly ahead.

"So long, Howard," he announced and braked the Honda.

"Charlie?"

"Yes."

"Have you—uh—had time to figure out any sort of plan?"

"Get out."

"I'm under a lot of pressure—from the *top*," Barringer appealed.

"Okay, tell the director I've got *two* plans. One for Spalding and one for McGhee."

"*McGhee?*"

"I can't move on Spalding till I've neutralized McGhee."

Barringer's stomach knotted at the word *neutralized*. It could mean anything from a negative memo in a personnel file to a piano-wire garrotte. Before he could say a word, Dunn reached across him to open the car door.

"Go away, Howard—*now*."

Barringer left the car and watched the Honda disappear into the flow of airport traffic. He stood there for a full minute, recalling other men whom Dunn had neutralized in a dozen countries. The chill wind was blowing even more strongly, but Howard Barringer didn't notice that at all. He was covered with sweat. He was still damp when he got home an hour later.

CHAPTER NINE

As soon as McGhee entered the large office, he realized that he was in trouble. He recognized the frigid wrath in Lieutenant General William R. Hartley's eyes. Hartley was the first black man to top his West Point class, the first to command U.S. Army Intelligence and first to serve as the director of Central Intelligence. Known for his cool competence and self-control, he was a brilliant soldier-executive whom Agency veterans spoke of reverently as the Iceman. This naked fury in his stare was most unusual.

Why was he angry? McGhee scanned the room for clues as he walked across the blue carpet toward the chair beside the big oak desk. He saw Barringer on the nearby couch, studied his face for some clue and found none. Then he noticed that there was a cardboard box—about six inches square and four high—and some wrapping paper on the desk itself.

"I believe this is *yours*," Hartley said coldly as McGhee sat down. He was pointing one long mahogany finger at the box.

"Would you like to know *where* I found it?"

he asked before McGhee could lean forward to study the container. "I found it under my bed, goddamn it! Take a good look at the wrapping paper. It's addressed to you."

The Counterintelligence chief found his name block-printed on the brown paper. Three inches above and off to the left was that of the sender—Charles J. Dunn. McGhee's jaw fell in shock.

"Shut your mouth, Mr. McGhee. There's more. Do you know *when* I found it?"

McGhee shook his head.

"When it went off at four this morning. It's an alarm clock. It could have been a bomb, *couldn't* it?"

Each sentence cracked like a whip.

"Yes, sir," McGhee said hoarsely.

"Barringer tells me that Dunn, who slipped past your security team guarding the home of the Director of Central Intelligence as if they were dumb-ass Boy Scouts, knows *a lot* about bombs—that he's an extremely *dangerous* and *ruthless* field agent. Did he *happen* to tell you that?"

"Yes, sir."

"Did he also tell you that the Deputy Director, Plans, *and* the head of the covert-action staff had decided that Dunn was the man best qualified to handle a *special* and *very high priority* operation—and did he ask you to leave Dunn alone?"

"I got that message, sir, but—"

"What about *this* message?" Hartley demanded fiercely, and pointed at the box. "That's what this is, you know. It's a very simple message. Get off my case, McGhee, or

I'll do something terrible such as blowing up the DCI and his wife."

"He wouldn't really do that, sir."

"How the *fuck* would you know what he'd do? Do you have any idea how frightened my wife was when this damn thing went off? Do you understand whom you're dealing with?"

The gloves were off. The mask of executive gentility was gone. A veteran bureaucrat, McGhee saw that he was facing raw power.

"I think so, sir," he answered. "General, there are two things I'd like to say. *First*, I'm not convinced that Dunn's story about the alleged attempt to hit him is true. At the very least, I'd want him brought in for a polygraph test."

"And the mole?"

"I'm not sure about that either. That's another strong reason for a poly. We are checking into the possibility of penetration, of course."

"What's your *second?*" Hartley demanded.

"Chain of command. Barringer and his people can't tell me what to do. They can ask, but they can't order."

"*I* can order."

"You certainly can, general. You're the DCI."

Now the brown finger pointed at McGhee's throat.

"This is an order—from the DCI to the head of Counterintelligence. That's from me to you, mister. You'll get it in writing—by messenger—in ten minutes. You'll get it in goddamn triplicate. Forget Dunn and find the mole."

"If there is one, I'll get him—or her—sir."

Hartley pressed a buzzer on the communications panel on the right side of the desk surface. When his secretary entered with her pad fifteen seconds later, he dictated the order and told her to have it delivered to McGhee by hand *immediately*.

"I'll want a signed receipt, Miss Seigenthaler."

As soon as she left, he turned to McGhee again.

"As to those *so-called* security men at my home—"

"They'll be replaced within the hour," McGhee promised through compressed lips. "The team will be doubled."

"Don't let me keep you," the DCI replied in curt dismissal.

"Good morning, general."

Hartley shrugged and looked down at a document on his desk. He didn't look up until McGhee was gone.

"What do you think?" he asked Barringer.

"You handled it very well, general."

Hartley shook his head impatiently.

"That's not what I meant. *Have* we been penetrated?"

Barringer nodded.

"Probably. Had to happen, general. Sooner or later, somebody gets through the finest security systems. Of course, I still respect McGhee as a technician. He has lots of experience and a good record."

"Bottom line. What the hell are you saying?"

"I'm saying he's as competent and compulsive as he is unpleasant. In his line of work, being compulsive is an asset. I'd expect that he'll find the mole."

"Unless he *is* the mole," Hartley thought aloud bitterly. "Maybe Dunn's right not to trust him."

"Charlie Dunn doesn't trust anyone, general. If he ever did, he doesn't anymore."

Hartley glanced down at the voucher for $185,000.

"But we're supposed to trust him with all this cash—just on his word?"

"His word is very good, sir. Dunn is the most honest man I know. That's part of what makes it so difficult to deal with him."

"He kills but he doesn't steal?"

"That's his past record, general. If there isn't anything else, would you mind signing the voucher now?"

Hartley looked at the piece of paper, and considered the risks to his future if it ever got into the hands of some hostile journalist or senator. Authorizing federal funds for a paid assassin might cause a certain stir. He decided that he could handle it as so many officials in this and other governments had dealt with awkward and ugly situations. He'd look earnest, talk about national security and lie in tones of utter sincerity. Hartley signed the voucher.

"*You* could be the mole!" he told Barringer a moment later.

"I certainly could."

Barringer took the voucher to "walk it through" the various steps of processing, and Lieutenant General William R. Hartley glanced at his desk calendar. In seventy-five minutes, he was due on Capitol Hill to testify in defense of the CIA budget before the watchdog committee. The chairman was a silky son of a bitch who despised blacks in general and detested Hartley in particular.

It would be a challenge.

CHAPTER TEN

There were no lovers strolling hand in hand along the Left Bank of the Seine. It was too cold and too gray for that. This was November 29, 4:00 P.M. on a gloomy Friday afternoon. There weren't even any tourists walking by the river, Spalding noticed as his taxi rolled along the Quai Voltaire toward the tomb.

Instead of looking at the famed river on his right, Spalding faced straight ahead. Neither Paris nor the Seine meant anything to the assassin. He was as devoid of romance as he was removed from patriotism. Now the signs signaled that the cab was on the Quai D'Orsay, and half a minute later Victor Spalding turned to eye the huge domed building that housed the crypt.

It was part of a grandiose assemblage of structures that the French called the Hôtel des Invalides. None of these was a hotel, though the first building put up had been a barracks for disabled veterans in the seventeenth century. Today the complex included a palace, two splendid churches and a sprawling military museum crowded with memorabilia that ranged from captured flags, crossbows and muskets to one of the vintage taxis that carried reinforcements to stop the Germans on the Marne in 1914.

Some of France's military greats are buried in the crypt of the Church of St. Louis des Invalides, but the greatest of all rests beneath the curved and gold-leafed roof of the nearby Church of the Dome. Spalding paid off the taxi driver and walked directly to the circular crypt—twenty feet deep and thirty-six feet in diameter—that holds the remains of Napoleon Bonaparte.

Everything about it is larger than life. Though he had been a small man physically, the honor of France demanded this massive tribute to his glory. The Little Emperor is not interred in one casket, but in the innermost of *six*. The outermost of these is safe within a sixty-seven-ton sarcophagus—thirteen feet long, six and a half wide and fourteen and a half high—hewn from a single immense block of red rock. A dozen huge statues ring the crypt.

Spalding barely noticed them. His attention was focussed on a heavyset Oriental in a tweed overcoat. Spalding didn't know whether this portly man was Chinese, Japanese, Manchurian or Mongolian. He didn't care. The Asian was only a messenger.

"Impressive, isn't it?"

"Only if you're interested in dead people," the assassin replied. "What do you want?"

The fat man handed him a folded copy of *Le Monde*.

"To pass on *his* schedule and itinerary for the next seven weeks—it's taped to page five—

and to ask whether your work can be done by mid-January."

"You just did," Spalding replied coldly as he took the newspaper.

"Well?"

"I don't like to be rushed—certainly not on a job this big."

"You're right," the Oriental agreed, "but something *urgent* has come up."

Now a uniformed guide led in a score of high-school students. As she began her singsong recitation, Spalding swiftly considered the timetable and the financial possibilities.

"*How* urgent?" he tested.

"An extra one hundred thousand."

No individual had ever been paid half a million dollars for a hit before. There must be a very special reason for them to commit this much money. The answer was probably in that schedule taped inside the newspaper, Spalding thought.

"Six weeks might be tight, but not impossible," he said.

"Excellent," the fat man celebrated softly.

"I'll finish that job in Sweden first," Spalding told him and saw the man's brow furrow in disapproval. "*Don't argue with me*. It's all planned, and it *has* to be done on a certain day."

He had a steely edge to his voice, a hard obsessive look in his eye. The portly Oriental made a mental note to emphasize these things when he reported to the general. The general would be irate. This might blunt his wrath. If Spalding was beyond reason, the Mongolian could not be blamed.

"But if something goes wrong in Sweden—"

"The way it did in Vermont?" Spalding jeered. "Don't sweat it, chubby. *Nothing's* going wrong in Sweden."

The fat man controlled his temper.

"We will eliminate Dunn—as agreed."

"Where is he?"

"No one knows, but we will find him—or his former employers will locate him for us—soon."

"*How* soon?" Spalding asked.

"*Very* soon. One man without funds or allies cannot hide from the two biggest intelligence agencies on earth for long. For practical purposes, he's dead already."

Spalding considered this for a few moments.

"I could take him myself, you know—*anytime*," he declared.

"Of course—but you have more important things to do—so forget about him."

Spalding nodded, and left the church. Late that afternoon on the Scandinavian Airlines flight to Stockholm, he eyed the bulging blouse of the efficient stewardess pouring his Scotch and smiled in appreciation. He was in good spirits. Sipping the whisky, he reflected on how he'd humiliated the CIA and Dunn three days earlier in Tangier. The next move was really up to Dunn. It was almost too bad that he wouldn't live to make it.

Spalding had never liked Charlie Dunn, and had always been annoyed at the way the Agency overrated Dunn's talents. He certainly wasn't a serious threat to Victor Spalding. Eliminating him was merely a routine precaution, a sanitary measure.

It would also be a pleasure.

Now Victor Spalding thought ahead to the Swedish capital where he'd be landing in thirty-five minutes. For several seconds he let his mind drift to the pair of sixteen-year-old prostitutes he'd met there ten days earlier. Aside from the needle marks on their arms, the twin sisters were quite attractive and they did their best to satisfy. It was too bad that he couldn't see them tonight.

This was strictly a business trip. He could indulge himself on the earlier visit which was primarily to study the target, his home and his habits. Now Victor Spalding had to concentrate completely on the execution of the plan he'd developed. The time for killing was at hand.

CHAPTER ELEVEN

The phone call didn't come in until nine minutes after noon. The delay was probably designed to give Dunn more time to check for possible traps, Barringer guessed as he pretended to study the poster glorifying Eastern's service to Mexico. He was right. The bell rang, and a redheaded ticket agent at the shuttle counter picked up the telephone.

"Is there a Mr. Lee Strouse?" she asked cheerily.

Barringer gestured and started towards her.

"Here he is," she said into the instrument. She smiled brightly as she handed Barringer the phone, and he braced himself to try to deal with Charles Jefferson Dunn.

"Strouse here."

"Sorry, I can't make it today. I'll be in touch."

Before Barringer could ask or argue, he heard the hum of a severed connection. What the hell was he supposed to do with the $185,000 in the Pan Am bag slung over his shoulder? When would Dunn make contact? Where? How? Why hadn't he kept the rendezvous? Was something wrong? Was Dunn sick or wounded or going half mad again?

"Jeezus," Barringer said and remembered the ticket agent standing a yard away. "Sure, that'll be fine," he forced himself to continue. Then he hung up the telephone and squeezed out a sham smile.

What would-should-could he do? What was he to tell the covert action people or the DCI? Frowning in concern, he made his way through the churning mobs of travelers. Somebody bumped into him. Someone else banged a suitcase against his left knee, and a chemical blonde cursed him in Spanish when he almost trod on her miniature blue poodle. Barringer was glad to get out of the terminal.

"Hey, Howard!"

It was Dunn. He was at the wheel of the same car, but the license plates were a different color. Dunn probably switched them as often as he changed his shirt. Controlling his temper, Barringer got into the sedan. Dunn stepped on the gas pedal immediately.

"Why do you do these crazy things, Charlie?"

"To stay alive. How's McGhee?"

"*Steaming*. The DCI has ordered him—in writing—to leave you alone. In case you're keeping score, you've got the director pretty worked up too."

"He should be grateful. I'm one of the few who still make house calls."

"You didn't have to do that, Charlie."

"Yes, I did. What else would get that paranoid off my back?"

Barringer decided that this was the time. He tapped the shoulder bag.

"Got your money," he announced, "and the names of those three most likely targets. Will you *please* listen?"

"Of course," Dunn replied pleasantly. Barringer instantly wondered what had changed. Why was he so agreeable now?

"Number one's an arms dealer named George Stamos—based in Lisbon. Ripped off the Costa Verde junta for nine million three on a phony tank deal, and they put out a contract on him."

"Number two?" Dunn asked.

"Retired Swedish colonel named Morelius. Sold the Sovs military information for two years, and then burned a whole KGB *apparat*. Seems he was a counterintelligence agent all along. Moscow's livid, and we figure they might buy a free-lance gun to get even. Their tricky relations with the Swedes won't let them risk using their own hit men."

Nothing—not even a flicker of interest—showed in Dunn's face. Barringer knew that he was listening-recording somewhere behind the mask, and decided to continue briskly.

"Third is President Makumba of the Republic of Twanzi. Nationalized his uranium mines, booted the Red advisers his predecessor imported and tossed four West German bankers into jail for trying to bribe him. He's survived two assassination attempts in the past year. Has some nut idea the Agency was behind them."

"Was it?"

"That's *ridiculous*," Barringer replied indignantly.

He could be lying. The whole operation could

be some kind of setup to camouflage something else.

"He's the prime target in my book, Charlie.
Lot of people hate him. He's just the sort
someone would hire Spalding to hit. We want
him alive."

"Why?"

"He's honest, and we think he could be a
stabilizing force in the region."

"That's horse shit," Dunn answered. "You
mean he's an improvement over his predecessor who was a crook and played footsie with
the Communists, and you want to buy his
uranium."

"This guy's worth saving, Charlie. Compared
to nine-tenths of the characters who run African states, this guy's a saint—a *complicated*
saint. Listen, I want you to meet James. James
grew up in Twanzi when it was British, is an
old friend of Makumba. Makumba's suspicious
of Americans, but he trusts James. That's
money in the bank."

They were out of the airport now. For a
moment Barringer wondered where they were
going. Then he refocused.

"James can get you in close," he pressed.

"Agency staff?"

"Private citizen. Never worked for the government. Very smart, very decent. Ready to see
you anytime," Barringer assured. "It's not far
either. Tomorrow? Next day? You pick it."

Dunn computed and decided.

"Now," he said abruptly.

"Right now?"

"Any reason why not, Howard?"

"Hell, no. Might be a good idea to phone

ahead—just to let the security men know we're coming."

"*Bad* idea. Save the taxpayers' dime," Dunn advised in tones that left no room for negotiation. Showing up where he wasn't expected was part of Dunn's survival system. Barringer gave him the address in Falls Church. When they reached the old house on the quiet tree-lined street twenty minutes later, Dunn did not stop the car. He drove around the block twice and then circled in a slightly wider arc before he returned to park. There was space directly in front of the three-story colonial residence that was their destination, but he chose a place across the street and forty yards from the white wooden building.

"Force of habit. Nothing *personal*, Howard," he assured as he stepped from the car. He looked up and down the street, and then hefted the pistols in his raincoat pockets to make sure that he could draw them quickly. The uniform Dunn wore now was not an army sergeant's but that of a Harvard-educated executive—gray flannel suit, buttondown shirt of blue Oxford cloth and sturdy cordovan shoes. As they walked to the house, Barringer braced for what he might say when he saw the small neatly lettered sign on the front lawn.

"*Doctor* H. James?" Dunn asked when he spotted it.

"Let's try the back door," Barringer said in evasive reply. Dunn would know soon enough. He might well be furious. When they reached the rear entrance, the Deputy Director of Operations rapped on the door twice, then once, and finally three times. The curtains behind the glass panel that filled the upper half of the door parted, and someone looked out for a few seconds.

"What kind of a doctor?" Dunn questioned abruptly. At that moment, they heard a lock turning. As soon as the door opened, Barringer hurried inside and Dunn followed immediately. The noise of the lock closing warned Dunn that someone was behind him. In reflex-defense, he spun on his heel.

The man he faced was about thirty, muscular, big featured and visibly startled by the twin pistols that Dunn was pointing at him. He'd never seen anyone draw weapons that quickly. They had blossomed in Dunn's hands as in some conjurer's trick. Barringer winced and shook his head ruefully.

"You can put those away, Charlie. This is one of our security people," he explained.

"He's *slow*," Dunn judged. He surveyed the large kitchen in which they stood and inspected the long corridor leading to the front of the house before he returned the guns to his pockets.

"Please tell the doctor we're here," Barringer said to the security man who was still staring at Dunn. The guard nodded, walked up the corridor and rapped twice on a door. When it opened, Dunn heard an odd sound that resembled an animal growl—something guttural and inhuman. It was a noise made by a beast in pain. Some thirty seconds passed before the security agent stepped back into the corridor and gestured. Dunn and Barringer were in the doctor's office a minute later, eyeing the patient.

"It's a nasty infection, but those pills should do it," Dr. James said.

"Thank you," the plump old woman in stretch jeans replied, and patted the patient. The patient was less than three feet tall, weighed 140 pounds and was covered with thick black fur. Four-legged and sad-eyed, the limping patient was a large Newfoundland bitch. The elderly woman led the sick dog away, and Dr. James closed the door before turning to face the two men.

Dr. James was wearing light blue trousers, a white surgical gown and almost a yard of silken blonde hair. Five feet one inch tall, she was pretty with splendid blue eyes and creamy skin. The T-shirt beneath her half-open surgical gown bulged under the pressure of breasts much larger than those of most women her height. She had perfect teeth and a quizzical smile.

"Sit down, gentlemen," she invited in a voice tinged with remnants of a British accent.

"What the *hell* is this?" Dunn demanded.

"Is he the friend you mentioned, Mr. Barringer?" she asked as the gown opened further to expose the entire Save the Whales legend on her T-shirt.

"Are you *crazy*, Howard?" Dunn questioned before Barringer could answer. "You want me to go into a tricky African country with *her* on a *covert* operation? *Shit*, I wouldn't walk to the corner mailbox with her. I'm not that suicidal."

Barringer had expected such a reaction. He hung his coat on a hook and dropped into an armchair before he answered in a carefully controlled voice.

"What's the problem, Charlie?"

"Problem is she's a walking target, self-propelled bull's-eye. With that hair and that body, everyone over six will notice her."

"Would you like a glass of water?" she inquired.

Her calm only irritated him more.

"You can *stick* your water. Maybe you don't understand this situation, doc. How much has he told you?"

"Mr. Barringer appealed to me on behalf of the federal government to help you protect President Makumba from a professional assassin. He said you were expert at such matters, Mr. Smith."

"My name isn't Smith. It's Charlie Dunn. Did he mention what branch of the government he's with?"

"I believe it's the Department of State."

"Don't believe *anything* he says. He's one of the great patriotic liars of our time. He's captain of the lying team at the CIA—a great *humanitarian*."

The shock showed in her face.

"Is that true?" she asked.

"We felt that—well, in light of your attitudes toward the Agency and the defense establishment ... This is a terribly important matter, and we weren't sure you'd cooperate," Barringer answered.

"How would you know about my attitudes?" she wondered.

"They investigated you, doc," Dunn said. "Right back to kindergarten. They know about the prize you won at Sunday school, and the middle name of your first boyfriend. They've got your dental X rays and income-tax returns, lists of all your long-distance calls for the past five years and your father's credit rating. If you ever had a traffic ticket, abortion or gay uncle in Indianapolis, they know it. They're taping your phone calls, opening your mail and sifting your garbage. Ten to one they're recording this conversation right now. The house *is* bugged, isn't it, Howard?"

"I'm not at liberty to discuss classified security procedures," Barringer said stiffly.

"That's outrageous!" she erupted.

"Not in the world he lives in," Dunn told her. "It's outrageous in your nice world where decent people worry about whales and clean air and violence on television. I suppose those things concern him too, but he's basically in the garbage business. He's got the shit detail, clearing away the mess. I was in the same line of work for years."

"I'll bet you were good at it," she accused.

"The *best*. That's why I'm breathing and some other people aren't. Didn't he tell you? I used to *kill* people to make the world safe for democracy."

Her hand went to her mouth in horror. Then she saw the hurt in his eyes.

"I'm sorry, Mr. Dunn. I didn't know. I'm *really* sorry," she apologized in a choked voice. Her compassion unnerved him, but only for a moment.

"I didn't mention it to get your pity, doctor. I'm trying to give you a realistic picture of the world Barringer wants you to enter. This operation will be nasty and risky. It will be very difficult and extremely dangerous to prevent this man from killing Makumba. He's a professional with the scruples of a vending machine. Put the money in, and a corpse drops out," Dunn said grimly, and took a cigar from his jacket.

"You know this man?"

"We both do. Howard, tell her what his code name was."

Barringer hesitated as Dunn lit the Corona.

"Okay, I'll tell her," Dunn decided impatiently. "They called him *Cleaver*. He kills without hesitation. He enjoys it. He has no inhibitions, no regrets. He'd kill a baby or a president—or even a lady vet—without a second thought."

"You're trying to frighten me, aren't you, Mr. Dunn?"

"Damn right. I've got two terrific reasons. The first is you're too useful and sexy to die so young. It's my duty to save your ass—for humanity."

"For Christ's sake, Charlie," Barringer protested.

"What's your other reason?" she asked calmly.

"To save *mine*. If you come along, we're both dead. Then who'll protect Makumba?"

She glanced at his cigar, and moved an ashtray to the edge of her desk where he could reach it.

"Don't be so damn helpful," Dunn said irately. "Be sensible instead. Stay out of this, doctor. Take care of your dogs and whales. That's your line. I have to stop this homicidal monster, but you don't. You have a choice. Use your head, damn it."

She smiled patiently.

"President Makumba is more than a close friend. I was made a member of his tribe when I was fourteen," she explained. "He is my brother. I cannot abandon my brother."

"You *believe* this, Howard?" Dunn demanded.

"Without me," she continued evenly, "you'd never get near enough to him to protect him. I have no choice."

Dunn stood up abruptly.

"Let's go, Howard."

"I'm sorry, doctor. *I* think you could help," Barringer said as he rose from the chair, "but I must respect Mr. Dunn's views since the responsibility is his. Don't worry. He's highly experienced. I'm sure he knows what to do."

She turned to look directly into Dunn's eyes.

"So do I," she said firmly. "I'm going to Twanzi."

"Not with me," Dunn vowed, and strode from the room. Barringer followed him to the car, braced for the verbal assault that would start the moment they were inside the vehicle. But minutes passed in silence. They were three miles from Falls Church when Dunn finally spoke.

"I've been thinking," he said in a calm voice that startled Barringer. "Let's get rid of those pretentious old code names and tell it like it is. That Cleaver and Excalibur crap is ridiculous."

He was up to something.

"Got anything in mind?" Barringer tested warily.

"We'll call Spalding—ah—Garbage. Suits him, don't you think?"

"Garbage?"

"And make sure everyone who knew about your wires to me hears of the change. I want it to reach Victor. Mr. Spalding is now—officially—Garbage!"

"He'll go wild," Barringer predicted, and suddenly understood. "Wild men make mistakes."

"One is all I need, Howard. In this game, second prize is a pine box."

He was the old Charlie Dunn all right. Every trick in the book.

"What do we call you?" the CIA executive asked.

"Something just as accurate. I'm a specialist, like those athletes they bring into baseball games in clutch situations just to hit. I hit people instead of balls. Baseball's the national sport and I'm the national assassin."

"What the hell are you saying, Charlie?"

"I'll settle for the same title. Designated Hitter."

Barringer shrugged in assent. It didn't matter what code name Dunn chose so long as he did the job.

"By the way, Howard, what does the H stand for?"

"What H?"

"Dr. *H*. James. Harriet? Hortense?"

"Heather," Barringer said stiffly, "and you were damn rough on her. That wasn't necessary."

"All I did was tell her the truth. You ought to try it some time."

Barringer ignored the taunt.

"And I think you're making a mistake," he argued as Dunn accelerated to pass a station wagon filled with nuns. "You need her on this. She may be eye-catching, but she's also essential."

Something that might have been a smile flickered across Dunn's face for a moment. Then it was gone.

"Okay," Dunn said. "We'll leave on Thursday. That's the twelfth."

"You're going with her?"

Dunn nodded, and again checked the rear-view mirror.

"When you're right, you're right, Howard. Tell her we'll be traveling light—one suitcase each. She won't need her guitar."

"How did you know she has a guitar?" Barringer asked, and wondered why Dunn had changed his mind so abruptly.

"What is she? Twenty-seven or twenty-eight? Hit puberty in the late sixties. Sincere young woman out of that period who cares about whales is almost *bound* to have a guitar," Dunn replied with a chuckle.

"Now about the hardware," Dunn continued. "Pack it in two canvas valises. We'll pick it up at American Express on the thirteenth and go to work."

"American Express in Twanzi on the thirteenth," Barringer confirmed.

Dunn shook his head and smiled benignly.

"American Express on Haymarket in *London*," he corrected. "Don't ask why we're not going directly to Twanzi, because I'm not going to tell you. It's—"

"Nothing personal," Barringer completed dourly. "I know. Anything else?"

"Tell me about Heather James."

Barringer reported that she'd been born in northern California, daughter of a gifted painter and a physician. She was eight when her mother died, and a year later her father took the family to Twanzi where he served as a medical missionary for a decade. She had a brother who was dean of the Harvard Divinity School, and two sisters. Willow was attorney general of the state of California. Fern was a widow with $48 million worth of Dallas real estate and a seat on the board of the American Civil Liberties Union.

"Father still in Africa?" Dunn asked.

"Brazil. Runs the World Health Organization team there. Heather's the youngest— twenty-seven, and maybe the smartest. IQ of one hundred sixty-three. Speaks French, Spanish, Swahili and Noro. The Noro are Makumba's people. Toughest tribe in East Africa."

"Let me know when you get to the personal stuff."

"You don't have to be nasty, Charlie. She doesn't smoke or drink, and she's never used drugs. Runs three miles every morning. No criminal record, no kinky sex, no current boyfriend. Was engaged to a poet, who dumped her last year to marry a Rothschild."

"Poets are tricky. I could have told her that."

As Barringer went ahead with his account, he noticed that they were driving on a road that would not take them directly to National

Airport where he'd left his car. A minute later, he saw the massive bulk of the five-sided building that housed the headquarters of the U.S. defense establishment.

"Hope you don't mind if I drop you at the Pentagon," Dunn said. "Could be somebody put another transmitter in your car, or somebody else spotted it in the parking lot. A whole gang of somebodies could be waiting for us at National right now."

The line separating paranoia and precaution was a thin one, Barringer thought. Then his mind focused on why Dunn would stop in London en route to Twanzi. It was part of some cunning complex plan, a devious Dunn design. Maybe he didn't intend to go to East Africa at all, the CIA executive brooded as Dunn navigated the concrete cloverleaf that led to the main entrance of the drably functional forty-two-year-old structure. Barringer glanced at his watch as Dunn braked the car to a halt. It was 6:55 P.M.—only a skeleton crew would be on duty at the motor pool.

"Show your ID and the guards will let you in to call a cab, Howard," Dunn suggested. "Now about the passports—"

"They're in the bag with the money."

"*Very good*, Howard. I'll be in touch."

"Suppose we want to reach you overseas?"

"The old Valentine code. Run the ads in the *International Tribune* on weekdays and the London *Daily Mail* on the weekend. Best to Heather."

As Dunn drove away, Barringer started up the steps wondering whether he should have wished him good luck. He was halfway up when he realized that it wouldn't matter to Charlie Dunn. Dunn didn't believe in luck. No man who did would start such a dangerous operation on Friday the thirteenth.

CHAPTER TWELVE

The rain had stopped but the streets were still wet, and when Willoughby stepped from the car the damp was almost tangible. It usually was in London at this time of the year. He immediately found himself in a bustling throng. Many of the pedestrians hurrying along the Haymarket were obviously foreigners, and that was no surprise either. This street was dotted with theaters, and banks where the currencies of other nations could be exchanged for pounds, and many visitors from the United States and Canada came to the American Express building to collect their mail.

Willoughby glanced at his reflection in the window of the Design Center, noted that the black bowler hat sat atop his long narrow head at the proper angle, and strode off with his neatly furled umbrella. Wing Commander Willoughby walked with a slight limp. His left leg had been amputated below the knee after a plane crash a dozen years earlier. He'd then been given an artificial limb and "seconded" to one of the most aggressive units of Secret Intelligence. On paper, he was attached to the telecommunications planning staff of the Ministry of Civil Aviation and that's why he dressed as a middle-level bureaucrat.

On the next block he paused to consider the tweed coats in the Burberry shop windows, professionally checked to see whether anyone might be following him and then crossed through the torrent of traffic to the other side of the wide street. At 10:40 A.M., he entered the lobby of Her Majesty's Theatre. Six minutes later he stepped out onto the roof and looked for the man he was to meet. There was no one in sight.

"You alone?"

The accent was definitely American. Willoughby's eyes searched the roof again, and this time he noticed the gun muzzle jutting from behind a corner of the chimney.

Dunn stepped forward with an iron bar in one hand and a P-15 pistol in the other. Willoughby observed that there wasn't the slightest trace of mental or physical weakness. Dunn looked as hard as the pieces of metal he held.

"*Awfully* nice to see you again, Charles."

Dunn did not answer immediately. He wedged the bar under the doorknob so the portal could not open, tested the barrier and only then put the gun in the right pocket of his coat. He took a pair of binoculars from the other pocket before he spoke.

"How's it going, Peter?"

"Busy as ever. *Delightful* surprise to hear from you. Didn't know you were in town, old boy."

Willoughby spoke in the soft but chiseled tones of an English gentleman. There was no trace of urgency in his voice, and nothing to suggest any curiosity about the field glasses, the meeting place or the reason Dunn was here.

"Just in for my Christmas shopping. Got a couple of presents for you too," Dunn announced and handed him the binoculars. "No, not the glasses. Down there. Take a look."

"What am I looking for, Charles?" Willoughby inquired politely.

"The man in the leather jacket standing by the green motorcycle ... *there* ... and the gray Triumph sedan just up the street ... *there*."

Willoughby peered down through the binoculars.

"Green, you say? ... Yes ... Burly chap ... and there's the Triumph."

"Two men in the car, plus the biker, and another inside American Express," Dunn said. "Short guy in a blue slicker. He's in the basement where tourists pick up mail and packages. Four men altogether."

Willoughby lowered the glasses and stroked his mustache thoughtfully.

"You're giving me the entire lot, Charles?"

"They're a matched set. Couldn't break them up. If they're not your size, you can always exchange them—for someone you want. Maybe Sid Lamb."

Lamb was a veteran British agent whom the KGB had captured three years ago near Leningrad. Willoughby had sworn to get him out. They had been friends for more than a decade.

"Who are these four?" Willoughby asked.

"I believe they're Sovblock agents. Probably Russians, possibly East Germans or Czechs and *surely* armed. They're carrying illegal guns. I'm almost certain they intend to kill somebody—today. They've been waiting for him down there since 8:45 this morning, ready to shoot him down as he leaves the American Express office."

The Briton looked up at the sky. It would rain again soon.

"Whom do they mean to kill?"

"Me, of course," Dunn answered briskly.

"Of course," Willoughby said as the stump of his maimed limb reminded him of the cold damp. He glanced down at the street once more before he handed the binoculars back to Dunn.

"You are telling me the truth, Charles?"

"Absolutely."

"But not *all* of it, of course?"

Dunn wondered why the British so often felt obliged to say the obvious. It was odd for a civilized people.

"Of course," he confirmed. Then he explained his plan designed to avoid a violent confrontation here in the heart of London. The Red agents would be watching for Dunn to pick up two suitcases at the basement service center inside American Express. Instead, a young woman with blonde hair would claim the baggage and leave by taxi. They would follow her with the hope that she'd lead them to Dunn. The cab would take her to a garage on a back street several miles away in Camberwell, where Secret Intelligence personnel could seize them with minimum risk of harm to innocent civilians passing by.

"And where will you be, Charles?"

"In the garage, with three or four of your gents right outside. I'd guess you'd want to trail them out with another four or five. You might need nine, plus yourself. That's just my opinion, Peter. I'm not trying to tell you what to do."

Dunn had always been a ruthless loner. Why was he offering this unusual "present" now?

"Is there anything else I should know?" Willoughby tested.

"Yes, she'll be here at exactly a quarter after four. That should give you time to check with Barringer on the scrambler circuit. I scheduled it that way."

Willoughby hesitated. Rushing into operations on such short notice was not his way, but the chance to do something—*anything*—to free Lamb was difficult to resist.

"Are you in?" Dunn demanded.

Willoughby nodded, and Dunn walked to the door that led down from the roof. He removed the bar, and then turned suddenly.

"Take good care of the woman," he said.

"We will."

Dunn gave him the address of the garage, and then left. Willoughby descended a few minutes later to assemble a team and reach a "secure" telephone for the call to CIA headquarters at Langley. He was back on the roof of Her Majesty's Theatre by 3:00 P.M. with his agents in place nearby and a walkie-talkie radio in one hand. It had not been easy to secure permission for every one of them to carry guns, but Lamb's name had finally prevailed.

Everything went as Dunn had predicted. At 4:15 Willoughby looked down and saw a young woman with long yellow tresses step from a taxi. When she entered the American Express office, he raised the radio to his mouth.

"Shepherd One to all units. I believe that Our Friend has arrived. Prepare to engage."

When Heather James reached the basement, she found two lines of tourists—many in their early twenties—waiting cheerfully for their mail. Several had backpacks, others cassette players and one a guitar. There were also older people, including two female teachers chatting about the splendors of their sabbatical respite from the University of Texas. The lines moved slowly. It was 4:29 before the blonde veterinarian reached the counter.

"Shepherd Four to Shepherd One. Our Friend has the bags," a British agent watching from a phone booth reported. Two minutes later: "Leaving now with the bloody Bandit in the blue slicker right behind."

From here on it was *all* timing, Willoughby thought. They had to protect her every second. Perhaps the Bandits wouldn't follow her to the garage. They might snatch her at any moment. The whole damn operation was a calculated risk. Willoughby looked at his wristwatch, saw that it was 4:33 and alerted his men to prepare to move.

Heather James emerged from the building just as a cab stopped to let out a passenger. Pleased by her luck, she got into the taxi and gave the address of the garage in Camberwell across the Thames. She had no idea that the driver was a Secret Intelligence agent with a submachine gun at his feet. The cab set off with the motorcycle and Triumph following, and British agents trailing them in a maroon Ford and a small truck bearing the name of a fictitious wine shop.

It took twenty minutes to reach the garage. The driver unloaded the valises, thanked Heather James for the tip and guided the taxi around the corner to an alley. He parked the vehicle, picked up the automatic weapon and radioed that he was in position. Some seventy yards away Dunn closed the garage door behind Heather James and took the suitcases from her.

"Thank you, doctor."

"You're welcome, Mr. Dunn. It wasn't any problem at all," she told him, and looked around the garage. It wasn't very large. A battered old Hillman filled nearly a quarter of the space, and beside it was a metal table heaped with wrenches, tools, lengths of pipe and greasy rags. Dunn carried the suitcases across the concrete floor to the car, and set them down near the rear door. Then he paused and cocked his head towards the street. He seemed to be listening.

"Would you do me a favor, doctor?"

"Certainly."

He pointed to the wall.

"Would you please stand over here?" he asked.

"What?"

"Behind the car—please."

Puzzled by the request, she hesitated for a

few seconds before she shrugged in compliance. Barringer had assured her that Dunn knew what to do, and she had promised to cooperate. She started towards the aged sedan.

"Bandits! Bandits!"

The voice was scratchy, not quite human. She guessed that it was coming from some radio or loudspeaker. There it was on a shelf, jutting from the wall. It looked like a walkie-talkie. Dunn suddenly ripped off his jacket, and she was startled by the sight of the twin P-15s in belly holsters.

"Mr. Dunn?"

His reply was swift and violent. He seized her by the right arm, dragged her across the chamber at top speed and threw her between the Hillman and the wall as if she were a large doll. She gasped under the impact of the metal and concrete, and she hurt as she struggled up from the floor.

At that moment the door that she'd entered exploded. It was difficult to tell whether it was a crash or a blast, and for a few seconds she thought a bomb had gone off. Chunks of the door hurled across the room. Then she saw that it was a car that had smashed into the garage—a gray Triumph sedan. The doors flew open as the auto bucked and shuddered to a screeching halt. Three men jumped out with guns in their hands.

Low in a tense shooter's crouch, Dunn fired first. One intruder in a blue rain slicker staggered as a 9-millimeter bullet shattered his left kneecap and another slug broke his right arm, knocking the pistol from his grasp. The man who'd driven the car dived to the floor, while another attacker in a black pea jacket swung a rapid-fire weapon in a wide arc as he turned to the man they'd come to kill.

He screamed as Dunn's bullet tore away his left ear, and then again when a 9-millimeter slug ripped through his stomach. Dazed and disoriented by pain, he slumped to his knees and squirted off several unaimed bursts that ravaged the metal roof and ruined cans of oil and paint on a wall shelf. He made more garbled sounds as the crimson stain on the front of his trousers widened. He couldn't see much, but he kept hold of the submachine gun until Dunn grabbed the weapon and rolled behind a fifty-gallon drum.

"Keep down! There's one more!" Dunn shouted.

He was wrong.

There were two.

The motorcyclist had broken open the rear door. The sound of his forced entry had been lost in the shooting, and Dunn was focused entirely on finding the third man who'd been in the Triumph.

"Look out!" she screamed, and threw a foot-long file that she'd seized from among the tools. As the leather jacketed foe took aim at Dunn, her missile hit him five inches below the throat. He looked down at the thing embedded in his flesh, and shuddered. He staggered back a step. Then he said something. It was a curse in a tongue she didn't understand. He turned to shoot her.

But the pain was too much. He made two frantic efforts to pull the file free before he fell back out the rear door. Now there was more noise from both ends of the garage. Dunn swiveled his guns left and right, recognized the British agents and yelled a warning.

"There's another one in here somewhere!"

Two of the SI team dropped to the floor, while others bent low with their weapons at the ready. One of those sprawled on the concrete pointed at the Hillman, and Willoughby understood. The fourth gunman was under the car.

"Perhaps I can reason with him, Charles," Willoughby said. "No need for unnecessary bloodshed."

Then he spoke in a much louder voice.

"Listen, you bastard. There are eight armed men out here, three with automatic weapons. We know you're under the bloody car. You've got no chance. Either you kick out your gun and crawl out now, or we'll shoot you to pieces. Will you come out in one lump, or do we pick up the mess with blotting paper?"

Five seconds later a .32-caliber pistol equipped with a silencer clattered out into view.

"Don't shoot. Coming out," the man under the Hillman said.

"Feet first and face down," Willoughby ordered. "He may have another weapon, men. Keep him covered."

Eight guns were pointed at the space beneath the car as the feet emerged slowly. One weapon swung to cover the wounded man in the blue slicker when he moaned, but the others were aimed at the body that was inching out from under the old sedan.

"Duckett! Cheetham! Take him!" Willoughby said and the two agents obeyed at once. The battle was finished. Some seventy-nine seconds had passed since Heather James entered the garage. Now she stepped forward, openly appalled.

"Take a *good* look at the world Barringer has talked you into, doc," Dunn urged grimly.

She had to swallow before she could reply.

"This is—I didn't *dream* that it would be—"

"No dreams in this world," Dunn interrupted. "That's the rule, and it covers everybody. No exceptions."

He was trying to intimidate her again.

She shook her head defiantly.

"I've called for ambulances, wing commander," reported the man who had driven her from the American Express office. "Two of them shot up, one losing blood from a hole in his stomach. Think he'll make it. There's another sod out back with a great ugly chunk of iron stuck in his chest, crying like a baby."

"She threw that. Probably saved my life. Thanks, doc."

"The Noro taught me to throw a spear accurately when I was twelve," she said.

"I forgot that—along with my manners," Dunn replied as he holstered his guns. "Dr. James, may I present Wing Commander Willoughby? The doc is a top notch vet and—as she mentioned—a member of the Noro tribe."

She probably *was* a veterinarian, Willoughby thought as they shook hands. Even Dunn wouldn't make up such an odd cover story. Whatever she was, she was extremely attractive.

"Pleasure to meet you, doctor," Willoughby told her. "Sorry we were a bit late."

"Don't *apologize*. We're lucky you just happened to be in the neighborhood," Dunn said sarcastically.

"We did our best, Charles," Willoughby declared stiffly.

"Does *late* mean you knew this would happen?" she asked. Then she recognized the agent who'd driven the taxi.

"You were in the cab! What's this all about, Mr. Dunn? Who are these men?"

She pointed at the two wounded on the floor.

"Not to worry. They'll get the best medical care," Dunn assured, "and then they're all going home to their mothers, *right*?"

"I certainly hope so," Willoughby said truthfully.

"*Who* are they, Mr. Dunn?" she pressed. "Are they connected with the man you call Cleaver?"

Willoughby blinked as he recognized the code name.

"He's called Garbage now," Dunn corrected, "but the answer to your second question is *yes*."

Then the "taxi driver" handed Willoughby identity papers taken from the captives, and reported that one had cursed in Czech. Willoughby scanned the documents swiftly.

"They appear to be foreigners, doctor," he said, "and I think they're with some Communist espionage unit."

Now he turned to Dunn who was putting on the jacket flung to the floor earlier.

"You didn't mention that Spalding was in this, or that he was working for the Sovs."

"He's working for anyone with cash. I really must talk to him about that," Dunn answered as he brushed a thread from one sleeve.

"Might be hard to find him, Charles."

"I'll find him."

Willoughby understood that this was a declaration of war. He hoped that it would not be fought on British soil.

"How long will you be in the country?" he asked.

Dunn smiled at the implicit eviction order. No one was rude as gracefully as the English, who still retained so many imperial skills.

"Give my regards to Sid," he said.

"I'll do that."

Suddenly the man with the bullet in his stomach moaned. Heather hurried to his side in compassionate response.

"Two more things," Willoughby said softly. "Barringer wanted me to tell you that the man in Lisbon has gone to his brother's house. I assume you know what that means."

Arms merchant George Stamos was in Athens.

"What's the other thing, Peter?"

"Thank you for the presents."

"You're welcome," Dunn replied, and went to get the valises.

"It's a terrible wound," Heather reported.

"I'm afraid this is a terrible business, doctor."

"That's what Mr. Dunn said," she recalled, "and he'd know—wouldn't he?"

Willoughby cleared his throat carefully before he answered.

"Absolutely."

"What—what sort of person is Mr. Dunn, commander?" she asked intently.

"Highly intelligent and immensely capable . . . and he lies less than almost anyone I know. Of course," the British agent warned wryly, "most of the people I know are rather—"

"*Terrible?*"

"Precisely. Returning to your question, I don't actually *like* Charles but I do respect him. I'd trust Charles Dunn to do *the right thing*—if at all possible. Rather unusual chap."

He stopped talking as Dunn arrived with the suitcases.

"More presents, Peter," he announced as he set down the valises. It would be difficult to move these weapons across frontiers, and he'd never intended to use them anyway. He had other plans.

"Thank you again," Willoughby accepted courteously.

Now Dunn pointed at the taxi driver in silent request.

"Of course, Charles. Safe home."

The farewells were brief. Dunn was in a hurry, openly impatient as they followed the driver around the corner to his parked vehicle.

"Move it, doc," he said brusquely. "You're in danger every second that you're near me, and don't forget it."

When they reached the cab moments later, he told the British agent to check under the hood for bombs rigged to the starter. While the driver was doing this, Dunn dropped to the street to look for explosive charges clamped beneath the chassis or fuel tank. Only after these security precautions did he open the door for her to enter the vehicle.

"Are we expecting trouble?" the Secret Intelligence man inquired.

"Why not?" Dunn answered and asked to be dropped at the Picadilly Hotel. They were on their way moments later. From time to time the driver glanced at his rearview mirror. If the situation was this dicey, it was only prudent. He did not notice the green MG that was following them. The Oriental woman at the wheel of the small coupe had a lot of experience at this work. She hung back and maneuvered expertly, using a variety of techniques and other vehicles to avoid detection. She was short, slim, pretty and very good at these things. She appeared to be about twenty-eight, but was actually a month short of thirty-five.

The pre-Christmas flow of traffic in down-town/central London clotted the streets, and turned a twenty-minute journey into a forty-minute crawl. It was after six when they left the cab to enter the Picadilly. Four minutes later, they emerged to take another taxi to the Hyde Park Hotel in the Knightsbridge section—the place where they were staying. The green MG followed.

CHAPTER THIRTEEN

Though its exterior was definitely old-fashioned, the Hyde Park Hotel was equipped with all the modern amenities. After they entered their third-floor suite, Dunn double-locked the door and opened a cabinet to expose a well-stocked bar. He took out two miniature bottles of Dewar's Scotch.

"Think of it as medicine, doctor," he said.

"I'm not sick, but serve yourself," she replied as she hung up her coat. Dunn poured both miniatures into a glass, sipped the smoky whisky and waited for her questions. Seated in the big armchair with her legs crossed, she seemed completely calm. Only her slightly disheveled hair reflected the recent violence. She had handled herself well, he thought. The questions did not come.

"Sorry I had to throw you over the car," he told her, "but it was necessary."

She nodded in agreement.

"I didn't understand the situation," she said.

"That's what I've got to talk to you about, doctor. Be safer for both of us if I filled you in on some things."

She recalled what Barringer and Willoughby had said about him, and relived his performance in the garage.

"I feel perfectly safe with you *now*," she replied. Dunn shook his head and sipped more whisky.

"I appreciate your confidence, doc. There's more to it. There are more gunmen where those came from."

"I'm sure that you'll deal with them. I've been on many hunts with the Noro, and I saw what you did in that garage. You set a trap, didn't you?"

"Yes."

"And I was the bait?"

He nodded, and braced for her angry outburst. There was none.

"It was a very good trap," she judged. "You do know what to do, and you're quick. You're a first-class hunter, Mr. Dunn."

"I've had a lot of practice. So has Victor Spalding."

"The man who means to kill Alfred Makumba?"

"Makumba and *me*. That's one of the things Barringer didn't mention. The number at the garage was Spalding's second try in a month," Dunn said and drank more of the Scotch. He suddenly realized that he was looking at her as a desirable woman. That was something he couldn't risk now.

"Why *you*?" she asked.

"Because he thinks he's got to kill me before I kill him. So does Barringer. That's something else you weren't told. Our government expects me to *terminate Spalding with* extreme prejudice. That's shoptalk for killing him."

Dunn finished the whisky, walked to the bar and reached inside.

"Will you?"

"Like some ginger beer, doc?"

"Yes, thank you."

He poured more Dewar's into his glass, filled another with the soft drink and gave it to her. She thanked him again and swallowed half a mouthful. Then Dunn took off his jacket to hang it over the back of a chair. She saw the twin pistols again. He walked to his adjacent bedroom and returned fifteen seconds later holding a small photo.

"That's Spalding. Take a good look; he's cute with disguises. If you see that face or one anything like it, sing out. He's about six feet, one hundred and seventy-five pounds and very fast. He's a goddamn snake."

She studied the picture carefully.

"There's *something* in his eyes," she said.

"He's kinky about sex and death—among other things. Actually he's fifty-three percent crazy."

She sipped more ginger beer before she spoke again.

"You know him well?"

"I taught him the trade. That was just before I had my breakdown. I was crazy too, you know."

"I didn't know."

"I was *scared* back to normal—if you call this normal. I was quaking and shaking up in Vermont when Victor's chums sent two hoods to blow me away. *Raw fear* succeeded where the shrinks, mind drugs and electroshock had failed."

She finished the soft drink and smoothed her skirt. Now the bitterness made sense. His professional self-esteem and male pride had been hurt by the fact that he'd been intimidated. There was pain as well as outrage in his anger.

"As a government employee, Mr. Dunn, I'm sure—"

"You're wrong. I was pensioned off as hopeless more than two years ago. I'm a free lance with a ninety-day contract. I'm a high-priced mercenary—like Spalding."

That had to be a lie. He just didn't act like a sick murderer.

"What did you mean when you said that you taught him?" she asked softly.

"Just that. He worked for the Agency. Now he's a renegade, a rogue out on his own," Dunn sipped the Scotch again. "My job is to put Victor Spalding out of business—permanently. He isn't a person anymore. He's a political embarrassment."

"What does *that* mean?"

"Some foreign officials suspect he still works for the United States, and there are Agency people bothered by what he knows and what he did before he deserted—and what he could tell the KGB or the Los Angeles *Times*."

He saw her brow furrow in concern.

"If you're keeping score, doctor, there are at least sixteen other governments doing the same kind of thing. Spare yourself the guilt trip."

His tone was hard and unpleasant. It was

as if he intended to offend her. She made up her mind that she would not be provoked.

"What about Alfred Makumba, Mr. Dunn?"

"I've got nothing against him, but I wasn't hired to protect your tribal brother. Nobody in Washington—or in Moscow or Peking—really gives a damn about Twanzi or any African country. Not a big damn anyway. It's what you might call a low-priority continent," he took a cigar from his shirt pocket.

"Mr. Barringer told me—"

"Don't believe anything Barringer says," Dunn interrupted impatiently. "He wanted something, so he told you half the truth. For him that's not bad."

"He *does* care about Makumba?"

He lit the Corona before he answered.

"Barringer cares *some*—more than most people. Hell, only six percent of the U.S. population ever *heard* of Twanzi. No more than one percent has any idea who Makumba is. Africa just isn't sexy."

"*Sexy?*"

"Come on, doc. Face the facts. When an epidemic or a famine kills one hundred forty thousand Africans, that's five inches on page ten in those papers that carry the story at all. Maybe ninety seconds on the TV news—generally on a Sunday night when they need filler."

He was right. He was also baiting her.

"*Is* somebody planning to kill Alfred Makumba?" she asked tensely.

"Barringer thinks so," Dunn answered, and puffed on the cigar.

"What do *you* think?"

"He's probably right. Saint Alfred has made himself a gang of powerful enemies. He's hardly got any friends at all."

"I'm his friend," she said.

"That's because you're an innocent, doc. This is a game of sharks—not whales. You still believe that the noble independent hero's going to win."

She nodded.

"That's why I'm here with *you*, Mr. Dunn."

"Well I'm here for money and to protect my life. I'm here for Charlie Dunn. That storybook stuff is a lot of crap. The age of romance is over, lady. The time of heroes is gone. Look around, will you?"

She looked directly at him with undisguised warmth.

"Commander Willoughby said you could be trusted to do *the right thing*. Was he wrong?"

"That's baby talk. Why don't you grow up, for Chrissakes? And stop being so goddamn nice. I'm not your friend. I don't want to be your friend. I couldn't be if I wanted to ... That's what I have to talk to you about."

He probably had very few friends, she concluded. He wasn't wearing a wedding ring either.

"I'm listening," she assured him.

"You could be bleeding," he said as he put the guns on an end table beside him. "You could be dead. You've got to do what I tell you as soon as I say it. You almost got killed by that car crashing into the garage because you hesitated. You say you trust me?"

"I do."

"Then follow my instructions—*immediately*.

We're playing cat and mouse with a professional hit man. There isn't a second to waste. Every move has to be planned—has to serve a specific purpose."

It was simultaneously a war of wits and a battle of nerves. Today's ambush confirmed that both the mole and Spalding had working relationships with Moscow. Dunn would amputate that connection. With the loss of four agents in a single day, KGB executives *had* to wonder whether it was worth risking exposure of their deep cover agent within the CIA to feed further information to the hired assassin.

"My plan is simple," Dunn told her. "I'm going to isolate Spalding—make him fight one on one. Then I'll take him."

"How will you find him?"

"That's the beauty of it. He'll find me!"

She recognized the look on his face. It was a hunter's smile.

"Think of this as a partnership, doctor," he reasoned. "Since this is my turf, remember I'm the *senior* partner."

"I wasn't raised to be the junior anything. Don't misunderstand me. I'm not giving you the liberated-woman speech."

"You don't have to, doctor. We both know who you are. You're a professional, like me. This deal happens to involve *my* profession— not yours. What do you say?"

She thought about Makumba and nodded.

"Okay?" he tested.

"Sure. There's one thing I'd like to ask you."

"Anything."

"When are we going to eat, Mr. Dunn? I'm *starving*."

Dunn reloaded his pistols with fresh clips while she washed up and combed her hair. He could not help noting that she looked splendid when she rejoined him. It was too bad that he couldn't allow himself to want this woman. Any sort of involvement would be dangerous. He certainly couldn't care about her. Any kind of commitment now would be impossible. The idea could only be a fantasy inspired by his many months of living alone. She was here for a charismatic president, not a ruthless mercenary.

The food in the hotel's snug Cavalier Room was excellent. Dunn watched as she downed half a dozen plump Colchester oysters. Then he suggested the Hyde Park's famed "mixed grille." It was a massive dish, but she ate it all with gusto. Between bites she answered his questions about the slaughter of the whales.

"One killed every twenty-five minutes—almost twenty thousand a year," she reported. "They hunt them with sonar and helicopters, destroy them with six-foot-long iron harpoons fired from a 90-millimeter cannon ... And there are substitutes available for everything they butcher them for. Six kinds of great whales are already 'commercially extinct' ... It's an outrage."

"Who are the bad guys?" Dunn asked as he speared a piece of pink lamb.

She told him that Japan, the Soviet Union, South Korea and Iceland were among the worst. It was half-past nine by the time they returned to the suite.

"We'd better get to bed soon," he announced barely ten minutes later. "We'll have to be up before six to make that early flight to Athens."

"Athens?"

"Trust me. Good night, doctor."

"Good night."

They walked to their separate bedrooms. She winced as she began to undress. When she was naked she saw why. There were large black-and-blue marks on her left thigh, hip, upper arm and shoulder, a result of being hurled over the car onto the cement floor. This was Charlie Dunn's work.

She looked at her body carefully, almost curiously. It was as if this full figure, these heavy breasts and cascading gold tresses belonged to someone else. Heather James had not eyed herself this way in a long time. Not *too* bad, she thought. Just a pound or two over her best weight. She filled the bathtub with very warm water, and settled in to luxuriate in the sensual experience. She closed her eyes and sighed.

Midnight. Dunn's eyes were wide open. Naked and wide awake, he lay in his bed—thinking. He was miles from sleep. There was so much to compute, so many possibilities to consider. There was Victor Spalding—out there somewhere. Free of either scruples or humanity, Spalding was busy scheming—or maybe killing at this moment. Now Dunn let himself think about Heather James, the whales and Alfred Makumba. They were all so vulnerable.

With an effort, he forced his attention back to the reality of Victor Spalding. Even fully awake, Dunn knew that Heather James was a dream.

When he heard the door click open, he reacted swiftly. He pulled out the twin pistols as he sat up—all in one motion. Silhouetted in the doorway with the light behind her, she was wearing a thin robe that concealed little. He stared and waited for several seconds before he lowered the guns.

"What is it?" he asked.

"*First*, I owe you an apology. You saved my life in that garage, and I never *really* thanked you. I'd like to do that now."

Dunn swallowed his desire and spoke.

"What's *second*, doctor?"

He tried to sound casual. She wasn't fooled. He saw her move, and the robe slithered to the carpet. Nude and sure, she began to walk towards him. This wasn't part of his plan. He could smell her perfume. She was only two yards away.

"Doctor," he began.

"You'd better call me Heather," she said. Then they made love for a long time before they fell asleep.

CHAPTER FOURTEEN

It was a very large room, well lit by over-head fluorescent tubes and cooled by an efficient system that maintained a constant temperature of sixty-eight degrees year round. There were no seasons in this place—no day or night either.

Everything was the same in this heavily guarded bunker all the time. At any hour of any day of any month, there were thirty-four carefully screened U.S. citizens manning the teletypes and other machines. The equipment in this underground chamber never rested—except when maintenance required. Even on Christmas Day, there were full crews of men and women at the machines inside and guards with automatic weapons at the single entrance.

The sound-absorbent material that covered the ceiling and walls reduced the noise of the machines to a bearable level, but the people who worked in this place spoke to each other only when necessary. They knew that was the official policy, and they were aware of the closed-circuit television cameras sweeping the room from hidden openings overhead.

This was the global communications center of the Central Intelligence Agency. Everything about it was TOP SECRET. Those who worked here under the Agency's massive Virginia headquarters did not tell anyone—not even their families. Each member of this signals staff was provided with a false story about a nonexistent job—such as electrical repair or switchboard servicing—and sworn to use it. They were also under orders not to mention the unit's code name outside the bunker.

Though one wall displayed large clocks showing the hour in Peking, Moscow, Cairo and four other capitals, time was merely a statistic in this chamber. When a teleprinter stuttered out a message, it was automatically marked with the day-hour-minute that it arrived. With Britain five hours ahead of Virginia, the report from London reached Langley at 4:20 P.M. eastern standard time.

Priority Green.

Standard procedures required that Priority Green messages be decoded within an hour and hand delivered promptly.

It was ten minutes after five when the messenger delivered the green envelope to Barringer's secretary. She signed the receipt, and immediately locked it in a drawer in her desk to await the deputy director's return from the working-group "D" meeting. He got back at 5:40; she handed it to him at once. He took it into his office, read it twice and called the Director of Central Intelligence.

When General Hartley studied the report at 6:05, his eyes narrowed in concern. It was a full ten seconds before he spoke.

"I thought he was only going to London to pick up his weapons," the director said-asked.

"So did I, sir."

"Full of surprises, isn't he?"

"Always was, general."

Hartley scanned the message form again before he eyed Barringer appraisingly.

"You think he planned this?"

"I'm sure of it, general."

"He *deliberately* staged a major shoot-out in the capital of a country with the toughest gun-control laws on earth?"

"He does *everything* deliberately, general."

"It'll be on the front page of every paper in Britain!"

"In Europe," Barringer corrected calmly, "and probably here too. Ought to make all the news broadcasts as well."

Now the Director of Central Intelligence stiffened.

"And that doesn't bother you?" he tested.

"No, sir. It did its job."

"*What* job?"

"Identifying the employers of our mole. Dunn has definitely established that it's the KGB, and he feels comfortable about that."

Barringer recognized the uncertainty in the DCI's face.

"Dunn *knows* how to deal with the KGB, sir. He *knows* how they *think* and how they *do* things," Barringer explained. Then he decided to spell out the rest of it.

"And, of course, he humiliated Spalding. That's part of his plan too, general. Round three clearly goes to Designated Hitter. This war is as much a battle of egos as of bullets. I *did* mention that, didn't I?"

"Twice. Well, maybe we should count our blessings. Our luck wasn't *all* bad," Hartley philosophized as he leaned back in the big leather swivel chair. "At least he didn't *kill* anybody—Wait a minute. Don't say it. He didn't *mean* to, right?"

Barringer nodded.

"Everything *deliberate*, general," he ratified. "He intended to wound them *seriously*, because he was sending a *serious* message."

"To Spalding?"

"To both Spalding and the KGB," Barringer answered. "He wants Spalding to know that he's on his way, and that nothing—not the mole or anyone or anything else—is going to stop him. The object is to intimidate Spalding, to frighten him into changing *his* plan—and making a mistake."

"Is he trying to scare the KGB too?" Hartley asked sarcastically.

"You could say that. It would be more precise to say he's *warning* them. He's announcing that he's hunting Victor Spalding, and inviting the KGB to get out of the way. He's asking them *nicely*."

"That's why he wounded and didn't kill?"

"Precisely. The choice is theirs, and they'd better make up their minds right away . . . That's as much as I've figured out so far," Barringer admitted.

"You think there's *more*?"

"There usually is with Dunn, general. Behind every number he does, there's *another* number. He's planning five moves ahead, and he never wastes a move."

Hartley glanced at the digital clock on his desk, and realized that he had to leave in ten minutes to attend the vice-president's cocktail party. Then he thought about the latest report from McGhee.

"Too bad Mr. Dunn can't help us find this damn mole," Hartley said. "Our Counterintelligence people could use some assistance."

"No progress at all?"

The black general shrugged.

"Nothing hard. McGhee's run a couple of computer scans—looking for everything and anything. He did one sweep on agent losses during the past five years. It looks as if our rate of 'breakage' started to inch up about three years ago."

"But the mole could be a sleeper," Barringer reasoned aloud. "Might have infiltrated years before that, lying low and doing nothing the least bit risky—maybe nothing at all."

The ebony face relaxed in a smile.

"Funny—that's what McGhee said too. He's looking for a pattern now, trying to see whether the mole has been working any special division or regional desk."

At that moment there was a knock on the door and Hartley's redheaded secretary entered to remind him that his car and driver would be out front in five minutes. He thanked her. A moment after she left the room, the

Director of Central Intelligence pointed a finger at the door through which she'd departed.

"Would you believe that McGhee's assistant—Philipps—put her through the poly yesterday? The executive secretary to the DCI taking a lie detector test?"

"My secretary gets hers Tuesday," Barringer replied.

Now Hartley rose to his feet and the two men started to walk towards the door.

"You know where Designated Hitter's going next?"

"No, general—and Victor Spalding doesn't either. Good night, sir."

At 6:25 Howard Barringer drove his car from the CIA parking lot and started on his way home. He had been followed every day and night since his confrontation with McGhee about the mole. This time the vehicle that trailed him was a green Chrysler with a mustachioed Latin male at the wheel.

The ride back to Chevy Chase was uneventful, and the evening that the Barringers spent as dinner guests of Admiral Craig of Naval Intelligence and his hard-drinking wife was simply necessary. It was shortly after Howard and Aline Barringer got home that a four-story apartment house on Pershing Road in Arlington caught fire. The flames spread very quickly—totally gutting three apartments.

According to the next morning's Northern Virginia *Sun*, the conflagration apparently began in or near apartment 2F occupied by the Philipps family. Joanne Philipps, a thirty-four-year-old computer programmer, died of smoke inhalation en route to Arlington Hospital. Her husband, Arthur, aged thirty-nine and a polygraph specialist for a federal agency, suffered extensive second- and third-degree burns. Doctors at the intensive-care unit described his condition as critical.

CHAPTER FIFTEEN

6:50 A.M. . . . Saturday . . . December 14.
It was thirty degrees below freezing, and
Moscow was covered with snow. Now more
was falling as the black Zis limousine turned
onto Dzerzhinsky Street—named after the first
head of the Soviet espionage and internal security service. Felix Dzerzhinsky's successors
had not been so honored, the burly officer in
the back seat of the big car recalled.

Menzhinsky had been poisoned in 1934.

Yagoda was executed in '38.

His heir, Yezhov, simply vanished a few
months later.

Then Beria took over until the bloody "re-
organization" of 1953. That year both Beria
and Merkulov were killed, and in '54 the huge
intelligence system was renamed the KGB.
General Semyon Temko had been a mere
leytenant in a frontier police until when the
Council of Ministers established the Komitet
Gosudarstvennoi Bezopastnosti—the Committee for State Security. Now he was in charge
of the KGB's American division, a powerful

man with a chauffeur-driven Zis and heavy responsibilities.

Still a bit surprised that he'd risen this far, Temko took his work seriously. Both a dedicated patriot and an effective technician, he worried a lot. At the moment he was troubled by the cryptic message he'd received over the car's radio-telephone eighteen minutes earlier.

Now he saw the nondescript Lubianka building and Detsky Mir—the popular Children's World—across the street. Some considered it ironic that Moscow's biggest toy store should face the KGB headquarters and special prison. To Temko—who had two grandchildren and a third due next month—it was a convenience. He wasn't thinking about gifts this frigid morning, nor were the uniformed sentries who recognized the approaching limousine as a VIP vehicle. They snapped to rigid attention.

The cold made Temko wince as he stepped from the heated car. Eight days ago he'd been perspiring in tropical Havana, and now he was back to the fierce reality of a Moscow winter. He shuddered, felt a twinge of sympathy for the half-frozen sentries and hurried into the headquarters building. He entered his office exactly at 7:00 A.M.—as usual.

"How bad is it, colonel?" Temko asked as he took off his greatcoat.

"Not *that* bad," his bespectacled deputy replied. Then he reported what had happened in London.

"Not that bad *yet*," Temko corrected, and sat down behind the elaborately carved desk that had once served a czarist admiral.

"What do you mean, general?"

"It was an ambush. Dunn was expecting them, and that means he knows we've penetrated Langley. The whole Ikarus operation is threatened."

Temko looked at his watch, then at the door. Where was the tea? Did that damn woman spend *all* her time in the lavatory? At that moment Sergeant Olga Neskin entered with the tray and an apologetic explanation that Temko ignored.

"Do you play poker, colonel?" Temko asked when she'd gone.

Polchasny shook his head.

"You might study it," the general suggested. "You'd understand American thinking better. In this poker game Mr. Dunn has just increased the stakes. The Americans would say *raised the ante.*"

"I don't quite understand."

"He's warning us we shouldn't risk our most valuable deep-cover agent—Ikarus—to protect a hired foreign assassin. He's trying to make the price of helping Spalding prohibitive," Temko sipped his tea.

"*He's* telling us how to run *our* business?" Polchasny erupted indignantly.

"He knows a lot about *our* business," Temko answered soberly. "You ought to read his file. *No*, don't bother. There's little in it you could apply to others. He's an *exotic*. Let's get back to Ikarus."

"Yes, general?"

"Priority signal to our *rezident* in Washington. Ikarus may be in acute danger. Must be protected at all costs. Ikarus is to pass on only most important information or even suspend contact temporarily if safety requires . . . Send that at once."

Polchasny left the office. When he returned a few minutes later, he found Temko looking out at the falling snow. He appeared to be deep in thought.

"It's being coded now, general."

Temko did not turn. He merely nodded.

"General?"

"Yes?"

"What did you mean by *exotic*?"

Now Temko slowly rotated the big chair to face him.

"Charles Dunn is extremely independent," he told his deputy. "He doesn't work smoothly in a large organization. You might say he's really in business for himself."

"A petty bourgeois mentality, general?"

"That's not quite right. There's nothing petty about this Dunn—and nothing predictable either. He has no standard procedures. Never does anything the same way twice. He's also both bold and clever. That's a *rare* combination, Polchasny," Temko pointed out.

"But he can't be much of a shot," the deputy reasoned. "Our agents in London—"

"Were spared for a purpose," the general broke in impatiently. "A *Dunn* purpose—something complex and devious. As for the shooting, he's one of the best anywhere—with either hand—and the guns of either side. And bows and arrows, knives, grenades, rockets—he's a weapons expert."

"At least he doesn't know about Spalding's primary target." Polchasny consoled.

Temko shrugged.

"He *can't* know," Polchasny insisted.

"Where's Spalding now?"

"Stockholm, I think—about to earn his money."

"He'd better move fast."

"You think Dunn's on his way there?"

"He will be," Temko predicted flatly. "He now knows that Spalding's linked to us, and the one man on that CIA target list we obviously care about is the Swede. Charles Dunn will eat his dinner in Stockholm tonight."

"Then we'd better alert our people there."

"To do what?" Temko asked.

"To cover flights from London arriving at Arlanda."

The general shook his head gloomily.

"You don't believe me, do you?" he said. "Arlanda's the airport where European flights to Stockholm come in. I know it and you know it, and Dunn is well aware that we know it. I have no idea how he'll get to Stockholm, but he won't fly into Arlanda."

"But General—"

It was depressing. Polchasny was worrying about how Dunn would reach Stockholm, Temko brooded, and Dunn was probably already planning how he'd leave.

"Very well, colonel. Do what you want."

Three hours later, teams of KGB operatives moved into position to start surveillance at both of Stockholm's airports. The shifts changed every six hours to reduce the risk that the watchers would be noticed. Warned that Dunn might try some trick, they covered inbound flights from Paris, Amsterdam, Copenhagen and Oslo as well as those from Britain.

All day.

And all the next day.

They studied every inbound passenger including portly nuns, African exchange students and twisted old men in wheelchairs.

It was entirely in vain.

No one who could possibly be Charles Dunn—not even in the most masterful disguise—arrived at either Arlanda or Bromma airports.

CHAPTER SIXTEEN

It was a chilly gray morning in London, but Heather James smiled throughout the taxi ride from the hotel to the airport. She had found a new lover—strong and sharing and very different from any man she'd ever known. Of course, there was a great deal about him that she didn't know. That would take a while.

Right now, every inch of every part of her felt *good*. She knew that she looked wonderful. She didn't have to study her reflection in the glass barrier—but she did. Her eyes glistened and her skin glowed, and her face was suffused with that soft primeval radiance of utter contentment. It was total physical fulfillment—and something more. She reached over to take Dunn's hand. He squeezed hers affectionately for several seconds. Then he stiffened and withdrew his grasp.

"Sorry," he said a moment later.

She understood. Some survival instinct made him want to keep both hands free. She had seen the twin 9-millimeter pistols. From what he'd told her about Spalding, every second might count. Until the threat of Victor Spalding was gone, she might never hold her lover's hand for more than a few moments.

Suddenly she found herself hating Spalding intensely. She could not remember feeling this bitter toward anyone in years. It wasn't just the fact that the assassin meant to kill Charlie Dunn. That seemed remote and unbelievable— an abstract concept. But the thought that Spalding could deny her the simple pleasure of holding her lover's hand filled her with fury. Dunn recognized the anger in her eyes.

"What's the matter?" he asked.

"I hate him."

"Who's *him*?"

"The man who wants to kill you. I really hate him, Charlie."

Dunn's fingers brushed her warm cheek gently.

"You don't hate anybody, Heather."

"Nobody but him. Do you hate him, Charlie?"

Dunn thought about the question carefully.

"No. I despise him, but I don't hate him. You shouldn't hate him either. If it wasn't for him, we'd never have met."

She smiled up at Dunn confidently.

"We'd have met, Charlie. Had to be. It's like something out of a schoolgirl's dream. A tall handsome stranger saves your life, buys you a great meal and makes marvelous love. It's *terrific*, Charlie."

"I'm not exactly a poet," he remarked.

"That's for me to judge," she said, and rested her head on his shoulder. They rode on in silence for nearly a minute. She could almost hear him thinking.

"It may not stay so terrific," he told her.

"You mean when we meet Spalding?"

"Maybe *we* shouldn't. Maybe you should go home now."

"Impossible. If I did, you'd never get to Makumba." She snuggled cozily into the hollow of his neck and shoulder, and he felt the silken softness of her fine golden hair.

"I've never worked with anyone else, Heather."

"And I never thought I'd go to bed with a man who carried two guns. *That* wasn't part of the dream, Charlie. But it'll be all right. As I showed you back at the garage, I'm not *quite* a schoolgirl. We can protect each other."

He wondered whether she'd feel so confident if she knew about his decision. No, this wasn't the time to tell her. He hadn't even mentioned it to Barringer. Once more Dunn considered whether she might be working for Barringer, whether her identity and history were fictions created for a CIA cover story. His instincts said that it wasn't so. He'd always trusted his instincts—but could he still be sure?

There were rules that governed, he remembered.

He'd lived by them for years.

She had no "need to know," so why take a chance?

"You're a terrific person yourself," he announced.

She recognized the male guilt and smiled again.

"Don't worry, Charlie. I'm not in love with you."

Her voice was firm and assured, but even as

she spoke she sensed the reservation deep within her. Whatever her mouth said, her heart wasn't nearly that sure. But it would be immature to confuse her reactions to yesterday's danger and last night's extraordinary physical experience with *love*.

Traffic was flowing smoothly on the multi-lane highway to London Airport, and they disembarked from the taxi a few minutes before eleven. It was starting to drizzle.

"I can hardly wait to get to Athens," she told him as they entered the vast high-ceilinged terminal. When he led her directly to the Scandinavian Airlines System counter, she realized that she'd have to.

"Change of plans, Charlie?"

"Weather's not that great in Athens in December anyway," he replied obliquely. She didn't ask any more questions. He appreciated that.

At noon they boarded SAS Flight 552. One hour and fifty-five minutes later the DC-9 jet touched down at the visibly new Landvetter Airport outside Goteborg, Sweden's major port and home base for the Volvo auto and Hasselblad camera firms. The temperature was fourteen degrees below freezing. Snow covered the low hills on both sides of Highway 40 as the taxi took them into the seventeenth-century city.

They reached the railroad station just in time to catch the 3:25 P.M. train heading eastward. During the first half of the four-hour journey through the dim and dismal afternoon, Heather James spoke of her years with the Noro in the jungles of Twanzi. She talked about Alfred Makumba and her other "brothers" now high in the young nation's government. She recalled the hunters and the herdsmen, the customs and the seasons.

"It's *summer* in Twanzi now," she reported accusingly as the trail clattered across the snow-covered Swedish countryside.

"And it still will be when we get there."

She sighed. She wanted very much to know what they were doing here instead of Athens or Africa, but she had made up her mind not to ask such questions. Dunn was the sort of man who would tell her only when he thought it was necessary—and then only the minimum. She knew very little about Dunn, but she knew that much. Suddenly it wasn't enough.

"Have you any children?" she asked abruptly.

"You mean *am I married*?"

There was an edge to his voice.

"I don't intend to pry—"

"I was married for three years," he interrupted. "No children."

"If you'd rather not discuss this, Charlie—"

"There's nothing to discuss anymore. Somebody killed her with a bomb. It was a mistake. They meant to get me."

"Oh, my God! I'm sorry, Charlie. I had no idea."

He nodded twice before he spoke again.

"That was fourteen years ago—fourteen next month," he said slowly. "Her name was Anna."

"I feel terrible, Charlie. I'm *really* sorry," she apologized.

He reached out to touch her cheek.

"No, I shouldn't have told you. It all happened such a long time ago, anyway," he said.

He saw the whole scene in his mind's eye a split second later. He looked at Heather James, but he saw only the burning shattered car and the bloody ruined corpse in the street beside it. It was very clear and bright and real. Then he blinked and it was gone.

"Probably be more useful to talk about Stockholm," he proposed. "City's about seven hundred years old. A big chunk of it consists of islands with lots of canals, bridges and parks. Pretty in the summer, but lousy this time of year. Should be freezing or colder all month," Dunn predicted, "and another foot of snow. The hotels are fine, and they've got seven McDonald's for fast-food freaks."

"You're joking?" she tested.

"No. Plenty of regular restaurants with excellent fish and seafood—and the beer's good. They're proud of their aquavit, but I prefer the yellow Norwegian Linie brand myself. Loads of hard drinkers, beautiful glass and ceramics and an intensely pious government that hasn't trusted the U.S. since the Vietnam war."

He noticed that she flinched.

"I see you're not so trusting either," he noted in a voice devoid of judgment. "It isn't relevant to us anyway. All you want is to keep Makumba alive, and I feel the same about Charles J. Dunn."

Then he took from inside his jacket a small photo and showed it to her.

"*He* may help. Maybe not voluntarily, but in his own way he could make a genuine contribution," Dunn told her wryly.

She looked at the head of the graying man

in the picture. He appeared to be in his late fifties. He had sharp features, and eyes filled with authority.

"His name's Morelius. Colonel in the Swedish Army till seven months ago," Dunn said.

"What does he do now?"

"Hides—because he's a walking target. Spalding's next target, if I'm right. I won't bore you with the details, but the good colonel made fools of some people who have no sense of humor at all. You've met them."

"In that garage in London?"

"Same crowd," Dunn confirmed. "I'd bet that Barringer never mentioned Stockholm, did he?"

She shook her head.

"Didn't want to worry you," he said. "Nothing to worry about. All I've got to do is find one man who's hiding somewhere in a city of about a million and a half people *before* Victor Spalding and the various espionage services of the USSR and all its allies."

"Don't you know where he is?"

"No, and if I asked the Swedes they wouldn't tell me. These noble neutrals aren't going to collaborate with the brutal CIA on anything."

"Shouldn't you warn the Swedes about Spalding?"

"I'm not sure he's here," Dunn replied, "and they'd be highly indignant about my meddling in their internal affairs."

"But Morelius could be murdered!"

"That's not the issue for anyone—except Morelius. The Sovs are only using him to make a point. The U.S. has no interest in what happens to him."

"What about you, Charlie?"

"I'm not responsible for protecting him. That's his government's job, and they're probably getting bored with it after seven months."

"Won't you do *anything*?" she appealed.

"Hell, I'm going to do just about *everything*. I'm going to find him . . . and I'm going to watch him . . . and I'm going to take care of Spalding when he shows up to hit him."

Maybe she had a right to know. Since she'd saved his life in London, it was unlikely that she served the Sovs and it didn't matter if she worked for Barringer.

"That's when it will be dangerous," he warned.

"You mean that you'll have to—" she began, and stopped in mid-sentence. It was difficult to say the word, to face the reality that her lover would *kill*.

"Commander Willoughby told me you'd do the right thing, Charlie. I believe him."

Dunn leaned forward as he told her.

"I'm not going to kill Victor Spalding. I'm not going to kill *anybody*."

Her eyes widened in astonishment.

"I had a long time to think about it in Vermont. Sitting alone in that little house—shaking and remembering, I made up my mind that I'd never kill again."

"Oh, Charlie!"

"Problem is," he continued with an odd smile, "that Victor will—in a flash. It's like a reflex to him. That's why I want you to go home."

She shook her head.

"Barringer didn't know this when he recruited you, hon. I never told him. He'd think I was crazy."

Her eyes were glowing with emotion.

"You'd *be* crazy if you thought I'd leave you now," she declared firmly.

"You don't understand. I have no backup on this. I'm out here alone and naked."

"You look good naked, Charlie—and you're certainly not alone. You've got a Noro spear chucker as a bodyguard."

Then she leaned forward and kissed him hard.

"What's that for?" he asked.

"That's for not killing anybody."

She kissed him again. He held her close for half a minute before he moved away.

"We're both wonderful—but don't go making me into some hero," he said. "I'm not a hero—never was. There's no such thing."

"You can be the first, Charlie."

He put the photo back into his pocket and clutched her shoulders.

"I like you, Heather. I like you a lot. It's going to get much uglier—and bloodier—from here on. Please go home."

"I can't leave you, Charlie. Don't laugh."

"I'm not laughing."

There wasn't anything more to say, and Dunn had a great deal of thinking to do. He'd read the Stockholm package—the CIA research report on Morelius—six times. Now he went over it in his mind again—and then again. At 7:15 P.M. they saw the lights of Stockholm ahead. Ten minutes later the train glided to a halt in the city's main rail terminal.

If Stockholm was celebrated for modern

design, this old stone building wasn't representative. It was something out of the pre-World War II era, drab and high roofed and devoid of even the grace of that period. Neither the central station nor those using it at this hour—mostly young people and swarthy foreign workers—had the elegance or glamor of the international airports Dunn had shunned. He paused only long enough to buy a copy of the *International Tribune*.

"That's it," he announced as they stepped from the building. Directly across the busy Vasagatan—less than one hundred yards away—was the Hotel Terminus with no pretentious architecture and 116 smallish but comfortable rooms. It was the kind of establishment favored by visiting engineers and Japanese delegates to antipollution conferences.

As soon as Dunn and James—Mr. and Mrs. William L. Frost of Toronto, according to their Canadian passports—were alone in room 502, he immediately turned his attention to the newspaper. The story of the London shoot-out was on page one. He scanned that swiftly before he found the classified ads. He read them much more carefully. There was no coded message from Barringer.

"We can hang up our clothes later," he said.

"Later than what?"

He took her in his arms, and they kissed. He stroked that long blonde hair and caressed her back, drawing her tight. He felt her body moving against his. Then she stepped back and smiled.

"A lot later," she announced as she began to unbutton her blouse.

At 8:40 they agreed to get up. He rose first. Sprawled luxuriously in curves of contentment, she studied Dunn as he reached for his suitcase.

"You look *very good* naked, Charlie," she told him, "and you feel good too."

"So do you. Get dressed."

She wriggled her hips provocatively.

"*Definitely*," he approved, "but not now. Move your tail, lady."

She rotated her midsection again, grinned and sat up slowly. They hung up their clothes, washed and dressed in time to leave the hotel by nine o'clock. The night was cold and raw, and the traffic was heavy. Dunn guided her through the flow of cars back across to the line of taxis in front of the rail station. Heather James shuddered and drew her coat closer as Dunn opened the door of the cab.

"Diana—Two Brunnsgrand," Dunn told the driver.

"You have women everywhere, Charlie," the blonde veterinarian joked.

"You'll like her."

Dunn was right. Diana was an excellent restaurant in the seventeenth-century house at Two Brunnsgrand, a short and narrow street in Gamla Sta'n. This was Stockholm's famed Old Town, simultaneously medieval and alive with small shops selling modern crafts. Like New York's Greenwich Village, it was home to successful writers and painters and, increasingly, advertising executives. Historic and fashionable, Gamla Sta'n had been a chic high-rent district for years.

Filled with fine food and drink, they left Diana at half-past ten. There was no sign of a taxi or any other kind of car. A light mist filled the cold empty street.

"Let's take a walk," Dunn said. He turned right before she could answer. They walked a block up to Old Town's main street—twisting Osterlanggatan. It was far from deserted. There were restaurants and cafés open on every block. Dunn spoke about the birth of Old Town, but something in his eyes said that he had contemporary events on his mind. He studied certain buildings, street intersections and alleys with undisguised intensity.

"You're a great guide, Charlie," she complimented, "but I have this funny feeling that our stroll through history has something to do with a certain colonel."

"Trust your feelings," Dunn advised.

"He's here?"

"Someone who might know where he's holed up is—a woman I mean to talk to. Don't scowl. My interest in her is purely *professional*."

"You *sure*?" Heather James tested.

"Of course. She's living with her psychiatrist. This is a very *progressive* country. Ah, there's the royal castle."

It was a grand and stately building, a massive square block structure constructed in the Italian Baroque architecture of the late seventeenth century. Dunn tried to remember whether it had 500 or 600 hundred rooms. He couldn't.

"This woman, Charlie?" Heather James began.

"What about her?"

"Will she tell you?"

Dunn thought about it as they started to walk left across the street from the palace.

"Her name is Kerstin," he announced as they headed towards the canal. "She's twenty-four years old, and she has no reason in the world to trust me. I'm not only a stranger but I'm a foreigner—an American. Why the hell should she believe an American?"

"You got a plan, Charlie?"

"Two," he assured, and squeezed her arm. They walked past the sentries on duty at the front of the palace, and started across the bridge. They could see the flames of the big gas torches that framed the entrance to the Grand Hotel 200 yards away. It was probably the city's most elegant hotel, and there were always taxis there.

It was the kind of place where Victor Spalding might stay Dunn brooded as they approached the line of cabs a minute later. The bastard might be in there right now, he thought.

Dunn was wrong. Spalding was four blocks away.

CHAPTER SEVENTEEN

Victor Spalding was in very good spirits as he strode north through the night towards the Chat Noir—Stockholm's most expensive "sex nightclub." The evening had gone well thus far. He had again walked every step of the escape route that he'd use, and he'd scouted the entire neighborhood for any sign of a surveillance team. Half an hour ago, he'd picked up the tape from the recorder attached to Kerstin Morelius's telephone line. Everything was fine. The rendezvous was on.

Now he looked forward to the erotic diversions of the celebrated Chat Noir. He probably wouldn't stay through all forty-five acts of "high class artists from all over the world in a luxury atmosphere." Even though the fleshy young women and men here were both attractive and assorted and their coupling showed a certain imagination, six hours of watching nonstop sex was too much.

The clever men who produced this carnal extravaganza tried to enliven the proceedings with bits of humor, but Spalding didn't find them funny. Some visiting German businessmen and officers off a Brazilian freighter laughed a lot more than he did. Still, Spalding enjoyed three or four of the lesbian routines and the heterosexual oral-sex demonstrations weren't bad at all. And the costumes were first-rate. The Chat Noir didn't stint on that sort of thing.

The assassin spent eighty minutes and forty-nine dollars in the smoky nightclub before he began to be bored. It was nearly midnight when he made his way out onto Dobelnsgatan. The cold fresh air cleared his head. He paused for a moment to recall the ample hips on the Turkish woman who'd made love to herself so artfully, and then he set off for his hotel.

"Harry! Dear Harry!"

Aware that he'd played the role of an Australian named Harry Meadmore on his previous visit to Sweden, Spalding tried to remember that female voice as he turned.

"It's Greta!" the slim blonde in the doorway reminded. "The show get you hot?"

Greta Blom and her twin sister were the sixteen-year-old prostitutes whose services he'd purchased when last in Stockholm. They were also two people whom he did not want to see. They could remember his presence in the city, and they could talk. For a few lines of cocaine or a shot of heroin, they'd tell anybody anything.

What were they doing in this neighborhood?

"Sure did," Spalding answered as he decided what he should do.

"I can fix that, *remember*?" the streetwalker smirked. "Lucky for you Ulla and I moved over this way last week. Damn police were bothering us so we found a new place—just a block from here. You'll love it."

Spalding hesitated.

"Come on, Harry. I know what you like. Let little Greta cool you off, and when Ulla gets back, the three of us can do things together. Any way you want, Harry."

Spalding smiled in anticipation and nodded. Then he turned up his coat collar and adjusted his cashmere scarf to shield the lower part of his face.

It was amusing how embarrassed foreign businessmen were about being seen with young prostitutes, she thought. So many of them were still ashamed, still weighed down with obsolete guilts about a perfectly natural transaction. They needed reassurance. She knew just how to handle them. Chattering about how glad she was to see him, she took his arm and guided him some 110 yards to the old building in which she lived.

Her apartment was on the second floor at the rear. As she unlocked the door, she hummed some melody that he couldn't identify. It was the prospect of a large tip that cheered her. The man whom she knew as Harry Meadmore demanded a lot, but he never bickered about price and was always generous after they'd satisfied his special needs. With any luck, the sisters might get seventy or eighty dollars from him.

Recalling what he had liked, she undressed slowly. She took several minutes to disrobe completely, giving him plenty of time to appreciate each step. She rubbed her breasts and stroked her thighs. Then she strutted and posed provocatively, making cooing noises to simulate sexual arousal.

"Want to tie me up now?" she asked, and licked her lips.

His response was another broad grin. She took the ropes from the bed-table drawer, and pretended to be frightened as he bound her wrists and ankles. He removed his jacket and rolled up his sleeves neatly. Now he'd take off his belt and hit her.

But he didn't. Not this time.

She was surprised when he suddenly said that he had to go to the bathroom for a moment. Then she was puzzled to hear water running for what seemed a long time. What the hell was he up to in there? Why was he returning to the bedroom with her blue washcloth in his hand?

"Harry?"

She couldn't say any more before he crammed the cloth into her mouth. She was choking. She gagged and shuddered. Her body arched in frantic spasms, but he held her firmly. She couldn't spit out the terrible cloth, and she couldn't break free. Thrashing in panic, she made desperate muffled sounds of appeal.

He ignored them.

He picked her nude and bound body up easily. He was extremely strong, and totally indifferent to her fear and suffering. No, he enjoyed it. She jerked and writhed, twisted her head and kicked out, to no avail as he carried her towards the bathroom.

Now she heard the running water more clearly. An awful thought jolted her like a massive electric shock. Suddenly Greta could taste the coppery bile of terror in her mouth.

No! She tried to scream out in protest. She told herself this was merely another of his sick games—that he was just trying to frighten her. But her body knew better. It was jackknifing like a hooked fish trying to tear loose. Sheer hysteria and mindless survival instinct ruled her completely.

"Be quiet, Greta," he ordered like an annoyed parent.

She squeezed out another shuddering moan before he pushed her face into the lukewarm water that covered the bottom of the tub. It was seven inches deep. Gagging on the cloth, she struggled and fought and sobbed silently. He kept her face submerged with one hand while his other probed her flanks.

"Make bubbles, Greta," he said cheerfully.

He was enjoying her agony. Now she was breathing in the water, coughing and choking and blind with terror. Sour vomit was surging up in her throat. She knew that she was doomed.

Then he raised her face from the water and pulled her half upright by her hair.

"Don't cry, Greta. There's nothing personal in this, you understand. *Understand?*"

Nauseous, glassy eyed and barely conscious, she somehow managed to force herself to nod in reply. She was alive. He'd stopped in time, and that was all that mattered.

"*Fine,*" he said and patted her head. "*Goodbye,* Greta."

The words struck her like a club. Her dazed eyes widened again in shock as he reached forward. She barely resisted as Spalding pushed her face back into the water. She couldn't fight any longer. Her physical and emotional reserves were exhausted.

The bubbles rose again—briefly.

Her body twitched two or three times.

Then it was over.

Spalding turned off the taps. He looked down at the corpse in the tub and noticed the yellow stain in the water. She'd lost control of her kidneys in her dying spasm.

"Disgusting," he said, and dried his hands with a towel. Next he used it to rub his fingerprints from the hot and cold taps. When he was done, he refolded it neatly and hung it back on the wooden bar. Returning to the bedroom, he rolled down his sleeves and buttoned the cuffs. He donned his jacket and started toward the hook on which his overcoat hung.

He paused as he reached a wall mirror, saw that his hair was disheveled and carefully combed it. Then he heard the key in the front door.

It had to be the sister.

Was she alone, or was she returning with a customer?

He loosened the .22-caliber gun in his shoulder holster and waited.

"Greta? You home? I scored some good stuff," Ulla Blom called out loudly.

She was alone.

It would be easy.

Spalding stepped into view. She recognized him as the Australian who paid so well for triangular sex games, but couldn't dredge up his name. She'd have to fake it.

"Nice to see you, luv. In town for some fun?"

"That's it," he answered.

Greta must have met him in the street, she guessed. They'd probably been to bed already. His face had a soft satisfied look.

"You two didn't wait for me?" she accused playfully.

"Afraid I couldn't."

She chuckled in knowing reply. She wondered whether she might sell him some of the cocaine she'd just bought—at twice the price she'd paid.

"Where's Greta?" she thought aloud.

He winked and pointed an index finger at the bedroom. She started towards the door, with Spalding just a step behind her. He decided that the scalpel would be a mistake. That weapon was his trademark. He had no wish to leave his calling card here.

"Ulla?" he said.

She stopped. Before she could turn, he broke her neck with a single savage karate chop. Ulla Blom was dead before her body hit the floor. He rolled the corpse over with his shoe, crouched down to test for a pulse and grunted when he found none. Her eyes were wide open, shiny with surprise.

"Good-bye Ulla," he whispered.

Then Spalding put on his overcoat and departed, taking care to leave no fingerprints on the doorknobs. He walked briskly through the icy night, spurred by the exciting awareness that Morelius would soon be even colder—in a refrigerated drawer in the morgue. In eighteen hours, the colonel would be as dead as those two stupid whores.

And then another $200,000. His heart beat more rapidly as he anticipated his victory. It was the thought of beating them all again that was most exhilarating.

Nobody could stop Victor Spalding. They were all fools—even the men who needed his expert and expensive services. He needed no one. He lived nowhere. He had no loved ones or ties of any kind that might make him vulnerable. He even changed his Swiss bank account twice a year. With a dozen passports and nearly $2 million to buy more, he could go anywhere and purchase any pleasure that he desired.

Dunn was probably on his way to Stockholm. Let him come. *Garbage?* What a clumsy effort! In a few weeks everyone would see—the *world* would see—who was garbage and who was the greatest assassin of the century. His next hit might even start a war, Spalding thought proudly as he reached his hotel.

A war?

That would really be *something*.

He was still smiling ten minutes later when he turned off the light in his room and closed his eyes. For a few seconds he let himself recall the sex show at the Chat Noir. Then he yawned and slid off immediately into eight solid hours of utterly restful sleep—just as he always did the night before or after he killed. It was actually quite logical that he feel so relaxed. After all, killing was what Victor Spalding did best.

CHAPTER EIGHTEEN

9:10 A.M. . . . Sunday . . . December 15.

Turning his glance from the big photos of nineteenth-century Stockholm that adorned the Hotel Terminus dining room, Dunn eyed the breakfast that Heather James had assembled from the buffet. Eight pieces of red salami, a mound of yellow cheese slices, a hardboiled egg, butter, jam and two kinds of Swedish flatbread covered her plate completely.

"You always eat this much?" he asked as she drained a glass of orange juice.

"Only when I feel good, Charlie," she replied. Then she took three cubes from the sugar bowl and dropped them into his black coffee.

"You've got a good memory," he complimented.

"I've been studying you, Charlie," she confided with a grin.

Her eyes glowed when he leaned forward to put two sugar cubes into her cup. He'd been paying attention to her too.

"Eat up," he urged abruptly. "We go back to war in about twelve minutes, and we're way behind. Victor's had weeks to find the

158

colonel and refine his plan down to the last detail. We've got a serious time problem. Hell, he could be hitting Morelius *right now*."

Between bites, Dunn told her more about Morelius and his daughter and the psychiatrist-lover with whom she'd lived for three years. The colonel's wife had died in a skiing accident when Kerstin Morelius was fourteen. With her father busy as a general staff officer and also coach of the army's famed riding team, she grew up alone—and fast. A series of highly sexed men in their forties helped.

"Father figures, Charlie?"

"Maybe. The doctor she's living with now is very active in the pacifist movement. Think she's punishing daddy for not being around?"

"It would be right out of the textbooks."

Dunn nodded. He'd read hundreds of books during the two years of his breakdown. He could do little else. The ancient Greek plays had been best. They said it all about fathers and children. Dunn found himself thinking about his own father, the quiet master carpenter who loved wood so much. He'd like a woman like Heather James.

It was too soon to speak of fathers, Dunn decided. The blonde veterinarian was a decent and attractive woman, but it could well be the danger and strange glamour of this exotic life-and-death world that drew her to Dunn's arms. Or maybe it was gratitude for saving her life. He looked at his watch.

"Are we late, Charlie?"

"Won't know till we get there. You finished?"

"Sure."

They left the hotel. As they walked through

the nearly deserted streets of this commercial part of the city, she got her first daylight view of the waterways and bridges that gave the Swedish capital its special maritime quality. They were halfway across the Norrbro span when she realized where they were going.

"Back to the Old Town?" she asked.

"Right. There's something I want to check at Kerstin Morelius's house."

"So you think she may help?"

"One way or another," he replied and she wondered what he meant.

"Maybe she's not home, Charlie."

"It doesn't matter. The only thing that counts is the plan. Not *my* plan—Victor's plan—if he's here."

Now she saw the sentries in front of the royal palace fifty yards ahead.

"You're trying to figure out Spalding's plan?"

"There's no other way to stop him. I trained him. I know his methods and his thinking. For this kind of operation, there are certain basic tactics for the first phase—and then there are options."

"Options?"

"Where to kill Morelius, how to do it and then how to get away. Technical stuff . . . wouldn't interest you," Dunn said, and pulled a polyester scarf from his coat pocket.

"Blue okay? I've got a tan one too," he announced.

"What are you talking about, Charlie?"

"Odds are that Victor knows about you and that great blonde hair, doc. Scarf might make you a little harder to spot."

"Or shoot?" she asked.

"That's it."

"Blue's fine," Heather James announced and covered her head.

"You can wear the tan one tomorrow," Dunn suggested. "Routine tactic to change your appearance."

"How many scarves have you got, Charlie?"

"Four. You mind?"

She smiled and squeezed his arm for a moment.

"I think you're very smart," she said. "How long have you been carrying these scarves?"

"Two days before we left Washington. Listen, this whole bit could be for nothing. Victor may not be in Sweden at all."

They walked on into the Old Town. There were few people in the narrow winding streets this Sunday morning. Even Osterlanggatan was almost empty. Dunn stopped several times to study shop windows. Twice he turned back to reexamine a restaurant menu and an alley. Since he continued the casual conversation seamlessly, it was several minutes before she realized that he was checking for possible followers.

"Anybody back there, Charlie?"

"Who knows?" he replied noncommittally. Then they turned down a narrow street and walked some eighty yards to a gray stone apartment house that was six stories high.

"That's it," Dunn announced.

"She lives there?"

He shook his head.

"Two buldings down. We can't just walk into her house," Dunn explained. "Victor could be watching. Or somebody else. Let's have a look."

When they reached the roof, he spelled it out simply. Take the high ground—basic military principle. This was the high ground—the tallest building on the block. If Spalding was watching, he'd probably be up here.

"Probably?"

"I'm playing the odds. Only thing I can do when he's so far ahead of us. I'm doing what he's likely to do in phase one—the recon phase."

He paced the roof slowly and carefully. Whatever he was looking for, he didn't find it.

"Doesn't matter," Dunn said as they started down. "He doesn't usually leave evidence anyway. I taught him *that*."

They descended to the street, made their way to the house where Dr. Ulf Holberg and Kerstin Morelius lived and scanned the street and buildings in both directions. Then they entered the small lobby of the five-story apartment house where the colonel's daughter made her home.

"Good," Dunn approved. He'd feared one of those damned electronic combination locks that opened only when the right sequence of numbered buttons was pushed. Such protective devices were popular in this high-rent district, but there was only a conventional key lock here. Three tries with his credit card did the trick, and he hurried her into the tiny lobby.

"She's in four-A," Dunn announced as he opened the elevator door.

"Are we just going to walk in on her, Charlie?"

"Certainly not."

He closed the door and pressed a button.

Not four.

Five.

They got out at the top floor. Dunn eyed the apartment doors, and studied the carpeted staircase leading down. Then he raised an index finger to his mouth to request silence. This was no time for questions. He looked around warily, and pointed to another door. The American Express Card prevailed once more.

Ten steps up . . . they were on the roof. Now he walked across every foot of the roof, sometimes studying adjacent buildings and often pausing to examine the roof itself. She wondered what he was looking for, but she didn't ask.

He led her back to the door and stopped. Dunn crouched to peer at the lock intently. He opened the door, rotated the knob several times and ran a finger over the cylinder and bolt. He touched the tip of his finger to his tongue, and something flickered in his eyes.

He'd found something. What? Dunn saw the question in her face, shook his head and led her back into the building. Now they took the elevator to the basement. Several minutes of cautious searching brought them to a locked metal door. It did not yield to his credit card. His lips formed a silent one-word oath.

Dunn reached inside his jacket, took out a fountain pen and unscrewed the cap. It wasn't a pen at all. It was a professional burglar's tool—a thin metal lockpick. Dunn smiled at her surprise, slid the probe into the cylinder and maneuvered it carefully. Four times.

Click.

It was done. He swung open the door with his left hand. One of the 9-millimeter pistols was in his right. It was dark beyond the threshold. He listened for several seconds, slid his left hand around the door frame and found the light switch. If Spalding was waiting in the blackness, he'd open fire as Dunn entered.

Dunn flicked on the light, dropped into a shooter's crouch and swung around into the room. It was a small chamber, lined with cables and fuse boxes and electrical panels. Dunn swiveled the gun in a wide arc swiftly. There was no one in the room.

"It's okay. He's not here," Dunn announced.

She entered the room cautiously, still uneasy.

Dunn pointed the gun at a black metal box on the floor. Wires from it were clamped to one of the cables whose protective sheath had been cut open neatly.

"Just the way I taught him," Dunn said.

"What is it, Charlie?"

"Tape recorder—voice activated. Hooked to a tap on somebody's phone line."

"Kerstin Morelius?"

"You can bet on it," Dunn replied grimly. "He's playing it right from the book. Came in over the roof. Oiled the lock up there so he can get in or out fast. Then the tap and the recorder. He drops by every day or so to find out whether daddy's called."

"So that's why you wouldn't phone her. You knew the phone was tapped?"

"The thought occurred to me," Dunn acknowledged wryly.

"Shouldn't we go up and tell her, Charlie?"

Dunn shrugged as he holstered the automatic.

"Can't risk it, doc. He's probably got a bug in her flat too. Victor's the tidy sort, you know."

He nodded towards the door.

"Aren't you going to disconnect it?" she wondered.

"No, that would warn him. Right now, the bastard isn't sure we're in town."

Dunn looked at his calendar wristwatch. It was 11:06 A.M. on December 5. He tried to remember what was *special* about December 15. Well, it would come to him.

"Let's take a walk," he said. "Don't worry. Victor probably won't be back until dark. That's part of the drill too."

They were three blocks away when Dunn spelled out what tactics the assassin was likely to use.

"The location will govern the choice of weapon, of course. Whatever he uses will be silent—or at least very quiet. Could be a bodyguard or two with the colonel. Victor may have to take them out as well," Dunn pointed out in a matter of fact tone.

"He'd kill *three* people?"

"Or nine. One would be better—and faster. Time's crucial. Weapon'll be something quick—something sure. No second chances—that's a fact. Hit and run is the name of the game.

She shook her head in silent revulsion.

"He'll have to get away fast," Dunn continued as he checked the mirror of a parked car to see who might be behind them. "He'll have the escape route—the timing—everything— worked out *very* carefully. Probably did a dry run or two already. Should be out of the country within three hours after the hit. Might be gone before they even find the bodies.''

Then he nodded suddenly toward an eighteenth-century building across the street.

"That's the Gyldene Freden—*golden peace*. Oldest restaurant in Stockholm. One of the colonel's favorites,'' Dunn recalled.

"You know a lot about him, don't you?''

"Sovs know more. You can bet Morelius hasn't eaten *there* in a long time,'' he said as they turned from the quiet Osterlanggatan towards the pulsing traffic of busy Skeppsbron a block away.

The Oriental woman followed patiently. She did not like this place or this weather. Both were alien to her. Bracing herself against the chill temperature that made her very breath condense as it left her half-frozen nostrils, she stubbornly trailed Dunn and Heather James through the snowy streets. She had no choice. She had her assignment and her sawed-off shotgun in the sling inside her coat. When the time came, she would do her duty.

CHAPTER NINETEEN

The three-masted warship was a remarkable ruin. It was extraordinarily well preserved after three and a half centuries beneath the waters of Stockholm Bay. Heather James could see why it had been raised and placed in a special museum. What she didn't understand was why Dunn had brought her here now.

"Built at royal command to strenthen Swedish naval power during the Thirty Years War," the guide said briskly, "the *Wasa* was to be the most powerful battleship in the Baltic. She carried sixty-four cannon, including two huge sixty-two-pounders ... three thirty-five-pounders and forty-eight standard twenty-four-pound guns. Some two hundred feet long, thirty-nine feet wide and one thousand three hundred tons in displacement, she was a giant."

There had to be a reason why Dunn had chosen this time to visit this place. Dunn always had a reason.

"Commissioned in 1625 and designed by foreign naval architects, she sailed on her maiden voyage on August 10th, 1628. On board were one hundred thirty-three sailors and three hundred armed soldiers who would fight from her decks when battle was joined."

Flashbulbs dazzled as a number of tourists—mostly Swedes—took photos. The high-ceilinged chamber was very humid. The guide had explained that the humidity was maintained to help preserve the old hulk that had been submerged so long.

"The *Wasa* left the pier near the royal palace and moved out into the harbor with all sails set and flags flying. She was three hundred meters from shore when she suddenly keeled over and sank immediately. Almost everyone drowned. No one knows exactly why this happened."

"It was the foreign ship architect," suggested a patriotic accountant.

"Some think so," the bespectacled guide replied and went on to describe the problems conquered in raising the vessel 333 years later in 1961. It was ten after one by the time that Heather James and Dunn walked from the museum out onto windswept Djurgarden.

"It was very interesting, Charlie. But why did we spend eighty-five minutes in a museum when Victor Spalding is getting ready to kill somebody?"

"Because I do some of my best thinking in museums. The Louvre's not bad, and the Prado in Madrid is terrific. The lousy lighting inside helps me concentrate. Places like the archaeological museums in Athens and Cairo are perfect. They display their stuff so badly that you've *got* to think."

She waited for him to continue. He didn't.

"You joking?" she tested.

"Dead serious. *Dead*'s the key word. If we don't alert Swedish military intelligence and Kerstin Morelius, Spalding's chances of killing the colonel are better. But if we do warn them, they might throw up such a security screen that Victor would put off the hit for weeks—maybe months. He's an egomaniac, but not suicidal."

Then he waved at an approaching taxi.

"If Victor backs off and runs," Dunn explained, "then I've lost him. That's bad. Finding him is never easy, and Victor's the person who counts most."

"Because he's out to kill you?"

"It's probably *us* by now."

The cab pulled over and stopped.

"So it's us or the colonel, Charlie?"

"Would have been simple for the *old* Charlie Dunn," he told her. "He'd have booby-trapped the recorder. When Victor came to check the tape, there'd be a loud noise and good-bye, Victor."

"I like the *new* Charlie Dunn," she announced as he opened the taxi door. They hurried into the warmth of the heated vehicle. The sudden change in temperature made them shiver. Time was running out, Dunn thought soberly. He'd have to decide on which course to take within the next few hours. Spalding might strike at any moment.

"Dunn's law," he announced. "When in doubt, eat."

He asked the driver to take them to the

excellent restaurant in the stately old Royal Opera House downtown.

Two miles away, Spalding was emerging from another taxi. The ferry terminal was large, bulky and modern in a dully functional way. It had to be big, for it handled a great number of passengers and cars every day. The vessels that sailed the Baltic from these docks were miniliners, equipped with swimming pools and saunas and little supermarkets overflowing with duty-free liquor, cigarettes and chocolates. Drinks at the busy bars on these craft cost half of what Sweden's heavily taxed citizens paid ashore, so the ships were always crowded. That suited Spalding's plan perfectly.

He carried his suitcase to the ticket booth, paid $97 for a stateroom on the overnight ferry to Helsinki and checked the valise.

He felt light and jaunty as he left the terminal. The anger that had swept over him earlier when he'd read the newspaper report of the London ambush was gone. It would be entirely different here—and very soon.

Timing was the key to the entire operation. Timing and ritual would make a corpse of Morelius within four hours. This was Kerstin Morelius's birthday. A proud man of habit and a slightly guilty father, the colonel had made a custom of taking his daughter to dinner every December 15 at the expensive and historic Gyldene Freden. First he'd come by her apartment at 5:15 P.M. with a gift in one hand and a magnum of cold Dom Perignon Champagne in the other. The dinner reservation was for seven o'clock. It was all on the tape.

It was good that Colonel Morelius was a disciplined soldier who was always prompt. Tardiness could create a serious problem for Victor Spalding. The ferry—which got much less attention from the police than the airports did—sailed for Helsinki at six. It would leave precisely on the hour, for the Swedes were as punctual as they were righteous.

Spalding's gold Rolex showed 1:19.

In three hours and fifty-six minutes, Colonel Iwan Morelius would be dead.

Then Spalding could proceed with his plans for the elimination of Charlie Dunn.

It had to be done. It had to be done soon, and it had to be done right.

This time Spalding would take care of it himself.

CHAPTER TWENTY

Dunn seemed to be completely relaxed.

He looked as if he were enjoying the splendid smoked salmon, shrimp and other delights from the Operakallen's famed "cold table."

He appeared to be genuinely interested in her account of what people could do to stop the slaughter of whales.

But there was something else—something different and distant—deep within his eyes. It had to be whether to sound the alarm about Spalding. Dunn was silently considering all the factors, weighing them on his private scales.

Heather James had never made such a decison, but she knew that it wasn't easy. There had been times when she'd reluctantly recommended that a hopelessly sick animal be "put to sleep." But it was the owners who had chosen, and those cases involved dogs and cats and birds. She loved those creatures, but this situation wasn't quite the same. This involved a healthy human and a wanton murderer.

It was almost certain that some human would die.

Which one?

Who had the right to decide?

And could there be a correct choice at all?

It all seemed impossible and insane. She realized that Dunn was taking the responsibility for the choice himself—that he was deliberately sparing her. Or perhaps excluding her because he felt she wasn't competent. Whatever his reason, she was grateful.

They returned to their room at the hotel at ten minutes before three. Snow was falling again—lightly but steadily. As she took off her coat, she felt sorry for him. From what she'd heard, her lover was one of the coolest, smartest and most experienced intelligence agents in the world . . . but no one should have to make such a choice.

Then she thought about Alfred Makumba and gasped.

"Oh, my God!"

"What is it?"

"It just occurred to me, Charlie. If we warn Kerstin Morelius and the Swedish police, we may save the colonel but Spalding might go on to kill—"

"Your blood brother down in Twanzi," Dunn finished, "or eight other people."

"How can anyone decide which life is more important?"

"I'm trying to save them all, doc—including yours and mine . . . Hell, I guess we'll have to start with Morelius. I'll see his daughter. Any objections?"

She shook her head.

"Is it always this bad, Charlie?"

"This is the *good* part; it gets worse," he replied as he went to the telephone.

Kerstin Morelius and Dr. Ulf Holberg heard the telephone ringing as they stepped into the elevator.

"We're almost late already," the graying psychiatrist reminded paternally. He was right, of course. This was an important meeting. Nearly one hundred progressive politicians, journalists, actors, playwrights, choreographers, labor leaders and artists were gathering at the home of one of Sweden's richest publishers to draft a declaration condemning American militarism. A prominent poet was coming from South America, and the envoy of the Palestine Liberation Organization was to speak on recent U.S. arms sales to the Zionist state. Press coverage might well be as extensive as it had been for last month's rally against international racisms.

"They'll call back later," Holberg assured confidently as he closed the elevator door. Within a dozen seconds they couldn't hear the distracting telephone at all.

Dunn let it ring and ring and ring. After a full minute, he hung up and shrugged.

"Try them again in an hour," he said.

When he called back at five minutes to four, there was still no reply. Perhaps they'd gone away skiing for the weekend, or maybe they were out at a concert. Dr. Holberg was a well-known devotee of contemporary chamber music.

By half-past four, Dunn was growing restless. The odds were that Spalding had no idea as to where the colonel was, but this was a Sunday and Victor Spalding liked to kill on Sundays. Yes, the code name Garbage suited him well.

The son of a bitch had an explanation, of course. According to the file that Barringer had provided, Spalding had said that it was easier to kill people of any faith on their religion's Sabbath because they were less on guard. So it was *logical* to hit Moslems on Fridays, Jews on Saturdays and Christians on Sundays. From a business point of view, that made sense. But killing was more than a business to Victor Spalding. It was a pleasure.

Dunn telephoned again at two minutes to five.

The phone rang twenty-six times. No one answered.

Dunn put down the instrument and found himself thinking about December 15 once more. Maybe it was in the microfilmed files. He set up the compact "reader," inserted the frames on Spalding and scanned them impatiently.

There was no reference to that date.

He grunted, thought and decided to check the microfilm report on Colonel Morelius. Nothing . . . nothing . . . nothing.

Jackpot!

Kerstin Morelius—this was her birthday. That might be just the thing to inspire a phone call from her father—one that Spalding could use or perhaps even trace. Or maybe the colonel—a little guilty about his daughter and a lot lonely after months in hiding—would try to see her. There had been no attempt to hurt him for more than half a year. Perhaps Morelius had persuaded himself that the KGB had forgotten.

Or maybe the danger was merely Dunn's feverish fantasy.

There was only one way to find out.

"Don't open the door—not to anyone," he instructed as he sprang to his feet. She was puzzled until he swept his coat from the hanger.

"I'm coming with you, Charlie."

He shook his head.

"Not *anyone*," he insisted.

Then he scooped up the phone and told the desk clerk to call for a taxi. The snow was falling more heavily now. It took several minutes before the cab arrived. Traffic moved slowly as cars and taxis cruised warily through the dark winter afternoon. Their headlights glowed eerily in this December dimness. It was compulsory here to drive with your lights on during these long gray months, Dunn remembered. Day as well as night—even if the sun was shining. The benevolent government was trying to protect the forgetful and careless.

Dunn looked at his watch.

5:08.

The colonel was probably enjoying the sun and a new identity in Morocco or Melbourne, far away and completely safe.

This urgency that Dunn felt—that gripped his throat and belly so ruthlessly—was unjustified, he told himself. That didn't help at all. The knots were still there and the goddamn cab was crawling at a ridiculous ten miles per hour.

They were on the bridge now. *Shit*, Dunn thought, that tap and recorder might not be Spalding's. Other people used the same methods and types of equipment. Maybe Dunn was panicking like some half-trained amateur.

5:12.

There was the building where Kerstin Morelius lived.

Dunn paid off the driver, hurried through the falling snow and used his credit card again to open the street door. He'd go down to the basement first to collect the cassette. *That* would convince the colonel's daughter that she was being watched. The elevator was waiting at street level. Dunn took it down to the basement, drew his gun and once more opened the door to the electrical room cautiously.

5:14.

He had the cassette. Now he walked swiftly back to the elevator and pressed the button. As he did, two men stepped from the elevator on the fourth floor and the car started down.

Both men were tall and dressed in the winter garb favored by thousands of other Swedes. One seemed to be in his late twenties. He was the burlier, and he looked around warily. The older man—somewhat more expensively attired—was cooler.

"Well, sergeant?" Morelius demanded.

"All right, colonel," Sergeant K. Arne Svedelid assented.

At that moment, a plump gray-haired woman in her sixties came down the stairs behind them. She was wearing rubber-soled rain boots and a woolen cape with a hood that covered most of her head. She walked very carefully—making no sound as she neared. She was almost upon them when she opened her left fist to expose an aluminum cigarette lighter. Morelius reached out to ring the bell beside apartment A.

Her right hand suddenly emerged from within the cape.

It held a .22-caliber pistol. There was a silencer screwed to the muzzle. Within the gun was a clip of Teflon-coated "killer" bullets—the kind that could penetrate almost all bulletproof vests.

"Excuse me," she said and coughed.

The two men turned. She thrust the cigarette lighter under Morelius's nose, twisted her head and squeezed the catch that released a five-second burst of cyanide gas. The colonel clutched at his throat, dropped the Champagne with a crash and fell. Sergeant Svedelid reached inside his overcoat for his Lahti M40 pistol. The bodyguard simultaneously opened his mouth to shout.

He didn't.

The old woman jammed her gun between his lips and fired twice. Pieces of the back of his head splintered against the wall in a pink spray. Then the assassin bent down, squirted more of the lethal gas into the colonel's face—and heard the elevator coming.

No more time.

Spalding spun on his heel, pocketed the cyanide weapon and sprinted up the stairs. He heard the elevator door open.

Dunn stepped out, saw the bodies and caught the bitter scent. He recognized it immediately, drew the twin automatics and listened. He heard the door to the roof open. As he ran for the stairway there was another sound.

Thump . . . thump . . . thump.

It was getting closer.

He knew what it had to be.

Dunn turned and hurled himself down the stairs. He was still tumbling when the concussion grenade exploded. He was on his feet a moment later, charging up the stairs. When he reached the roof, the door was open and there were fresh footprints in the snow. Dunn hesitated, aware that Spalding might be waiting out there to shoot him.

He dived out and rolled over with an automatic in each hand. Now he saw that the tracks led to the edge of the roof. Crouching low, he advanced to the parapet and found what he expected. A rope and hook had been bolted into place. Dunn looked down. The snow was falling more slowly, and he got a clear look at a man in black leather hunched over a big motorcycle.

Just for a moment.

The engine thundered as Dunn swung his weapons to take aim.

Too late.

The heavy machine roared down the alley and vanished around a corner. *Right out of the goddamn book, Victor,* Dunn thought angrily. Then he put the twin automatics back in their holsters and hurried to leave the building. There was nothing more that he could do here, and the police would arrive in force within minutes. Charles Dunn had no desire to spend the next week explaining to them who he was, why he carried twin 9-millimeter P-15s and what he was doing here.

He didn't have a day, let alone a week.

He had to find Victor Spalding.

Dunn noticed the woman's clothing and wig that the assassin had discarded as he'd rushed for his escape rope. He'd probably rappelled right down the back of the apartment house—exactly as those Special Forces instructors had trained him to do in the escape and evasion course.

Quite a monster they'd help create.

A sort of federal Frankenstein creature.

Dunn took the elevator down. As it passed the fourth floor he saw the corpses again and the blast effect of the grenade. The door to apartment 4A was a splintered wreck. Another portal hung from one hinge. People were shouting. They'd be out in the hall within seconds.

Dunn turned right when he reached the street. He walked slowly to the corner, and then turned right again. Trudging through the snow, he moved more quickly now that he was out of sight of those in the building where Morelius had died.

The cyanide had been *cute*, Dunn thought.

Only Sovblock agents used that gas. It was for *special* hits like the job they had done on the Ukrainian exile in Munich who'd been organizing an anti-Communist network. Spalding had chosen the weapon for this execution deliberately. He *wanted* the Swedes to know who'd paid for the job.

The Swedes would go crazy—in about twenty-three minutes. It would take them that long to appreciate fully what had just happened. This was peaceful-neutral-progressive Sweden, where citizens were taken care of from womb to tomb. Dunn wondered what kind of tomb Morelius would get. Would he receive an official funeral with full military honors—or would they hush up the whole affair?

Now he heard a distant klaxon. Ambulance or police car. He walked more quickly, striding along Storanygatan toward the imposing Riddarhuset—the historic House of the Nobility—and the Supreme Court beside it. Just beyond and a block to the left was the Central Bridge that would get him off this island. Once he was across he'd be out of the Old Town and much less likely to be noticed.

The klaxons were getting louder. Two police cars passed him as he walked onto the span. Not a cab in sight. This wasn't a city where taxis cruised on a snowy Sunday afternoon. They'd be waiting for radio or telephone calls at their stands, or lined up at busy places.

It was cold, and Dunn felt it both in his feet and face. Spalding wasn't walking. He was miles away by now, grinning at his victory. He'd won this round. Dunn had come *that close* to catching him. *That close* wasn't good enough.

He entered the hotel room at 5:39—his face grim and half-frozen. He strode straight to the telephone.

"*Ten* goddamn seconds," Dunn announced bitterly. "I missed the son of a bitch by *ten* lousy seconds."

"The colonel?"

"Dead," Dunn replied and dialed the hotel operator.

She stared at him in shock.

"Operator, would you please get me SAS reservations?"

She walked to her suitcase, put it on the bed and opened it. Where were they going? Her arms were filled with sweaters and underwear a few seconds later when she heard him ask about about the next flight to *Copenhagen.*

Shouldn't it be Twanzi?

What about Alfred Makumba?

She wondered for several moments before she resumed her packing. It was 5:58 P.M. when they checked out of the Hotel Terminus. The ferry sailed for Helsinki two and a half minutes later.

CHAPTER TWENTY-ONE

The message from the mole reached KGB headquarters on the afternoon of the twentieth. The first four paragraphs relayed information that pleased General Temko. It was the fifth that disturbed him profoundly. He swore a soldier's oath, glared at Polchasny and thrust the signal aside.

"Have you seen this?" Temko demanded angrily.

"Yes, general."

"We should have left that fucking Dunn alone. What a stupid mistake!"

The whole damn operation was a mistake, Temko thought. He wouldn't say that aloud—not in this building. The project had been conceived by the head of the entire KGB, a ruthless and dogmatic man who tolerated no disagreement. He was one of the last of the brutal "old guard," the driven fanatics who held grudges so well. The mission for which they were paying Spalding half a millin dollars was rooted in ideological idiocy and a personal feud that went back more than thirty years.

"Dunn would never have returned to the field if we hadn't sent those hoodlums to Vermont," Temko continued.

"Spalding thinks—"

"Spalding's half-crazy. He's got an obsession about Dunn. I told Spalding *to let sleeping wolves lie,* but he couldn't."

"It's hard dealing with undisciplined Americans," Polchasny sympathized.

"Life is hard—but death is harder," Temko quoted. "My grandfather used to tell us that. Spalding would be wise to keep that old Russian proverb in mind."

"Yes, general. By the way, our *rezident* in Copenhagen—"

"Is wasting his time," Temko broke in harshly. "I'd bet one thousand rubles Dunn left Denmark an hour after he paid for the advertisement. Speed is part of his game. He probably went there only because he wanted to leave Sweden quickly and there are many flights from Stockholm to Copenhagen every day."

Now the aide's face brightened with a cheering thought.

"At least we know from the advertisement he'll be in Athens tomorrow," Polchasny reminded.

"Because he wants us to. It's a trap—a clever one. Dunn expects Spalding to recognize it as a trap, and he's counting on Spalding's ego to make him go to Athens anyway. Mr. Dunn should have been a psychiatrist—or an Israeli. Games within games . . . he's full of tricks."

"Spalding's very capable too."

Temko drummed his stubby fingers on the antique desk.

"Is he still in Washington, major?"

"I think so. Should I notify him about Athens? You said you'd keep him informed on Dunn's whereabouts."

"If I do, Dunn may destroy him and the operation," the general analyzed aloud. "But if I don't, Spalding may not proceed with his mission . . . We may have to go to the emergency plan."

"It's very professional," Polchasny agreed. "I don't think that Dunn or anyone else can stop this operation."

The general thanked him perfunctorily, and asked him to bring in the new satellite photos of the U.S. listening post in Turkey. When the aide had left, Semyon Temko sighed and looked across his office at the large—and definitely romanticized—painting of V.I. Lenin. People said that it had all been easier—well, *clearer*— back in those early days when Lenin ran the government. Some called it a golden era—the time when the revolution was fresh and virtuous. It must have been wonderful before Stalin began his reign of terror and the power-hungry took charge, Temko brooded.

Now he deliberately turned his mind to the urgent and immediate question of Spalding's mission. This was undoubtedly the most secret project that the KGB had. No more than five men in the entire Soviet security apparatus knew the identity of the target—the global figure whom the head of the KGB had code-named Running Dog. Only a few key members of the Council of Ministers were aware of

the operation, which had been cleared by the
highest authorities.

Or had it?

Temko froze as he realized suddenly that
the chief of the KGB could be lying. He'd said
that "for security reasons" not a word about
this mission would be put in writing. What if
the bitter seventy-one-year-old man had fabri-
cated the "approval by the highest authorities"? Could this assassination be a *personal*
vengeance rather than an act of national
policy?

January 15—a week before Temko's birthday.

If the operation actually was unofficial, the
general would never live to see it.

Either the KGB chief would order Temko's
death and put all the blame on him, or the
Council of Ministers would have him executed.

The unauthorized assassination of Running
Dog would bring the most immediate and extreme punishment. Only the highest authorities could make such major foreign policy
decisions.

There was no chance that they'd tolerate a
private adventure that involved killing such a
major international figure. After all, Running
Dog was one of the most important men on
earth.

CHAPTER TWENTY-TWO

"So it *was* arson," McGhee thought aloud.

"Yes, sir.

"Are you sure, Mrs. Axt?"

"The Virginia fire marshals are, sir. So are our own technicians," she answered carefully.

McGhee encouraged this precise way of speaking among his staff. Absolute accuracy was his watchword, and a key consideration in his choice of special assistants. Emily Axt had been a computer security expert, Patricia Bonomi a statistical analyst and Gregory Keller a crack cryptographer before joining the Counterintelligence division. They were—like their chief—sober, mathematical and dedicated workaholics. Sixty- and seventy-hour weeks were common to those whom other Agency executives furtively called "McGhee's robots."

"Is there anything else, Mrs. Axt?" the CIA security chief asked.

"Yes, sir. Arthur Philipps died in the hospital an hour ago. It was two-fifty-five, to be exact."

McGhee blinked in approval. He liked his staff to be exact. Facts were important in this kind of work.

"Shall I notify the personnel department, Mr. McGhee? They might want to get moving on the insurance-claim and termination procedures."

Staring past her at a spot on the wall, McGhee considered the suggestion. "That's a useful idea," he approved. "It'll save time to start the paperwork."

He looked down at the report she'd just given him.

"Do the marshals have any leads as to who might have started the fire?" he asked.

"Not yet, sir," the thin brown-haired divorcee answered earnestly, "but they're working on it. They're trying to track the timing device used."

McGhee put his hand on the report.

"I'll inform the DCI right away," he announced. "No one else is to know about the arson investigation."

"Yes, sir."

"Philipps was a Counterintelligence employee and this is an internal security matter. It's our business, and ours alone."

Then he took out his wallet and extracted four dollar bills. He counted them twice.

"Please add this to whatever the division collects for flowers, Mrs. Axt. Philipps was—ah—very capable."

"People liked him."

It took McGhee several seconds to absorb the idea that Agency employees might have such positive and personal attitudes towards professional colleagues.

"Were you—ah—*friends*?" he asked gingerly.

"Acquaintances. Bob Dwyer and Tess Lipson were much closer to him."

McGhee's clouded eyes signaled her to continue.

"Dwyer works in the signals unit," she identified, "and Miss Lipson's executive secretary to Mr. Barringer."

Tess Lipson was on the list of people who'd known of the telegrams to Dunn.

"She passed her polygraph test the day before the fire," Emily Axt added.

But the machine could be beaten.

All the major powers possessed drugs that could defeat it.

A deep-cover agent as important as this mole would surely have them.

"Miss Lipson is among those under investigation," McGhee recalled.

"Around the clock. Visual and electronic monitoring. Home and office phones, car wired and full mail cover. Clean as a whistle—so far, sir."

The expression made the chief of Counterintelligence wince. It wasn't merely that it was an obsolete cliché. It was that it couldn't be entirely true. McGhee believed profoundly—he *knew*—that nobody was "clean as a whistle." Sin and imperfection were part of the human condition. He'd learned that at the age of six in parochial school.

"Continue the surveillance," McGhee ordered. Then he thought about the good nuns who had taught him so much—especially Sister Angela. He'd never forget *her*. She'd been a wonderful woman.

CHAPTER TWENTY-THREE

10:00 A.M. . . . Saturday . . . December 21
There was hardly a cloud in the sky. The temperature was fifty-eight degrees Fahrenheit, fourteen degrees Celsius. They used the Celsius scale here. It was a cool, clear, sunny day in Athens.

"Take a look," Dunn invited, and stepped back.

Heather James moved forward to peer down through the telescope.

"It's magnificent!"

"Has been for almost twenty-five hundred years. Makes me feel good just to see it . . . to know that we're capable of such things."

There it was—perched on a 400-foot hill about a mile away. She had seen photos, but was unprepared for the impact of the Parthenon itself. It dominated more than the ancient marble complex called the Acropolis. It dominated the entire city of three million sprawled around it.

"It's fantastic, Charlie. It's *glorious*."

"Lamartine called it 'the most perfect poem

in stone,' " Dunn said. "I read a lot of poetry in Vermont—and he's right."

She turned to look at him.

"Did you write any, Charlie?" Dunn did not reply.

"Let's get to business, doc. We're up here with the tourists on top of Mount Licabettos— nine hundred and ten feet above the town— because this is—"

"The high ground," she finished for him.

"You're learning. Right down near the bottom is the section called Kolonaki. High-rent district. One of those fancy houses is the residence of Mr. Peter Stamos."

"The brother of the man from Lisbon?"

"*Very* good," Dunn replied. "Yes, the man from Lisbon whom somebody will probably try to blow away soon."

"*Somebody?*"

"Spalding," he said, and moved forward to the telescope. Now he bent over the instrument and began to rotate it slowly. It took him forty seconds to find the house.

"Got it," Dunn announced.

He studied the building and the streets around it until the timing device ended his observation. Then he put in more coins and continued his careful reconnaissance.

"You said *probably*, Charlie?"

"What?"

"Are you sure Spalding's coming here?"

Dunn peered intently at the house for another ten seconds before he answered.

"Fairly sure. I made him an offer he's not likely to refuse."

"What did you offer him?" Heather James asked.

"*Me.* This time I'm the bait, doc. I sent him word that I'd be here to protect George Stamos."

The timer sounded again as he turned to face her.

"I don't like it," she told him.

"If you've got a better idea, let me know," Dunn replied, and took out a cigar.

"Let's fly straight to Twanzi. After all, Makumba's number one on the list."

He lit the Corona and shook his head.

"Suppose the list is wrong, doc?"

Her eyes widened in shock.

"Do you think it is?"

"I'm not sure," he admitted. "It's my head and instincts against Barringer's computer. I've got this feeling that there's *something* that doesn't add up right."

"With the list?"

"With the whole deal."

Even with the uncertain look on her face, Heather James was beautiful and desirable. Dunn could not help thinking of their ardent lovemaking the night before, and the way she'd cuddled against him from head to toe. For a moment he saw her—flushed and naked—again.

"Then I don't understand any of this, Charlie. Why are we in Athens protecting a crooked arms dealer?"

"We're not protecting him at all. He's only an address—the place where Spalding will come to hit me."

"*Please* don't do it."

At this point, three blue-haired and impatient widows from Miami pressed forward to use the telescope. Heather James glared at them. Then she joined Dunn as he walked towards the small café fifteen yards away.

"It'll be all right," he assured her.

"Don't humor me. Listen to me. I lied to you, Charlie. This is not just a pleasant, civilized affair. I care about you—a lot. I didn't intend to—and I'm not quite sure how it happened—but it did. Do you hear me?"

He nodded gravely.

"Good," she continued. "I have been waiting a long time for you to show up, Mr. Dunn. You are a *worthy* man, and I don't think you're afraid of a *worthy* woman. I want you alive and I mean to have you. What do *you* want?"

Dunn kissed her before he answered.

"I've got to stop him."

"You're as crazy as he is. How can a man who's sworn never to kill stop one of the most deadly professional assassins on earth?"

Dunn puffed on the cigar before he answered.

"I've been thinking about that."

"And you've got a plan," she said sarcastically.

He nodded and blew a smoke ring.

"What kind of plan? I've got a right to know."

"I'll talk to him—very frankly."

She stopped walking.

She looked at Dunn warily.

"*That's* the whole plan?"

"Basically—yes. I think that it'll work," he said and tapped the ash from the Corona.

"I think that you're either lying to me or having another breakdown."

"It's the truth, doc."

They walked back to the cable car and rode it down to the bottom of the small mountain. When they reentered their room in the businessman's hotel two blocks off fashionable Constitution Square, Dunn turned suddenly to take her in his arms. They kissed—again and again.

"Nobody's going to kill me," he told her firmly.

"Charlie!"

"And nobody's going to come between us. You asked me what I want. I want to be with you."

She pressed closer against him.

"How do you feel about making love at ten-thirty in the morning?" he asked softly.

"My watch shows midnight."

They were naked a minute later. They looked at each other with pleasure, and then began to kiss and caress. It was twenty minutes before she felt his weight upon her. Now he entered, and she began to gasp. He started to move. As she locked her legs around him she heard him whisper her name.

She rested in his embrace for what seemed like a long time afterward. Then they kissed again and rose to dress. Twice he stopped her to embrace again. When she was fully clothed, Dunn reached into the closet to take something from his Burberry hanging inside.

It was a .32-caliber Beretta automatic.

"You know how to use these?" he asked.

She nodded.

"One of my friends in Twanzi was a game

warden. He had such a weapon." She took it, checked the clip and the safety catch and put the weapon in her purse.

"There's a small chance—just a possibility, you understand," Dunn said, "that the Garbage Man might try something cute."

"Like shooting me?"

"More like grabbing you for some kind of hostage number. You know, *leverage*. Killing you wouldn't do anything but get me angry. He knows that I'm already angry."

Dunn paused to slip one of the heavy P-15s into his belly holster.

"I thought you were going to *talk* to him," she reminded as he buttoned his jacket.

"I will. There's one problem with Victor though. He's a very confused person. He doesn't listen well. It's hard to get his attention."

"And a .32-caliber Beretta ought to get his attention?"

"It always has."

Six minutes later they were at the office of an auto-rental company. Dunn invited her to select the color of the car. She chose dark green.

CHAPTER TWENTY-FOUR

"Those are the *evzones*," Dunn announced as they drove around the minipark that was Constitution Square.

She looked out at men with rifles, guarding an imposing building that was obviously official. They were tall—all at least six feet—and wearing most unusual uniforms. Red beretlike headgear, black shoes with pompoms, white tights similar to a ballet dancer's and what appeared to be white miniskirts.

"Don't let the outfits fool you," Dunn advised. "They're hard as nails. That's the Parliament they're guarding."

The traffic was heavy and the drivers fierce. They gave no quarter in these crowded downtown streets. The dark green Mercedes that Dunn had rented barely crawled as he slowly made his way towards the Kolonaki section of the city. The Stamos house was only half a mile from the former royal palace that now served Greece's legislature, but it seemed much further in the midday mobs of cars and trucks that clogged this central area of the capital.

"They may have streets named after Pericles,

196

Euripides and Apollo," Dunn said as he braked
to avoid colliding with a Metaxas Brandy truck,
"but Athens also has all the modern inconve-
niences of home. There's even air pollution
chewing on the Parthenon. Maybe we'll come
back some time—like normal human beings—
and see it all."

"I'd like that, Charlie."

"The summer would be good. They light up
the whole Acropolis at night with spots. It's
unbelievable," he told her, and loosened the
gun in his belly holster. He was wearing a
blue wool fisherman's cap and the upturned
collar of his jacket covered part of his lower
face. Her golden hair was concealed beneath
a gray scarf.

"Next right, doc. Just look straight ahead
and keep talking as we go by. It's only our
first run through the neighborhood."

"Anything you want me to look for?"

"People who might be cops or guards. Ped-
dlers or nursemaids where they shouldn't be.
Anything out of the ordinary on your side of
the street."

He turned the car onto an attractive residen-
tial street. Most of the buildings were expensive-
looking apartment houses. There were only a
few private homes. The four-story residence
of Peter Stamos was one of them.

"Pete's worth a few million himself. That's
U.S. dollars," Dunn reported as he pretended
to look straight ahead. "He's got a couple of
tramp freighters. Sometimes he hauls George's
guns. Okay, there's the house—number forty-
one."

"I don't enjoy this, Charlie. I hope you don't

think I'm a coward, but this riding around as a moving target gives me the five-star creeps."

"You're not a coward and you're not a moving target either. You're an intrepid scout."

"That's you—not me," she corrected. "I'm one of those normal human beings you mentioned. I've gone hunting lions with the Noros. Spears against lions. It was *much* better than this. *This* gives me a stomach ache."

"See anything?"

"There's a woman pushing a fancy baby carriage . . . a chauffeur waiting in a maroon Bentley and a chemical blonde walking an Irish setter. Her skirt's too tight."

"The setter?"

"Don't be funny, Charlie."

He drove to the corner and turned the wheel to circle the block.

"What did *you* see?" she asked.

"A teenage boy in a gray sweater and black pants delivering flowers . . . 'eighty-one Alfa Romeo, tan . . . last three numbers of the license plate two thirty-six . . . man about seventy in brown tweed suit, silver-headed cane and a stiff right leg . . . and the door of the Stamos house is steel, painted to resemble wood. So are the shutters."

"You do card tricks too?"

"No tricks. Lots of practice. Victor could do it just as well."

He felt her tensing as he turned the Mercedes again.

"Easy, doc. We're not going back," he assured. "Not till after lunch."

They had lunch twenty minutes later in a small restaurant facing the harbor in Piraeus,

Athens's busy port. He drove past the car ferries, a cluster of cargo vessels and a handsome cruise ship named *Jupiter* to the quiet Tourkolimano area where scores of private launches and sailboats bobbed in the sun. From their table near the restaurant window, the scene was a pure Aegean idyll.

"*Ouzo, parakalo,*" Dunn said to the swarthy mustachioed waiter.

"It's an anise drink with a good kick—like Pernod," Dunn told her. "Drink it with three parts water and you're a Greek god—or goddess."

The gnarled waiter returned with two tumblers and a tall, thin bottle of colorless liquid adorned with a red-and-black label. The number twelve on it caught Heather James's eye.

"Twelve years old?" she asked.

"Probably twelve weeks," Dunn chuckled. "Twelve is the brand name. Lord knows why."

Now the waiter produced a pitcher of water, worn but clean cloth napkins and a handful of cutlery.

"*Barbouni? Garides? Kalamaraki?*" he asked.

"Red mullet, shrimp, squid," Dunn translated. "He's offering the catch of the day— the freshest. The mullet's very good."

"So's your Greek," she complimented.

"You just heard about a quarter of it," Dunn answered as he unscrewed the cap on the *ouzo* bottle.

"I'll try the mullet," she said as he poured the pungent liquor.

"*Barbouni,*" Dunn told the waiter and held up two fingers.

"*Meze?*"

Dunn nodded. The *mezedes* that restaurants in Athens served were an hors d'oeuvres assortment that included tidbits of meat, cheese and other items. In this seafood restaurant ten yards from the Aegean, the *meze* were octopus chunks, clams, sea urchins, oysters and little *marides*—shiny silvery whitebait.

It was all delicious. So was the mullet and the yoghurt topped with honey they had for dessert. Dunn's glance roved past her several times as they ate.

"Expecting company?" she asked between swallows.

"Tell me about Irish setters—like the one you saw in town," he responded.

"They're like you, Charlie—active, aristocratic hunters. Both bold and gentle, lovable and loyal—and tough. *Very* tough."

Dunn smiled and lifted another spoon of the excellent yoghurt to his lips.

"There's more, Charlie. They've got fine personalities. Really cheerful. Once you've got them trained, they're wonderful companions."

"Hard to train?"

"Worth it," she assured with a smile. Then Dunn looked past her again.

"Hippo," he said.

"What's that?"

"That's me," a husky voice behind her announced. She turned to see a short grinning man of about forty or forty-five, wide shouldered but trim and muscular.

"Dr. James," Dunn introduced, "may I present Mr. Hippocrates Soloyanis—known to friend and foe as Hippo?"

"Got no foes," Soloyanis protested affably.

"Nice to meet you, doctor. Any pal of Charlie's is a pal of mine."

"Count your teeth," Dunn advised her, "and keep your legs crossed."

The man he called Hippo laughed.

"Don't believe him," he told Heather James. "We're old buddies. Talking of teeth, I've got a sore one—here in the back. Maybe you can help me."

"I'm sure she can," Dunn said. "She's a vet."

Soloyanis winked and lowered himself onto a chair.

"Sit down, Hippo," Dunn invited.

"Thanks."

At that moment, the waiter arrived with a bottle of Delamain *grande Champagne* Cognac and three brandy snifters.

"For friends, the *best*!"

"Business must be good, Hippo," Dunn tested.

"It's not easy for the small businessman, Charlie—but what the hell?"

Dunn saw the question in her face.

"Hippo has several businesses—all profitable," Dunn announced and sipped the excellent Cognac.

"I live by my wits," Soloyanis replied modestly.

"And he's very witty, doc. He owns this place—and two others."

"I stay afloat—which is more than some people can say."

"Some people can't say anything, Hippo," Dunn pointed out.

"I know. Heard about what happened to

Ken Perry in Berlin. Smashed to a pulp—that's a lousy way to go."

"Do you know of a *good* way?" Heather James demanded fiercely.

Hippocrates Soloyanis studied her more carefully.

"She with—ah—your firm, Charlie?"

Dunn shook his head.

"She's with me."

"Why do you need a vet?"

"Because we're looking for a son of a bitch," Dunn explained.

Soloyanis sipped more of the Cognac and chuckled.

"Now *that's* witty, doctor. Charlie was always funny. Not too many guys like that. You stick with him, doctor."

"I intend to."

Now the waiter gave Dunn the check.

"That seems reasonable—eight hundred and twenty-two dollars," he said, and took out his wallet.

"The Cognac's on me," Soloyanis volunteered.

Dunn began to count out the currency.

"Eight hundred and twenty-two dollars?" Heather Jones asked in a shocked tone.

"Includes the tax," Dunn said, and continued counting.

"I didn't charge tax to an old friend," Soloyanis corrected. "It's twenty-one dollars for the meal—including drinks and fifteen percent for the waiter—and eight hundred for the package."

"What package?" she wondered.

"It's in the trunk of your car, Charlie. Took

the liberty of picking the lock. Hope you don't mind."

"Not a bit, Hippo," Dunn said cheerfully, and drained the last delicious drops of the dry and delicate Delamain.

"I figured that you'd prefer an American model," said Soloyanis, "so I managed to find one that was en route to the Egyptian forces. It—ah—got lost on the docks in Alex."

"Those things happen. You finished, Heather?"

She swallowed the last inch of sweet strong coffee in the demitasse, picked up her purse and rose. Dunn was on his feet moments later.

"Thanks for your help, Hippo," he said, and the two men shook hands.

"Nice to meet you, doctor."

"And to meet you," she replied. "The lunch was excellent."

Hippocrates Soloyanis's face lit up with proud delight.

"I've been waiting for someone to say that. She's quite a lady, Charlie. You didn't mention her when you phoned three days ago."

"Knew you like surprises. So long, Hippo."

When the Mercedes was thirty yards from the restaurant, Dunn told her what was in the package. It was a three-pound Star-Tron "night vision" device that Smith and Wesson made for the U.S. Army. This was a second-generation model that amplified available light 60,000 times so a soldier could literally see in the dark—and at considerable distances. There was a larger version with intensification of 85,000— but that weighed forty pounds and was too bulky.

"For what?" she asked.

"For *whom*. For a man sitting in the dark partway up Mount Licabettos watching the damn Stamos house."

"Tonight?"

"And tomorrow and the next night—if necessary. Can't tell when Victor'll show."

"Charlie?"

"Yes?"

"Is it possible that Spalding will have a Star-Tron too?"

"No, it's *certain*."

They drove on in silence. Shortly before three, Dunn began another reconnaissance sweep through the Kolonaki section in the Mercedes. As they neared the block where Peter Stamos lived, Dunn gave her a green scarf and a pair of large-frame sunglasses to alter her appearance.

"Let me know what you see," he requested.

After they passed the house, Dunn drove straight ahead for two blocks instead of turning at the corner as he had earlier.

"Three little girls coming home from school . . . an old guy sweeping the street . . . four empty cars . . . one was a Caddy . . . and my stomach hurts again," she reported.

"How tall was the street sweeper?"

"Five feet five or six."

"No cigar. Victor's just over six feet," Dunn told her. "All I spotted on my side was—*wait a minute!*"

He sounded excited.

"What is it?" she asked urgently.

"Son of a bitch! I should have expected it.

Well, I'm not going to put up with this crap!
No way!"

Her right hand tightened around her purse.
She could feel the .32 through the soft
leather.

"Do we have a problem, Charlie?" she questioned in as controlled a voice as she could
muster.

"We *certainly* do," Dunn replied.

Then he began to swear.

CHAPTER TWENTY-FIVE

The name of the problem was Melendez.

Ernesto Herman Francisco Gomez Melendez was forty-three years old, a good-looking and notorious womanizer and a former major in the late General Somoza's Nicaraguan army.

He was a connoisseur of fine wines, an alumnus of the U.S. Special Forces School at Fort Bragg and an outstanding marksman with various weapons. Shrewd enough to leave Nicaragua nine months before the Somoza dictatorship fell, he was now a well-paid mercenary.

"And there's one more thing he is," Dunn said as he stopped the Mercedes for a traffic light.

"Here?"

"You got it. He isn't sitting in the window of a chic little bar two and a half blocks from the Stamos house because he likes the stuffed olives. He's here on business. He's here to hit brother George."

"Can you be sure, Charlie?"

"Only ninety-nine percent," Dunn replied. "He's worked for half the dictators and juntas south of the Rio Grande, and a few in Africa too. He's an absolutely logical choice for the hoodlums who run Costa Verde to send—and I don't believe in coincidences."

The light changed and he stepped on the gas pedal.

"What has he got to do with Spalding?" she wondered.

"Not Spalding—me. He's in my way. He's an extra complication in an already tricky situation. There's no telling what trouble he could cause. Ernie Melendez has to go."

He felt her wince beside him.

"Take it easy. It's Victor who kills people. I'm just going to talk to him."

At five minutes to four, Ernesto Melendez packed a fresh load of that excellent Dunhill pipe tobacco into his $110 briar and applied his sterling silver lighter carefully. He puffed contentedly as he watched the people and vehicles go by. He was getting the feel of the neighborhood, and timing the police patrols.

He was in no hurry. It would be stupid to be in a rush in this business. It might well be disastrous. Yesterday he'd met a maid who worked in the Stamos house. Tonight he'd get to know her a lot better. *Biblically*, he thought, and smiled in anticipation. After a night or two of his superb lovemaking, she'd be his eyes and ears within Peter Stamos's house.

The odds were that George Stamos would soon be getting bored and restless inside the mansion. He'd probably come out in a few days. If he didn't, the expertly seduced maid would provide the information for Melendez to slip in somehow. No security setup was perfect. Every professional knew that.

Now there was a beautiful woman.

The woman rippling down the street had a magnificent body, and that cascade of spun-gold hair was dazzling. What a splendid animal! Just looking at her through the bar window made Melendez tingle.

She was crossing the street toward him.

It was fantastic.

He'd see her up close in a few moments. Even a brief look from a short distance would be a wonderful piece of luck. After he'd slain the arms dealer, Ernesto Melendez would get himself a lush and elegant blonde like that one.

She was entering the bar.

Melendez swallowed, felt the surge of desire in his arteries and turned to give her his finest and most appealing smile. It was a combination of lust, macho confidence and reflex action.

It was also a mistake.

"Put both hands on the table, major," a strong male voice behind him ordered.

He hesitated, shrugged and obeyed.

The splendidly endowed blonde stopped. She seemed to be looking right past him.

"So long, doc," the man he couldn't see said firmly.

The beautiful young woman left. Melendez could not help staring at her wonderful figure as she walked out of sight.

"Glorious," the Nicaraguan declared.

"I'll tell her you said so. Turn around—slowly."

The ex-soldier complied. He found himself facing a man in North American clothes—

someone he'd never seen before. The gun in the stranger's raincoat pocket was obvious.

"I believe that you have the advantage of me, sir," Melendez said courteously.

"I mean to keep it until we've had our chat."

Melendez smiled and puffed again on the briar.

"I referred only to the fact that you appear to know who I am, while I do not have the honor of your acquaintance."

"My name is Dunn."

"A pleasure to meet you, Mr. Dunn. What sort of chat would you like?"

"A civilized and sensible one. How does that grab you, major?"

"That's fine," Melendez assured, and decided that the stranger was definitely a *Yanqui*. Then another thought filled his mind.

"You wouldn't be *Charles* Dunn by any chance?"

"By my parents' design."

"How splendid! I've heard much about you, Mr. Dunn. What a delightful surprise! May I offer you a drink?"

Dunn nodded.

"I'd avoid the wines," Melendez advised in a confidential whisper. "Greece is a noble and ancient land—but the alcoholic beverages are not quite suitable for a gentleman."

Dunn gestured with his left hand. A waiter arrived.

"Cognac. Delamain," Dunn told him.

Melendez beamed. It was appropriate that such a fine talent should order this little-known but elegant drink.

"I thought you'd left the field, Mr. Dunn," Melendez said as the waiter departed.

"I did. Would you mind if we got to our chat? I've heard about you too, major, and I realize that you're a busy man."

"Not too busy for Charles Dunn."

Dunn took his hand from the raincoat pocket.

"I hope that I didn't offend you, major, but I've found it prudent to be careful meeting strangers."

"So have I. I respect your caution. Now let us chat," Melendez invited as he wondered why Washington had sent Dunn here.

"I'll begin by telling you that you and I have no quarrel—no conflict of interest. Neither I nor the United States has any concern about Stamos's health or welfare."

"Stamos?"

"*George* Stamos—the man you're in Athens to hit."

The mercenary took the pipe from his mouth and reached for the glass of Amontillado sherry on the table. He lifted it—and stopped.

"Excuse my manners," he apologized. Then the waiter brought the Cognac, and Melendez raised his glass in courtly salute to his guest. Both men sipped.

"I don't care *what* you do to Stamos," Dunn continued, "only *when*. You see, I have business with a man who expects to find me near the Stamos house. Your presence in the area could cause serious problems."

"I'm not sure I understand."

"The man is complex and hostile. Dealing with him will require maximum concentration on my part. The presence of a third player might seriously confuse the situation."

Melendez began to puff on the briar again.

"This man?"

"One of your competitors—perhaps the worst. He has an awful temper, and he's often violent. Why, you might be in personal danger if you're here when he is."

Dunn's voice gave no clue as to whether this was a warning or a threat—or both.

"When is he coming?" Melendez asked.

"He may be here already. There could be a most unpleasant confrontation at any moment. That would attract the police—lots of them. They'd be sure to question every stranger and foreigner in the area."

This was a threat.

"What are you suggesting, Mr. Dunn?"

"That you consider staying away—say, half a mile—from Peter Stamos's house for the next five or six days. If you could make it a week, I'd be very grateful."

The arms dealer probably wouldn't come out for several days anyway, Melendez thought. Still there were the risks that came with delaying the entire operation. That was always dangerous.

"I'd like to help you, Mr. Dunn. But this extra week in Athens—which isn't exactly heaven in December—would disturb my whole schedule. I have other commitments—in Africa—for January."

"Maybe you could change your schedule," Dunn answered in a low voice that was as hard as steel.

"If there weren't other people counting on me—"

"Tell them it's a matter of *health*," Dunn urged, and slid his hand back into the raincoat pocket.

He was probably bluffing, the Nicaraguan calculated. It would be nice to be sure.

"They wouldn't like it," Melendez stalled.

"A person's health is important. You ought to take care of yourself, major. Nobody else will."

"I certainly agree. Fortunately I'm feeling fine."

"But you could be very sick tomorrow— maybe *critical*."

Melendez felt perspiration beginning to sheet his back.

"Lot of germs in Athens," Dunn warned. "This is the pneumonia season. Somebody died of it early yesterday."

It might take a week to win the maid's mind as well as her body, Melendez told himself. Pushing her too swiftly could be a serious error. Hurrying any part of the operation would be unprofessional.

"Just five or six days?" he tested.

"Seven at the most. You're at the Grand Bretagne?"

"The King George," Melendez replied, and regretted it immediately. It probably didn't matter though. If Charles Dunn wanted to find him, he would.

"Right. As soon as I've had my talk with this fellow and settled things, I'll phone you there. It might be only a day or two. I really appreciate this."

"My pleasure."

Dunn finished his Cognac and said good-bye.

"Thanks again, major. I won't mention our meeting to anyone, of course. Wouldn't want the local cops to bother you."

Another gracefully delivered threat.

If Melendez didn't keep to the bargain, Dunn would tip off the Athens police that there was an armed foreign assassin at the King George Hotel—preparing to kill the brother of a rich and probably well-connected taxpayer. That could lead to jail or deportation—both extremely bad for the Nicaraguan's reputation.

Mierda!

Controlling his annoyance, Melendez found himself admiring how stylishly Dunn had performed. He had won his goal and still left his opponent with honor. Not many *Yanquis* were that deft.

"It's been—interesting meeting you, Mr. Dunn," he acknowledged.

"Call me Charlie."

When Dunn got back to the Mercedes, he told Heather James what had happened. He expected her to be pleased. She wasn't.

"He said his next stop was *Africa*?" she asked with a worried frown as Dunn started the car.

"Yes, but he could be lying. People in this line of work often lay false trails. It's practically a trade practice."

"Twanzi's in Africa!"

"Let's not leap to any conclusions, doc. There are a gang of countries in Africa." He swung the Mercedes out into the late afternoon traffic.

"Twanzi's the only one I'm thinking about right now," she told him.

"I can understand that, doc," he said in an effort to ease her tension.

"Being reasonable won't help. I'm *scared*, Charlie. Maybe your *talk* with Spalding won't save Alfred Makumba. Maybe it's this Nicaraguan who's being sent to kill him."

"Hard to say," Dunn responded evasively.

There was no point in telling her that he'd already thought about this.

It wouldn't help anyone.

"Charlie, is it *possible* that the assassin who's been hired to murder my blood brother is sitting back in that bar sipping sherry?"

Dunn thought for several seconds as he shaped a careful answer.

"I don't believe that it's *probable*, but it *is* possible."

"You've got to do something," she appealed.

"After I've had my talk with Victor, I'll—"

"*After?*"

"Has to be—unless you want Victor to shoot me in the back outside Makumba's house," he explained patiently.

"I don't want anyone to shoot you anywhere, Charlie."

He did not reply. His mind had already moved on to tonight. It would be cold sitting up on the mountain in the darkness with the Star-Tron. He'd have to crouch up there—almost motionless—for hours. His muscles would be tense, his bones stiff and his eyes hurting from the hours of squinting and utter concentration.

Maybe it would all be for nothing.

Or maybe Spalding would be up there waiting for him.

It was going to be a long night.

CHAPTER TWENTY-SIX

Step by step.

That was the only way that Spalding could make it work.

The arrangements in Washington took a day more than he'd planned. Now it was all in place. He had the weapon, the explosive and specific ideas on how he'd strike. He liked both ideas a lot.

Spalding was pleased as he boarded the TWA jet to Rome. He had accomplished what had to be done in the District of Columbia, and he was on his way to destroy Dunn. *They* had not been eager to tell him where Dunn was, but *they* had grudgingly yielded to his firmness. He'd never doubted that *they* would, of course. After all, he was the best and *they* needed him.

Everything was ready for the hit that would change history. He would take care of that on January 13th or 14th. He'd kill Dunn now, however. It was to be Victor Spalding's Christmas present to himself.

Flying high over the stormy North Atlantic, Spalding smiled in his sleep as he dreamed of how he'd use the scalpel on Dunn's throat and face, belly and hands and groin. There would be blood everywhere. He thought about blood as much as he thought about sex. For some reason that he'd never identified, they seemed to be equally arousing.

Of course, he'd never discussed this with anyone. Those prying fools whom the CIA employed as psychiatrists had asked a lot of stupid questions after he'd taken their tests during the screening. He'd lied repeatedly about the idiotic ink blots and given bland answers to every one of their obviously tricky inquiries. He had completely defeated their insolent efforts to probe into his private world. His feelings, thoughts and dreams were only for Spalding himself.

He was still smiling when he awoke, and the buxom brunette flight attendant who served breakfast wondered whether this attractive man might be a featured actor on some television series. He had that macho look, the strong even features and air of confidence. His clothes said that he had plenty of money. She had a two-day layover in Rome. Perhaps he'd ask her to dinner.

He didn't. When they reached Rome, he collected his suitcase and caught the flight for Rhodes eighty minutes later. Rhodes was a Greek island with a large tourist business. Foreign visitors were both welcome and necessary, and entry formalities were kept to a minimum. As Spalding expected, the customs officials didn't even open his bag.

Now he was in Greece. There'd be no more checkpoints or police barriers between this airport and the capital on the mainland. That was where he'd fight his duel with Dunn. It had been an error to put it off, but now he'd correct that. It would be like two medieval warriors—jousting to the death.

The Dunn myth would perish with the man.

Victor Spalding would be the undisputed monarch, the King of Death.

Respect and fear. Money and power. He'd have it all. He'd earned it, Spalding thought as the taxi pulled away from the Rhodes air terminal. It would look strange if he simply took the next plane to Athens. It wasn't normal for people to spend only four hours on this scenic and historic Dodecanese isle. So Spalding checked into a half-empty hotel near the walled city built by Crusader knights in the fourteenth century, slept for an hour and then walked the cobblestone streets between buildings put up by the Knights of St. John of Jerusalem.

It felt good to pace this historic Street of the Knights. Spalding saw himself as one of those armor-clad legends, riding a powerful black stallion and carrying a mighty lance. Yes, he was the dreaded Black Knight—always feared and alone. It was not a new fantasy. Spalding had played this role since the age of seven when his fists had intimidated the other boys in the orphanage.

Confident that no one would be watching Olympic Airways' domestic flights, he caught the next afternoon's jet to Athens. In the clerical garb he'd worn several times before, Spalding registered as Father John Baker of Manchester, England.

Night came early here in December. It was almost dark by the time Father Baker—carefully padded to seem forty pounds heavier—walked down the street on which the Stamos house was. He did not approach the mansion itself, but kept at least a block away on this initial probe. After testing the neighborhood for some twenty minutes, he chose his observation post for tomorrow—a fairly new apartment house six stories high.

The temperature was down to fifty-two by the time Spalding returned to the King Minos Hotel on Piraeus Street. It was several degrees colder when he finished dinner and loaded the Star-Tron and partially disassembled sniper rifle into a cheap plastic suitcase. He wore a lined raincoat when he left with his equipment at ten o'clock.

He could not watch from the side of Mount Licabettos during daylight. He would be seen by the people who lived in the houses, ate in the restaurants. But in the blackness of this late December night he would be safe. Unlike many other children, he had always felt at home in the darkness. It was the natural habitat for a Black Knight . . . a comfortable realm for the King of Death.

Spalding made his way some 200 yards up the small mountain, found a thick clump of shrubbery and crouched low to screw together the long gun. He'd already slain five men with this 470 Weatherby Magnum. Hurling its massive slug at 2,700 feet per second, it could drop a bull elephant in his tracks. One round

would take off half of Dunn's head. The first
shot had to do it, and it had to be a head shot.
At this distance, there was no sense in risking
what bulletproof clothing might accomplish.

Spalding put on gloves, turned on the Star-
Tron and began to scan the streets and roofs
of Kolonaki directly below. He swung the
night-vision device slowly and carefully, peer-
ing and squinting as he searched every square
yard for any trace of Charles Dunn.

Nothing. Not a sign.

He felt stiff and uncomfortable. He wondered what Dunn might be doing. Where was
he? What was he planning? He was a fanatic
about planning, Spalding recalled.

Plan. Ambush. Escape.

Basics.

The temperature was still dropping. Spalding never let physical discomfort bother him
when he was preparing a hit, and with the
target Charlie Dunn the cold didn't matter at
all. Spalding actually felt warm as he contem-
plated the impact of that high-velocity slug
devastating his enemy's skull. Comforted by
this prospect, he continued his search with
the Star-Tron.

Zero.

The minutes ticked away with almost painful slowness. Where the hell was Dunn? Spalding glanced at the fluorescent numerals on
his wristwatch. It was eight minutes before
midnight. There was very little activity around
the Stamos house. Maybe Dunn wasn't down
there at all.

And the time crept by. Spalding's neck muscles hurt. His calves were sore, his eyes strained from staring so intently.

Now it was 12:37 A.M. on December 23. Spalding decided to continue his vigil until a quarter after one. The odds were that Dunn wasn't anywhere near here, but maintaining this watch was Spalding's way of reaffirming his toughness and self-discipline.

By 1:05, Spalding realized that he would not see Charles Dunn tonight. Still Spalding would not leave his post. It was a question of pride. He'd said 1:15 A.M. and he would keep his commitment. Bored with what he'd observed below, he now started to sweep the night-vision device across the slopes of Mount Licabettos itself. Perhaps there would be something to look at in one of the houses on the slope. Most windows were shuttered.

There were few lights on at this hour. That was to be expected on a winter night. Spalding peered into one window, saw an elderly woman pouring liquor into a glass and moved the night-vision scope on to another house. A couple was kissing and embracing. Both were men. Spalding watched them undress and observed their feverish intercourse. He'd seen better in a gay "exhibition" in West Berlin, he thought. Of course, the German performers were experienced professionals.

At 1:12 the duo slumped back in completion and Spalding turned his Star-Tron to a different house 200 yards away. There was no one in the lit window. Annoyed, he slowly scanned towards a third house further up the slope.

He stopped halfway and sucked in his breath.

He was looking into another Star-Tron.

Someone was watching *him*.

He couldn't quite make out who it was, but he *knew*.

It had to be Dunn.

In automatic self-defense, Spalding sprawled headlong and rolled into the brush for cover. As he dived, his body tensed for the impact of a bullet. Dunn would have a high-velocity sniper gun of his own, and he'd fire instantly.

But there was no crack of a rifle.

No heavy man-breaking slug rocketed through the December night.

Spalding swung his own weapon, squinted through the night sight and prepared to squeeze the trigger. He didn't. There was no target. He swept the section where he'd spotted the other Star-Tron. He couldn't find it. Whoever it was had shifted his position. Now he was somewhere else on the slope, about to squeeze off *his* shot.

And Dunn almost never missed.

His marksmanship was close to inhuman. Twenty-nine bull's-eyes out of thirty in night shooting. Sixty-nine out of seventy in daylight—at 200 yards. Those were typical Dunn scores. His field shooting in actual combat operations was nearly as good.

All that flashed through Spalding's mind in three seconds. He was in acute danger. He might not live out the *minute*.

Where the hell was Dunn?

There was no time to think of that.

Spalding had to find cover, or shelter behind some heavy boulder or thick metal that a big high-velocity slug would not penetrate.

The trunks of the pine trees that dotted this slope would barely slow down the large-caliber bullet.

Spalding found his throat and stomach knotted, his breathing short and fast. He could hear his heart beating. It was anger—not fear, he told himself. He had to stay calm, to plot his next move instantly and rationally—and to get away. Circling a first-rate shooter in the dark on unfamiliar terrain would be foolish. Dunn had probably scouted it thoroughly for several days and nights. That was Dunn's style.

Spalding had to get out of range. He must change the field of battle now—or it might be too late. There were no second chances in this war. Then he hesitated, wondering whether he was being tricked.

Why hadn't Dunn fired?

It wasn't like him to waste an opportunity. There had to be a reason. It must be something devious and brutal. Dunn had to be furious at being stalked. Perhaps he had something more terrible than a swift bullet in his plan for vengeance.

Maybe he meant to make Spalding sweat before he shot him. Maybe he intended to cripple Spalding, to leave him a wheelchair case for life.

Rigid with grim anticipation, Spalding crawled back five yards—paused—and slithered another few yards. He moved in a zigzag pattern, crawling at irregular intervals so the sniper could not plot his direction and position, just as Dunn had taught him. The surface was cold, covered with rocks and bushes that scratched and bruised. Spalding barely no-

ticed them. He must get away. It took more
than fifteen minutes of these evasive tactics to
find refuge behind a car parked outside a low
house.

Panting and damp, Spalding still didn't dare
to stand. He wasn't safe yet, and he knew it.
Dunn might be circling above him on the slope,
preparing to blow off the back of his head. Or
waiting higher up with a crossbow that would
hurl an eight-inch bolt between his eyes. Or
hiding with piano-wire garrotte or razor-edged
commando knife to sever his windpipe.

It could be acid in the face to leave Spalding blind and disfigured for life.

It might be a surgically precise blow to the
spine or neck that would make him a quadri-
plegic—denied the use of arms and legs and
with no hope of recovery.

Spalding knew these things because he had
done them all. He couldn't afford to wait here
while Dunn made his choice. Spalding had to
plan his own tactics at once. Taking the initia-
tive was the first big step towards taking command of the situation.

Dunn had taught him that too.

Spalding scanned the area around him, and
decided to retreat up the passage between
two homes. He was halfway through when he
heard *something* ahead. He dropped into a
combat crouch immediately, raised the sniper-
scope and sought his target.

It was not Dunn.

It was a large black Labrador, advancing
slowly and growling at the stranger. The Labrador had to be silenced. The growls might
draw Dunn. Spalding knew that the dog would

make more noise if he moved. He didn't. He waited—motionless—until the animal moved closer. Then he drew his throwing knife and hurled it with all his strength into the dog's chest.

The Labrador groaned once before it died. Still crouched low, Spalding advanced to pull his blade from the corpse. Then he stabbed the dog again to make sure, freed the knife and wiped it on the flat black fur. He listened for any sound that might signal Dunn's presence. He heard none.

Still moving warily in irregular patterns, Spalding took nearly twenty minutes to reach the bottom of the mountain where he disassembled the gun and put the parts under his coat.

But he wasn't safe yet. Dunn might be down here in another ambush. Dunn might be anywhere.

He had to find Dunn's base—to locate the place where Dunn felt safe.

Making his way cautiously through the almost empty streets, he walked seven blocks before he found a telephone booth shielded by two parked cars. There were dozens of hotels in Athens where Dunn and the blonde woman might be. Spalding couldn't check them all. Only a large intelligence organization could do that within twenty-two hours and ten minutes. At the end of that time it would be Christmas Day, and Dunn must not be alive to see it.

Spalding entered the booth and dialed the secret number that was manned twenty-four hours a day. Some fifteen minutes later he entered the lobby of his hotel. The night clerk on duty at the King Minos was too polite to ask what was wrong, but he could see that the poor priest was not well. A healthy man's whole face would not be glistening with sweat in late December.

CHAPTER TWENTY-SEVEN

Dunn blinked in surprise.

George Stamos was coming out.

Dunn had been watching the house from his rooftop observation post for five and a half hours. His binoculars had ranged across the neighborhood more than thirty times, probing every street and window and possible site for a sniper.

It was 2:20 P.M. on December 24.

He was tired and he was cold and he was curious. Why was the arms dealer leaving the safety of his brother's fortress-residence now?

There wasn't time to speculate. As two men who were obviously bodyguards scanned the street in either direction, Stamos strode impatiently to the big black Cadillac to open the rear door himself. It seemed clear that he didn't really expect any trouble here.

Dunn ran down the stairs as fast as he could, sprinted to his own vehicle and gunned the engine of the Mercedes as he started it. He had to stay close to the arms dealer's limousine, for Spalding might attack at any instant.

It was a block and a half to the Stamos

house, and the damn limo was already rolling. Dunn cursed as traffic blocked him at an intersection, and hoped that other cars might be slowing the Cadillac too. He sounded the Mercedes's horn. Two expensively dressed women in their late thirties glanced at him haughtily—and continued to stroll across the street in defiance of the traffic lights.

When Dunn reached the street where the limo had been, it was nowhere in sight. Could he catch it? Which way would it go? Probably towards the center of the city on some business, Dunn guessed. It was a crap shoot. Well, an educated estimate. He stepped on the gas, passed two cars at a rate of speed that was definitely illegal and narrowly avoided a collision with an Olympic Airlines cargo truck.

He'd lost the black Cadillac.

But Spalding might be closing in on it right now with a rocket launcher on the seat beside him. Bulletproof glass and light armor plate wouldn't stop a missile engineered to kill tanks. Either the 66-millimeter M72 weapon of the U.S. and Canadian forces or the 85-millimeter rocket hurled by the Sov RPG7 would penetrate the Caddy as if it were a paper bag and turn it into an incinerator.

It was foolish to have tried the surveillance alone, Dunn told himself as he drove on wondering what to do. The job required three or four vehicles and a dozen agents. But Dunn had no team and no choice. He had his wits, a few guns, the Star-Tron and Heather James.

Then he saw it.

There was the Cadillac—twenty yards ahead. Dunn followed it for three more blocks until it stopped in front of a large apartment house. Stamos and the bodyguards left the limousine and entered the building. Dunn parked up the block where he could watch the apartment house door in his rearview mirror.

Who was the weapons dealer visiting?

It had to be someone very special on some business that could not wait.

Why else would he expose himself to danger on the afternoon before Christmas?

Dunn felt exposed himself in the stationary Mercedes. Even checking the mirrors and turning to scan the street and pedestrians gave him no comfort. There was no telling what disguise Spalding might be wearing, or when he'd strike. It would probably be something elaborate. The crazy son of a bitch was a showboat with an ego as large as it was sick.

It was ten minutes after three when the bodyguards stepped out into the street. This time one of them opened the rear door of the Cadillac. George Stamos wore a strange pained expression as he left the building. He stopped for a few seconds to rub his jaw—and Dunn had his answer.

The someone very special he had come to see was a dentist.

The business that could not wait was a toothache. Day before Christmas or not, it demanded immediate treatment and dentists did not make house calls.

Dunn trailed the limousine back to the Stamos house. He returned to his rooftop nearby and resumed his vigil. Tomorrow he'd have to find another observation post. It wasn't safe to use one for more than a few days.

It was already dark by five o'clock, and he suddenly realized that he hadn't bought Heather a Christmas gift. It should be yellow and beautiful to match her hair—simple and classic. It had to be splendid like the woman.

He reached the Lalaounis shop-gallery just ten minutes before closing. It took him only four minutes to choose a graceful hand-sculpted pin of eighteen-karat gold. He felt good signing the sheaf of $100 traveler's cheques. This was his own money, and he'd never had so much before.

When he entered the hotel room, he found her seated in an armchair reading an illustrated guide to the National Museum. They had agreed to spend a day in that treasure house of ancient wonders when Spalding was no longer a threat. Dunn began to smile at the prospect. Then his computer-mind thought of something else.

"Have you been out of the room?" he asked.

"Just to buy *this* at the bookstore across the street. The color pictures are fabulous."

The telephone rang. She rose to answer it. In an instant, the smile on his face turned to something cold and urgent.

"Don't touch it!" he ordered.

"What?"

"Stand still. Keep away from the window."

The telephone rang and rang.

"What is it, Charlie?

"I think it's a bomb. Don't panic. It'll be okay."

"A *bomb*?" she blurted.

"In the phone. He's watching, and he'll detonate when one of us picks it up to talk. In five seconds I'll open the door—fast. I want you to go through it like a bat out of hell—staying as low as you can."

He didn't wait for an answer. He started counting.

"One . . . two . . . three . . . four . . . GO!"

As she began to run, Dunn saw—reflected in the wall mirror—something move in the window across the street. He hurled himself after her, knocking her out into the hall. As they fell into the corridor he pushed her sharply to the right—away from the open door.

Then the bomb went off.

The blast smashed the windows, mirror, lamps and much of the furniture. Pieces of the telephone and the table on which it had rested scythed across the room like shrapnel, slashing and gashing everything they touched. Chunks of wire, metal, plastic and wood sprayed out into the hall—ravaging the wall across from the doorway.

The door itself was ripped from its hinges. It spun and fell. Dunn's body took most of the impact, but not all. Heather James screamed as one corner of the ruined portal crashed against her left shoulder. She felt something break.

Dust and plaster were everywhere, filling the corridor like choking smoke. People were shouting, but Dunn couldn't see them. He coughed and spit and coughed again as he leaned down over Heather James. She was all that mattered now. He turned her limp body over gently, wondering how badly she was

hurt. She couldn't be dead, he told himself.
She couldn't.

But she didn't move.

"Heather! Heather!" he called desperately.

Then her left eye opened—very slowly.

She was alive.

Eight or nine seconds later her right eye—
just as glassy—peered up at him. Her face
was covered with plaster, and there was a cut
on her forehead oozing blood. The right sleeve
of her silk blouse was half-ripped—as if by a
razor. She struggled to breathe, coughed on
the dust and winced.

"I think my collarbone's broken, Charlie,"
she said softly. Then she coughed twice more,
and he saw the pain in her face.

"It'll be okay, Heather," he whispered.

"I like that. *Heather's* better than doc . . .
Thank you, Charlie."

She coughed again and gasped. There were
tears in her eyes.

"It hurts a *lot*. I don't like your damn world,
Charlie."

"Neither do I."

He took a handkerchief from his pocket and
used it to staunch the blood.

"I think I'm going to faint," she announced.

She lost consciousness ten seconds later.
When she awoke it was 6:58 the next morning.
She was in a hospital room, and her left shoul-
der and upper arm were in a plaster cast.
There was a shadowy figure at the foot of the
bed. She blinked, and recognized her lover.

"It still hurts, Charlie."

"And will for six weeks—but there's nothing to worry about. Doctors say it's a nice

clean break. You'll be out of here in forty-eight hours."

Church bells began to toll nearby.

"What time is it?" she asked weakly.

"Seven A.M. on December 25th. Merry Christmas, Heather."

She'd lost more than twelve hours. That explained why she was so hungry. Now he was coming closer with something yellow and shiny in his hand. She focused her tired eyes and saw that it was a splendidly crafted gold pin.

"It's beautiful," she sighed.

"So are you."

She shook her head, and that was painful. The blast effects were not entirely gone.

"Thank you, Charlie."

"You're welcome," he replied, and leaned over to kiss her lips gently. She sighed, closed her eyes and reopened them.

"How did you know it was a bomb?"

Dunn held up three fingers before he answered.

"I didn't. The three things I knew were—*one*, he's used radio-controlled bombs in phones—*two*, you'd gone out so he could have rigged one—*three*, I wasn't expecting a call because we haven't told anyone we're at that hotel."

She nodded—and winced. Then she noticed his rumpled clothes. They were the same ones he'd been wearing when the bomb exploded.

"You been here all night?" she asked.

"I was out in the hall for an hour lying to the local cops. There are two of them on guard right now."

It took her several seconds to understand.

"They think he might try something else?"

Dunn nodded.

"You think so too?"

Before he could reply, a uniformed police-man entered to announce that Lieutenant Rossides had just arrived and would like to ask a few questions. Dunn kissed her again before he left the room.

He hadn't answered her, but his eyes had.

Spalding would attack again.

At 3:10 P.M., on December 26th, five people walked out of the rear entrance of the American Hospital in Athens. One was a blonde-haired woman whose draped raincoat did not conceal the bulk of a cast that encompassed her left shoulder and upper arm. Another was a lean man with restless eyes and a pair of 9-millimeter pistols beneath his foreign-cut sport jacket. The other three were uniformed members of the municipal police.

There were two more police waiting outside. One of them held a short-barreled submachine gun flat against his right trouser leg. None of the uniformed men said a word or showed any emotion as Dunn carefully helped Heather James into the Mercedes and closed the door. He nodded to them in farewell. They did not respond at all. He got into the car and started the engine.

"Not too friendly, are they?" she asked as he drove the Mercedes onto the quiet street.

"Cops never are with people who cause trouble—and bombs are trouble."

"But we were the targets!" she protested.

"They really hate bombs," he explained.

"Bombs mean sophisticated criminals. Bombs mean politics and headlines that get the government tourist office furious."

"We almost got killed, Charlie."

"That's too bad—those cops are thinking—*but why here?* Why stick us with your mess? They know there was a reason for that bomb," Dunn told her, "and they didn't buy my story for a minute."

She stiffened in pain as her shoulder throbbed again.

"Then why did they let us go, Charlie?"

"Because they want us out of Greece—fast. If we're going to be blasted, they'd like it to be in another country. They practically said so."

"What did *you* say?"

"That we'll fly out the day after tomorrow. That seemed to do it," he reported, and glanced at the rearview mirror.

"So they'll leave us alone?"

"Not *exactly*," Dunn replied. "They'll cover us every second till our plane takes off. There's a carload of plainclothes cops tailing us right now—and some more on stakeout at our hotel."

"I don't like being watched, Charlie. This morning I remembered there was a woman watching me when I went to that bookstore. She looked Japanese—or maybe Chinese."

"A female who's either Japanese or Chinese? That covers about a billion people."

"I'm serious," Heather James insisted. "Isn't it possible she helped Spalding find us?"

Dunn nodded.

"Certainly is. He needed more than luck to

track us down. He needed an organization,"
Dunn thought aloud.

Which organization?

That was the critical question. Was it the
KGB—or devious people high in the CIA? Not
the mole, but another person or unit engaged
in some operation that required a diversion.

Was it really believable that they'd pull a
burned-out agent with the shakes from retire-
ment to go after a tough, skilled and younger
assassin? Maybe they'd sent Dunn out into
the field again as a smoke screen. Maybe Spalding still had some link to the Agency and
was carrying out a top-secret mission that
must never be traced to the U.S. government.
Maybe the Agency wanted Dunn to fail.

There was another possibility. It wasn't any
better. Perhaps the mole had slyly maneuvered the Agency into pinning its hopes on
Dunn—confident that he had no chance to
stop quick and deadly Victor Spalding. A mercenary such as Spalding could be doing jobs
for both countries—and others. What others?
The Chinese? Some oil-rich Arab state?

The mole was tied to the Sovs.

Spalding was bound exclusively to no one.
He believed in nothing but money and death.
No, there was one more obsession. He was
committed to the death of Charles Jefferson
Dunn.

It was like some bizarre jigsaw puzzle—or
maybe a Rubik's Cube designed by a homicidal maniac. Dunn switched the pieces and
rotated them in his mind, but he could not
find the pattern. It was there—just out of reach.
He shook his head in anger.

"What's wrong, Charlie?"

"I'm not quite sure—but I'll handle it."

There was a hard-edged finality in his voice that barred further questions as effectively as a stone wall. Heather James did not like being separated from her lover by this barrier. But she had come to know and accept Dunn's ways —including his sudden retreats into himself. He was in there now—barricaded and alone. He was fighting that special kind of war with his mind—a key weapon in the arsenal that had kept him alive. It was her intelligence and trust that shaped her reply.

"You'll do the right thing, Charlie."

"As soon as I figure out what it is," he responded wryly.

They were at the hotel a few moments later. It was not the one where they'd been bombed. The management of that establishment had been delighted when Dunn moved out on the previous evening.

"We've got a much nicer view," Dunn assured her as they entered the new hotel. Walking slowly through the lobby, she noticed a pair of muscular men reading newspapers. They might be police.

"Those two?" she asked softly.

"Those *three*."

There was another Greek security agent whom she had not seen. And two more in the room across the corridor from theirs on the fifth floor. It wasn't difficult to see them. They had their door ajar, and one was sitting with another of the stubby submachine guns across his lap.

"I don't like this," she said.

"That's the idea."

Inside their own room, Dunn took off her coat and watched her settle gingerly into the armchair. She closed her eyes, and he hoped that she might fall asleep. In a little while he would have to tell her about his decision on what to do next. She wasn't going to like it.

CHAPTER TWENTY-EIGHT

She did not sleep. She dozed fitfully for a mere ten minutes before she looked up and saw the tension in his eyes.

"Could we get some coffee?" she asked.

"Sure you don't want to rest?"

"I'm sure."

Dunn phoned for a large pot of coffee and today's *International Tribune*. They were savoring both a quarter of an hour later. She noticed that Dunn ignored the front-page stories about world crises to flip back to the classified section. His glance moved over the small advertisements as if he was looking for something important.

"*Bingo*," he called out suddenly in a low voice. Then he excused himself and adjourned to the bathroom with the newspaper. His face had an almost somber expression when he rejoined her four minutes later.

"How do you feel?" he asked solicitously.

"Not great—but not nearly as grim as you look. You can say it, Charlie. Whatever it is, I won't faint."

Dunn studied her for several moments.

"Okay, we'll take it from the top," he began. "You remember that I said something didn't add up? Well, I can feel a lump like a grapefruit sitting in my gut."

She nodded, and sipped her coffee.

"I've been thinking about it some more," he continued. "I've figured out what's wrong—what doesn't add up right any way you count it. To put it simply, you don't kill a fly with a cannon. A cannon's for a ship or a fort or a battle tank."

"What cannon?"

"The mole. There's a Soviet deep-cover agent who's penetrated the Agency. No one knows who, how, where or when. It's very serious and very secret. This mole is a heavy weapon—a terribly valuable one. Could be worth a squadron of bombers or an infantry division. There's no telling how many scores of lives—or maybe hundreds or even thousands—he's already cost. Whole networks of agents may have been betrayed or entire operations blown, and the Agency would never know who did it. In today's world, this mole could have lost us—literally—a small *nation* such as one of those wobbly African or Central American states. You don't use—you don't risk exposing—a mole inside the CIA to help take out an African president."

"Makumba?"

"Makumba or any other," he said. "It has to be someone else—someone much more important. This is a *big* deal, Heather."

"So's Alfred Makumba."

Dunn shook his head.

"Not big enough. This target has to be a

major figure—twenty-two feet tall. Makumba's just a seven-foot-high saint," he told her gently. "The KGB doesn't believe in saints, so it isn't likely to invest this much in destroying one."

"Do you believe in saints, Charlie?" she challenged.

"What I believe doesn't matter. It's what I *know* that counts. I *know* Victor Spalding's main target—almost surely his *next* target—must be a genuine world leader. It has to be a person who really counts."

"The pope?" she demanded.

"Possible—but not likely."

"How about the president of the United States?" she offered bitterly.

"I've thought of that, but I'm not sure," Dunn admitted. "I am sure it's not the president of Twanzi. I'm sorry, Heather."

She sipped more coffee before she spoke again.

"So you don't want to go to Twanzi?"

"I'm not going."

Her collarbone hurt as she put down the cup, but it didn't seem important.

"Then who'll protect Alfred Makumba from Major Melendez, Charlie? The week's almost up. He'll kill Stamos and move on to Africa. *He said so, Charlie!*"

"Old Hippo has a contact or two in the police here. He'll pass them the word that Melendez is part of some hit team, and they'll hold him for at least a month of not-too-gentle questioning. Whatever Spalding is planning should be over by then—one way or the other."

Her right hand went to her abdomen.

"I've got that stomach ache again, Charlie."

"You'll feel better when you're home tomorrow night."

It took her a few seconds to grasp his meaning.

"Where will you be?" she asked.

He tapped the newspaper.

"Tokyo. Barringer reports Spalding was spotted getting off a plane there yesterday. The Japanese security people are looking for him now."

"*Tokyo?* You think it's the emperor?"

Dunn shrugged.

"I don't like this, Charlie. I think we should stay together."

"I *know* we should—and we will when I've stopped Spalding."

With some effort, she leaned forward in the armchair.

"There's no reason I can't come to Tokyo," she argued.

He held up his right hand with fingers spread wide.

"I can think of five—for openers. *First*, you don't know the city and you couldn't contribute anything to the operation. *Second*, it would be better for your health to get back to your home and family doctor and lots of rest."

"I'm feeling good."

"You're lying badly," he scoffed. "*Third*, it would be better for *my* health. Worrying about you would cause me a loss of focus. *Fourth*, that damn cast makes you even easier to spot and more of a walking target. You'd make it simple for Victor to find us."

He took a cigar and lighter from his pocket.

"What's the *fifth*?" she demanded.

"You'd slow me down. All my instincts tell me we're coming to the final turn in this race—the last lap. I'm going to need all my speed as well as a fair chunk of luck."

An odd expression came over her face as he carefully bit off the end of the Corona and lit it.

"It's probably the effects of the blast—but I just had the most terrible thought. My shoulder wouldn't be broken—we wouldn't have any of this—if that night you saw him on the mountain—"

She couldn't continue.

"If I shot him right between the eyes," Dunn finished. "Would have simplified everything. We'd go home, collect a big sack of cash from our grateful government and have a nifty wedding. You'd look swell in white."

"I didn't mean it, Charlie," she swore.

"It's okay. The same idea's occurred to me—about four times. I'm a practical fellow. I'd have done it—if I could. *I can't.*"

There was something grim in his eyes as he puffed on the Don Diego.

"Is it high principle or the tail end of my breakdown?" Dunn wondered aloud. "Killing isn't that hard, you know. Thousands of people do it every day. In a war, hundreds of thousands kill and there's always a couple of stupid wars boiling. Why are so many ordinary folks out there killing with hardly a second thought—often *with pride*—while a genuine expert can't? Think I've lost my nerve?"

"You've found your senses."

He did not reply.

"You're right—about everything," she said.

"I'll go home tomorrow. Make the reservations."

Heather James left for New York the next afternoon on the Olympic 747 nonstop that departed at a quarter after one. Dunn's SAS jet for Tokyo lifted off fifty minutes later.

CHAPTER TWENTY-NINE

10:40 A.M. . . . December 28.

Norita Airport, very large and very modern and a preposterous forty miles from Tokyo.

Dunn was stiff and tired after the long journey, but he wasn't surprised when he walked out of the customs area with his suitcase and saw Leonard Fischer. He'd anticipated that someone from the local CIA station might be there. Sandy haired, short and extremely earnest, Fischer was a CIA veteran who operated with diplomatic immunity as an assistant cultural affairs officer at the U.S. embassy.

"How's it going, Len? How's the family?" Dunn asked amiably.

"I was divorced two years ago and you know it," Fischer accused.

"Never heard—but I wasn't hearing too well then. Anyway, it's nice of you to meet me. I suppose the Athens cops wired the flight number."

Fischer shrugged noncommittally.

"I've got a car outside. Let's go, Charlie."

The vehicle was a green Chevrolet. Embassy

officers were probably encouraged to drive American cars.

"You know what this is about?" Dunn asked.

"All I know is that the station's been ordered to help you locate a former Agency employee named Victor Spalding—who was described as armed and extremely dangerous."

"Anything else, Len?"

"It was designated a Priority Red mission, and top secret—of course."

"*Of course.*"

"Naturally we have given it immediate and substantial effort," Fischer announced in his best bureaucratic jargon, "and enlisted the cooperation of Japan's internal security organization."

"Well?"

"The results have been positive."

"What the hell does that mean?" Dunn demanded impatiently.

"He was seen last night in a car near the Imperial Palace, and pursued at high speed by three mobile police units. He nearly got away."

"Do you have him?"

Fischer pursed his lips and smiled a tight little smile.

"*We* don't. But he is in custody at a hospital—under guard. There was some accident in the chase, I believe."

It was ironic—almost unreal—that Spalding should be captured after a car crash. The assassin had prided himself on his expert evasive driving. *This* was surprising, but Dunn had no time to dwell on the strangeness of fate and the imperfection of man. He had to concentrate on his imminent "talk" with Spalding.

When they reached the Yomuri Hospital shortly after noon, Fischer stopped the car some thirty yards from the front entrance of the seven-story building.

"He's on the sixth floor. Carrying an Irish passport in the name of Eamon O'Brian. Ask to see Dr. Takeda," Fisher said.

"Aren't you coming with me?"

Fischer's attempt at a cordial smile failed utterly.

"Not a great idea, Charlie . . . Might be some press around. . . . Could be sticky if my name got into the papers on this."

Was it the truth—or was Dunn being set up?

"I'm sure you can take it from here without me," he continued quickly. "So long, Charlie."

"For now."

Fischer understood. If something went wrong, he'd see Dunn again—quickly. As soon as Dunn stepped out and closed the door, Fischer stepped on the gas pedal and fled. Eight minutes later, Dunn faced a bright-eyed Japanese of about thirty who wore the white jacket of a hospital physician.

"Yes, I'm Dr. Takeda."

"My name's Dunn. I'd like to speak to a patient who was brought in a few hours ago by the police. Auto accident. Mr. Eamon O'Brian?"

"I can't help you."

"Doctor, this is a matter of some urgency. If you can't authorize—"

"No one can help you, Mr. Dunn. The car burst into flames on impact. Your friend suffered extensive third-degree burns over much of his body. I've never seen a worse case."

"How bad is it?"

"It's beyond *bad*. It's *over*. It was finished before he reached our emergency room. I'm sorry, Mr. Dunn. Your friend is dead."

It took Dunn about five seconds to absorb the impact.

"Are you sure?" he asked.

"Yes, I'm sure," the physician replied politely. "He has been pronounced dead after examination by two doctors on our staff. I can assure you that they are quite competent."

Now the foreigner shook his head.

"That's not what I meant, Doctor. Are you *absolutely sure* of your patient's identity?"

"That's not my affair, Mr. Dunn. I can only state for certain that a male Caucasian of about six feet and one hundred seventy-five pounds—age approximately thirty-five or thirty-six—was dead when he reached us nearly three hours ago. His passport and other documents say Eamon O'Brian of Dublin in the Republic of Ireland."

"They could be forged."

Takeda nodded as he took out a cigarette and lit it.

"That's for the police to determine. Why don't you talk to them?" he proposed.

"I will—but can I see the body first?"

"No harm, I suppose," Takeda assented. "But if it's the face that interests you, don't bother. How good a friend were you?"

"We weren't close."

Takeda sighed. That made it easier.

"Then I can put it rather bluntly," he announced. "This body has no face at all. Come along."

It didn't necessarily matter, Dunn thought as he trailed the doctor down the corridor to the hospital's morgue. There were other ways to achieve a positive identification. Dental work, fingerprints and X rays of bones known to have been broken earlier were among the best.

Dr. Takeda was right. Two-thirds of the body was ravaged by fire, and there was still the awful stench of charred flesh. There was no face—not even an ear.

But one hand was—somehow—intact.

And looking into the gaping ruin of what had been a human head Dunn could see all the dental work—completely intact.

If this carcass had been Victor Spalding, Dunn would know it within thirty-six hours. The identification must be absolute. Dunn explained that twenty minutes later to a chubby man in a plaid suit who was attached to Section Nine—the special-security unit—of the National Police.

"I don't mean to pry," Inspector Gaifuku assured, "but might I ask who you think this Irish gentleman might be?"

"Probably neither Irish nor a gentleman. More likely a murderer for hire."

Gaifuku nodded almost casually.

"That would explain the weapons he was carrying. I assume that there was something special about this murderer to *interest* your government."

The Japanese was much too tactful to ask what that might be. Dunn was much too professional to answer the unspoken question.

"Interest and *concern*," Dunn evaded.

Gaifuku did not press the point. He was used to half-truths and lies in these political cases.

"Is there anything that I can do to help?" he asked.

"If it wouldn't be an imposition, I'd like to see his clothes and possessions—and the accident report."

"We have them all here. Not much survived the fire, I'm afraid. The rented Datsun was largely destroyed when the gas tank blew up, but we saved what we could."

A charred Irish passport.

The disassembled parts of a sniper rifle with scope.

The melted remains of an eighteen-karat gold wristwatch—a Rolex.

A .22-caliber pistol with screw-on silencer.

A wad of half-burned currency—48,900 yen and 23 U.S. $100 bills.

A .357 Magnum automatic.

And a stainless steel surgical scalpel.

Dunn looked at all these for several minutes, and then listened as Gaifuku translated aloud the police report of the pursuit and crash.

"Thank you, inspector."

"You're entirely welcome. Would you please excuse me now? I have to talk to one of my colleagues who deals with the media. The press is always interested in these *drunken driving* cases. We're having a drive against alcoholism, you know."

"It's a problem everywhere."

Gaifuku picked up the passport and carefully wrapped it in a plastic bag.

"We'll have this checked to see whether it's forged," he announced.

"And could you send over a technician to take a set of fingerprints? The hospital can handle the dental X rays, but prints are for police specialists."

"No problem," the inspector assured and bobbed in a quick half bow of farewell.

The technician arrived at two o'clock. He was a bit puzzled by Dunn's instructions, but he did what was asked. The X rays were completed an hour later. Both the prints and pictures were in the sealed U.S. diplomatic pouch that left on the evening flight for Los Angeles. They arrived at the headquarters of the Central Intelligence Agency at 4:00 P.M. on December 30.

They were studied immediately. Highly experienced men and women checked and rechecked before they certified the identity of the body associated with these prints and dental works. Word of their findings was coded and relayed to the CIA station in Tokyo before midnight. As a result of the international time difference, it was only 10:00 P.M. on the thirtieth when Fischer told Dunn.

There could be no question about it.

The corpse was that of "Garbage."

The mission was over.

Whatever Dunn felt on hearing this, he showed nothing. He bade Fischer a perfunctory good-bye, and returned to his hotel to pack. He was among the passengers in the first-class section of the Pan American 747SP that headed east across the Pacific the next morning. He slept most of the way.

CHAPTER THIRTY

General Aleksei Kholkov was not sleeping. It would be improper for the fourth highest officer of the Glavnoye Razvedyvatelnoye Upravlenie—the Chief Intelligence Directorate of the General Staff of the Soviet Army—to nap at 2:30 in the afternoon.

Now he heard the icy wind sweeping up from the frozen Moscow River rattle the windows of his office. The huge main building of the Ministry of Defense occupied more than a block of rivershore here at 34 Maurice Thorez Quay—named after the French Communist Party chief who'd died in 1964. Blindly loyal to the Kremlin, Thorez had never questioned any policy or deed of the men who ruled the Soviet Union.

White-haired Kholkov was also a committed Marxist, but it was his duty to question. His job in the GRU was to keep an eye on the KGB for the Red Army. The field marshals who ran the General Staff remembered the dark deeds and imperial ambitions of such power-crazed KGB despots as Lavrenti Beria.

They had destroyed him, and they still didn't entirely trust his heirs.

As their vast mechanized armies and missile brigades indicated, they believed that safety—for the Red Army and the USSR itself—lay in numbers. No one man could be allowed to make key policies. There was a delicate and complex balance of military-civilian power in Moscow that worked. It would be maintained at any cost. That was why Kholkov's force of agents assigned to watch the KGB numbered more than 900.

The marshals had picked Kholkov because he was a worrier. Right now it was a report from one of his clandestine operatives that troubled him. The agent was a pretty GRU *leitnant* named Anna Rokosovsky who was passing as a physiotherapist. For five months now she'd been "treating" a KGB major named Polchasny whose wife believed that he worked late a lot.

"Exactly what did he say?" Kholkov asked.

"That he was a very important man doing very important work . . . That one project he was handling was so secret that not a single word had been written down—anywhere."

"Do you believe him?"

"There are men who boast or exaggerate or even lie to impress a woman, general," the shapely brunette replied earnestly. "I think he was boasting. He was in a very *relaxed* condition. We had just finished a *treatment*."

"So you think it's true, *leitnant*?"

"I do."

"Of course you couldn't ask about it."

"I felt that might be imprudent. If he says more, I'll report immediately."

Kholkov thanked her and watched her leave.

What could the U.S. section of the KGB be up to that was so extraordinarily sensitive?

It must be something big.

Whatever it was, Aleksei Kholkov had to find out—and soon. That was his job.

CHAPTER THIRTY-ONE

5:40 P.M. on January 1.

Following the great American tradition, 82 percent of the population of the United States was either nursing a hangover or watching one of the championship "bowl" games on television. Or both.

Among the nonconforming minority was a blonde-haired veterinarian in Falls Church, Virginia, who sat listening to an LP of Ella Fitzgerald singing the incomparable songs of George and Ira Gershwin. Leaning back in her grandfather's rocker with her eyes closed, Heather James nodded to the rhythm and wondered where Charles Jefferson Dunn might be. She was an intelligent, successful, and very attractive young woman whom any man would be fortunate to know—and who needed Charles Jefferson Dunn.

"Happy New Year."

She opened her eyes and beamed. His smile was just as large.

"Happy New Year, Charlie," she replied fervently a moment before he kissed her.

"Your clothes look as if you've slept in them,"
she told him.

"I did."

Then they kissed again. Suddenly he stood
up—alert and wary.

"Where's the security team?" he asked.

"They left yesterday. They said everything
was all right now."

He removed his jacket. She saw that he was
still wearing the twin automatics.

"It is all right, isn't it, Charlie?"

"Sure," he answered.

"Spalding?"

He sat down and told her what had happened in Tokyo.

"Did he have any family?" she asked.

"No, but a lot of people he killed did. If
you're feeling sorry for anyone, you can start
with Ken Perry's wife and two kids."

"I'm feeling sorry for everyone, Charlie—
except us."

Then he saw the bottle of Delamain Cognac
and two snifters on the coffee table beside a
heap of Washington *Post*s and New York
*Times*es.

"I've been waiting for you, Charlie."

"You weren't worried?"

"Hardly at all . . . and the shoulder's hurting much less. Pour us a drink, will you?"

She moved to the couch as he uncorked the
grande Champagne Cognac, and then they sat
side by side as they sipped.

"How are you managing?" he asked as she
rested against his left shoulder.

"I'm coping. I've hired a housekeeper who
comes in every day and leaves after dinner,

and neighbors and friends stop by with cakes and other goodies."

"Bill them for everything," he advised.

"Who?"

"The red, white and blues. Barringer and Company. Whatever you pay the housekeeper, all the income you've lost and will lose before you're back to work—and every cent of extra expenses you have because you were injured on a federal project."

"I make a lot of money, Charlie. Five or six thousand dollars a month."

"You earn it," he corrected, "and you've earned this. You risked your life for the government. Think of it in terms of hazardous-duty pay. You're a highly skilled professional. They don't work cheap."

"It might come to ten thousand dollars. That's a lot."

Dunn finished his Cognac.

"They owe you a lot, and they've got it. Why do women underprice themselves so much? Are you so rich that you want to subsidize the federal government? You're going to need every penny—to support me. I'm practically unemployable, you know."

She smiled dreamily.

"I'll find something for you to do," she promised. "You can be my financial adviser—and bodyguard."

"Will you follow my advice?"

"Absolutely. Tell them that it's ten thousand dollars," she agreed and sighed. "I guess we'll never know who's the Mr. Big that Spalding was supposed to kill, will we?"

Did she feel Dunn's shoulder stiffen—just for a second—or was it her imagination?

"It could be extremely dangerous to have that kind of information," he said soberly. "Anyway, it's nothing for you to worry about."

"I'm just curious."

"Now I've got a question," Dunn announced. "I think that I ought to stay here for a couple of weeks to help out and keep an eye on you. Would you mind?"

"I'd be furious if you didn't, Charlie."

The record ended. Dunn walked to the player, turned the album over and went out to his rented car. He returned with the suitcase and another question.

"Where's the guest room?"

"You're not my guest. You're my lover. This way," she commanded. She led him to what was obviously her room. It was dominated by a large brass bed.

"Side by the window's mine," she announced.

"I was trying to be considerate," Dunn explained. "With your shoulder and everything, I thought you'd prefer—"

"It's *only* my shoulder that's broken. As you'll discover shortly, the *everthing* is fine. Now hang up your clothes in that closet and stop being so damn genteel."

Dunn followed her instructions and then found out that she was right—twice. Afterward, they ate cold roast beef and drank a bottle of rich red Bully Hill Baco Noir '80 wine. Then she listened to her favorite Joan Baez LP and an album of Mozart horn concerti while Dunn caught up by reading the previous four days' newspapers. He seemed to be looking for something as he skimmed most pages but read one or two intently. She was surprised that he showed no interest in the sports, entertainment or style sections at all.

Just before 10:00 P.M. she glanced over when she heard him grunt. If Dunn had been looking for a specific item in the papers, he'd found it.

Five minutes later he made her a cup of Red Zinger tea, and they went to bed before eleven o'clock. Yielding to lack of sleep and jet lag, Dunn succumbed to exhaustion immediately. He slept deeply for ten hours.

When he made his way down to the kitchen at 9:20 the next morning, he looked much less weary. The middle-aged woman at the stove eyed him curiously.

"Mrs. Parrish, this is Mr. Charles Dunn," Heather James said as she finished eating a slice of stoneground whole wheat toast.

"He's a federal agent," the housekeeper declared.

"How did you find out?" Dunn asked with a smile.

"Two guns. Big ones. And you're too well dressed to be a gangster. Matter of fact, you're a lot better dressed than those other federal agents. Coffee? Sugar?"

She rattled it all off fast, like a burst of machine-gun fire.

"Yes, three lumps—please," he answered gravely.

"Better lookin' too. Don't you think so?" the peppery housekeeper asked Heather James.

"Definitely," the blonde veterinarian agreed. Then she leaned over and kissed him.

"Mr. Dunn saved my life," she explained to the plump housekeeper.

"Toast or muffins?" was Mrs. Parrish's only reply.

"Both."

When he'd finished breakfast and complimented the housekeeper on the food and coffee, Dunn went upstairs to collect his clothes. He descended with an armful of them a few minutes later.

"What tailor do you use?" he inquired.

"Falls Church Cleaners over on MacIvor Road. I could show you the way," she offered.

"No, you couldn't. You've got to rest here. I won't be back for a couple of hours anyway. Got some things to do. People to call. Appointments to make."

"About my money?"

"And mine too, Dr. James. They still owe me a bundle. Now where's that tailor?"

He listened attentively to her instructions and kissed her gently.

"We're like an old married couple," she joked.

He didn't smile.

"One more thing. Have you got the .32 I gave you?"

"*What?*"

"The Beretta automatic?" he pressed.

"I have it."

"Keep it handy."

It took a moment for her to understand.

"I thought it was finished, Charlie."

"There's still the question of the mole."

"But that's none of your business. Leave it alone," she appealed.

"All I'm going to do is pass along an idea I had."

"Please stay out of it, Charlie. Just collect the money and come home," she pleaded.

"I'll be back before five o'clock," he promised.

Some sixty seconds later she heard the engine of his car outside, and she felt sick to her stomach.

"It isn't over. It isn't over," she repeated. Then she went upstairs and found the .32 automatic.

It was all insane.

When would the madness end?

CHAPTER THIRTY-TWO

After he'd dropped off his clothes at the tailor and been assured that they'd be ready by four, Dunn got back in his car and drove into adjacent Arlington. With the help of a gas-station manager, he had no difficulty finding the shopping mall that housed Video Plus. The large store was well stocked with an impressive variety of television sets, video-cassette players, video-disk machines, blank tapes and prerecorded cassettes.

There was also a salesman who wore a button that read Al. Radiating confidence and a lot of Brut aftershave lotion, he smiled broadly as he approached Dunn.

"Biggest stock in Northern Virginia, friend. Whatever it is in the very latest video wonders, we've got it."

"I want a lightweight ... high-quality ... video camera ... battery pack ... half-inch tape."

"I like a man who knows what he wants, sir. And you're in luck. We're having our famous January sale. Biggest January video sale in

Northern Virginia," the salesman enthused. "I suppose you've seen our ads."

"No, but I'd like to see the cameras—*now*."

It took six minutes and $861 to buy the camera and a trio of two-hour blank cassettes. Three minutes and $907 more took care of the player unit.

"I'll take the camera, and I'd like the player delivered to a friend in Falls Church—before five o'clock," Dunn told the salesman.

"How about tomorrow, friend?"

Dunn put a pair of $20 bills on the counter. They disappeared immediately into the salesman's pocket.

"Before five? You *got* it, friend," he assured.

Dunn printed Heather James's address on an order form and handed it to Al.

"Say, we've got a sale on Ataris that'll knock your socks off. Three brand new games that are *dy-no-mite!*"

"I don't play games," Dunn called over his shoulder as he exited.

Dunn carried the loaded camera, pack and extra cassettes out to his car and locked them in the trunk. He drove half a mile toward Washington and stopped the vehicle at a pay phone. He had two calls to make.

At 11:05 Howard Barringer returned to his office in a better than usual mood. The Caribbean Task Force meeting that he'd just left had been productive—for a change—and McGhee's agents had stopped following him.

"You won't believe this, Mr. Barringer," Tess Lipson blurted. Barringer looked at his secretary, wondered why she'd been so tense recently and guessed that it might be hormonal. He'd be compassionate.

"Try me," Barringer invited.

"*He* called. *Charles Dunn*—he phoned you less than fifteen minutes ago."

She nodded triumphantly when she saw the shock in her supervisor's usually composed face.

"Charles J. Dunn!" she celebrated.

Maybe it wasn't Dunn, Barringer thought. It could be a trick.

"Are you certain it was Mr. Dunn, Edna?"

"He said he was, and that he wanted to see you tomorrow. He's going to phone in the morning about when and where. He was very polite."

Dunn *polite*?

"He said that he'd prefer tomorrow—*if your schedule permitted*—but if you're *all jammed up* the next day would be fine," she continued, "and he asked that you give his regards to Mr. McGhee."

Why a call on a nonsecure line? What was Dunn up to now?

"Did he leave a number?" Barringer tested.

"No, sir," she replied, and handed him message slips covering four other phone calls. Even as Barringer thanked her, he wondered where Dunn might be.

Dunn was in the District of Columbia, driving cautiously through West Potomac Park and eyeing the Lincoln Memorial only a few blocks away. It was a chilly January day. Temperatures along the Potomac were in the mid-forties, and that was good. In warmer weather the nation's capital would be flooded with tourists and buses crammed with high-school students—and it would be damn near impossible to find a parking space near the imposing white marble shrine.

Framed by a colonnade of thirty-six lofty Doric columns that represented the number of U.S. states during Lincoln's presidency, the building reminded Dunn of those classic Greek temples. He remembered that was the architect's goal, and he thought about the dramatic nineteen-foot statue of white Georgia marble inside. A sculptor named Daniel French had created the seated masterpiece.

He parked his car and took out the video camera. When he was some sixty yards from the memorial, he began to tape the front of the building and adjacent areas. Then he slowly walked around the 189-feet-long shrine, pausing regularly to tape both the exterior and the approaches. When he'd completed his circuit, Dunn started around again—this time in the opposite direction. Now he videotaped with his back to the memorial, facing away from the shrine.

He never entered the memorial. When he'd completed his second tour of the perimeter, he returned to his car and drove to a parking lot only four blocks from the White House. He bought a button that read God Bless America from a vendor and put it on the left lapel of his coat. It would help identify him as a patriotic and harmless tourist.

When he reached the White House, he repeated what he'd done at the Lincoln Memorial—and more. There were many buildings—some quite high—on three sides of the White

House. Dunn carefully taped their upper floors and roofs. He stopped to chat with other tourists who were taking pictures ... he smiled ... he even waved amiably at a uniformed guard manning the Pennsylvania Avenue entrance.

It was almost 1:00 P.M. by the time he finished. He was hungry, but it was probably better to leave the heart of the city. He'd rather not run the risk of meeting anyone alert enough to be curious about the video camera. It was wiser to drive across the Twelfth Street Bridge over into Arlington for a bowl of New England clam chowder and a rare hamburger.

He wasn't completely rid of the jet lag. But he wouldn't yield to fatigue. He had a plan and a timetable. He had things to do this afternoon—not far away. He had to get it all right. Dunn consumed two cups of coffee with his meal and left.

The Arlington National Cemetery was only three miles away, 420 acres filled with row on row of graves. Soldiers, sailors and marines, generals and admirals and political leaders—including the murdered Kennedy brothers—rested here. Dunn taped the Kennedy graves first, and then went to the famed Tomb of the Unknown Soldier. Again he aimed the camera at both the places and their approaches.

At a quarter after four, Heather James heard a car move down her driveway and stop behind the house. Her right hand went to the .32 in reflex action. It happened so quickly that it was disturbing, for guns were not part of her way of life. She slipped off the safety catch and looked toward the rear door.

Dunn entered carrying an armful of clothes on hangers and covered with the plastic bags used by tailors. There was nothing in his manner or expression to suggest that he was the least bit worried.

"How are you feeling?" he asked.

"All right."

"Anything new?"

"There's a big box in the living room. The men who delivered it said it's a video-cassette recorder."

"*Good*. Excuse me while I hang these up." Dunn returned a few minutes later, and he kissed her.

"You know about the box, Charlie?"

"I sent it. It's a get-well present. I was going to buy three pounds of chocolates—but they're fattening."

"And you're not such a great liar either, Charlie."

"I must be out of practice," he answered and went out to the car. He came back with a videotape camera and two cassettes. He put them down on a large end table. Then he took off his coat and jacket.

"We didn't open the box, Charlie, because I thought it might be another bomb. How do you like that?"

Dunn looked directly into her troubled eyes.

"I give you my word ... that there's no reason for anyone—*anyone*—to do *anything* to hurt either of us now," he told her.

"Then why am I scared, Charlie?"

"Anyone who's been bombed on the day before Christmas has good reason to be scared."

He strode to her and stroked her face reassuringly.

"Everything's going to be fine, Heather," he promised. "We'll have our money in a week or two. We can go away to some quiet place with great beaches. Barbados?"

Aware that he was evading and smoothing over, she nodded. Dunn opened the Video Plus carton and set to work connecting the VCR to her television set. Pausing only to check instructions in the manual, he was finished in ten minutes. He tested the new machine. It worked.

"Not bad, huh?" he demanded.

"Fine."

Announcing that she felt weary, she went up to their bed and slept for seventy minutes. Then she washed her face and carefully made her way down to the living room. He was staring at the television set. No sound came from it. The pictures on the screen seemed unedited—like amateur movies. What station would transmit this puzzling footage of a cemetery?

"What is it, Charlie?" she wondered.

"Arlington."

"I don't understand."

"Arlington National Cemetery. See, there's the Tomb of the Unknown Soldier."

She glanced at the video camera still on the end table. Then she turned her attention back to the TV set.

"Did you take those pictures?"

"Sure."

More pictures of the famed cemetery. And more . . . and still more.

"Charlie, why did you tape so much at Arlington?"

"Business," he replied instantly.

"What kind of business do you have with a military cemetery?" Heather James wondered.

"It's just an idea right now. Could make us a lot of money if it works. I may go back in a day or two to tape some more."

Before she could ask any more questions, they heard the footsteps of the housekeeper approaching. The veterinarian was startled when Dunn immediately turned off the set. Why wouldn't he want Mrs. Parrish to know that he'd videotaped the Arlington National Cemetery?

When dinner was over and the housekeeper had left, they returned to the living room. He had sounded absolutely sincere and totally confident when he'd said that there was no reason for anyone to hurt them now. She believed him—and yet she felt uncomfortable.

He was back at the video player.

"Hope you don't mind," he said and inserted a cassette.

"More cemetery pictures?"

He shook his head. She found herself looking at various views of the Lincoln Memorial—all outside shots. Then came eleven or twelve minutes of the area around the Grecian building. After that the screen was filled with pictures of the White House. Next came all the buildings and rooftops around it. There were many close-ups taken with a zoom lens. It was

five minutes to ten when he turned off the VCR
and yawned.

"When are we going to Barbados, Charlie?"

"Couple of weeks. Say the seventeenth or
eighteenth—to be on the safe side. I'll bring
some brochures home from a travel agency
tomorrow. Aaah," he yawned again. "That jet
lag's got me."

She stood up slowly.

"I'm tired too," she reported, and started
for the staircase. She was only a step away
when she turned.

"I trust you, Charlie," she said simply. "I
don't know what the hell you're doing—but I
trust you."

"I'm doing what I always do. I'm doing *the
right thing.*"

When they were in bed, she thought some
more about what his nameless business might
be. She didn't speak until just after he turned
out the light.

"Charlie?"

"Yes?"

"When we're in Barbados, will I still need
to keep the Beretta handy?"

"Of course not," he assured.

"Good," she sighed and drifted off into a
deep sleep.

CHAPTER THIRTY-THREE

3:05 P.M. . . . January 3.

"What did he want?" the Director of Central Intelligence asked.

"Money," Barringer replied. "He says we owe him two hundred thousand dollars—the rest of his fee."

Martin McGhee nodded. He'd learned how much the Agency had promised Dunn. McGhee enjoyed finding out things. All the bits of information gave the counterespionage executive a sense of well-being. McGhee glanced to see how the DCI was reacting. General Hartley's ebony face showed only impatience.

"I know what his fee was," Hartley said quickly. "What did you tell him?"

"That I'd pass along his message. I—uh—took the liberty of pointing out that he hadn't actually finished the assignment—that Spalding's demise came in a car crash while Dunn was one thousand miles away. Then I mentioned that our legal people believed that the contract died with Spalding."

"Was he furious?" Hartley asked.

"He was quite calm. I was surprised, general."

"Well, he did get two hundred thousand up front," Hartley reasoned. "That's not bad for about a month's work. Anything else?"

"Yes, sir. He's requested ten thousand dollars for Dr. James—to cover her medical costs and loss of income."

The DCI drummed his fingers on the desk.

"What do you think?" he asked.

"Pay it."

McGhee nodded in agreement.

"I thought *you* didn't like him," Hartley said.

"Liking has nothing to do with it," McGhee answered. "She's entitled to it—and it's entirely *cost effective*."

"Would you translate that?" the DCI demanded.

"It's a lot cheaper than the price we'd pay if there's a stink in the media, sir."

"You really believe she'd go public?" Hartley tested.

"Dunn would, general."

"He might very well do that," Barringer ratified, "or something else."

"What?" the DCI challenged irritably.

"I'd rather not find out. That's why I'm recommending that we pay her the ten thousand immediately. You see, there was a look in his eyes when he spoke of her that hinted he might *care* about Dr. James."

Another fact for McGhee's collection.

"Very well. Let's get it over with," the general ordered briskly. "Send her ten thousand—

through one of our dummy companies—for research and consulting services."

Now Hartley looked at his watch, signaling that they could go. Barringer and McGhee rose.

"There's still the matter of Dunn's final two hundred thousand," Barringer reminded stiffly. "He said he'd phone me on the seventh for word on when he'd get it. I'll need your decision by then."

"Are you saying our legal people are wrong?" Hartley asked in an icy tone.

"No, general. I'm suggesting that it might be—to use Mr. McGhee's phrase—*cost effective* to maintain friendly relations with Dunn."

"Are you *afraid* of him?"

"I'm simply trying to look ahead," Barringer explained evenly. "The time may come when we'll need the services of Charlie Dunn."

This wasn't a subject that the DCI wanted to discuss. Even though the righteous atmosphere of the Carter years was fading fast, there could still be problems with the Congress or the press about certain kinds of covert action operations. Hartley represented the smart new breed of general—the kind who dealt well with politicians and media types.

"I doubt it," the DCI dodged cannily, "but we'll think about it sometime."

His face gave no clue as to whether he was stalling or signaling that he didn't want to be told about—or involved in any way in— such controversial and therefore dangerous matters.

"He's pretty good, isn't he?" McGhee said half a minute later in the corridor outside Hartley's suite.

"A highly capable executive," Barringer replied in automatic ambiguity. He certainly wasn't going to discuss the DCI with someone as devious as the head of counterespionage.

"By the way, where's Dunn staying?"

"He didn't tell me. You're not still looking for him, are you? He might find that very annoying."

"I thought he was in a good mood," McGhee teased.

"He is. Relaxed ... cheerful. You're still under orders to stay away from him, remember?"

"Think that applies now Spalding's dead?"

"It applies until it's revoked in writing. Leave Charlie Dunn alone."

Dunn was alone—in a large building at the intersection of Constitution Avenue and Sixth Street Northwest in the heart of Washington. There were hundreds of other people in the National Gallery of Art, but Dunn didn't notice them. He was alone with the El Grecos. It was a splendid exhibit—superb paintings, spaced, lit and mounted as well as anyone could desire.

For a presentation of the masterpieces of the late Domenikos Theotokopoulos—the genius known as El Greco—it was close to perfect. It was also good for planning. It might have been a little easier if the works hadn't been displayed so well, but Dunn had overcome that within ten minutes. He spent almost two hours with the El Grecos, and then went on to the Air and Space Museum of the Smithsonian Institution a few blocks away.

That was part of his plan too.

The last act.

It rained all day on the fourth. Dunn didn't seem to mind. He asked the housekeeper to stay out of the living room because he "had some work to do." He closed the door and ran his cassettes.

Over and over.

He stopped the machine a hundred times to study some particular view, rewound the tape to peer at that footage intently and took notes on a yellow legal pad. He'd bought five of them at a stationery store before he'd gone to the National Gallery.

He paused only for lunch—and briefly. Making certain that the housekeeper was busy upstairs, he made two chicken sandwiches and a mug of Colombian coffee and took them back into the living room. Dunn closed the door, sat down and ran the tapes once more as he ate. When he was finished at half-past four, he tore all his notes into tiny bits and burned them in a large marble ashtray. Then he ripped off the next three blank pages from the pad and burned them too. He tamped the ashes into powder before he flushed them down the toilet.

Dunn left the house at twenty minutes to five. It was nearly six when he returned. He was carrying a green plastic shopping bag that carried a Merry Christmas from Ben's Grog Shop legend.

"You didn't go out in the rain just for liquor?" Heather James asked.

"Of course not."

He took off his raincoat and emptied the shopping bag. Two bottles of '78 Bordeaux, a '79 Bernkasteler and a bottle of Glenfiddich malt Scotch now stood on the kitchen table. Then he reached inside his jacket and drew out an envelope.

"Afraid we'll have to change planes in Miami," he apologized, "but nobody flies directly from Washington."

"Where?"

"Barbados. I *told* you," he said with mock indignation as he gave her the envelope. She opened it and saw the Eastern Airlines folder. Inside were two first-class tickets for a January 17 flight to Barbados, and the receipt for a $500 deposit towards two weeks at the Coral Reef Club.

"It's a nice hotel. Good beach and some of the best food on the island. You'll like it," Dunn predicted.

"You did it, Charlie," she said happily.

"Of course. I wouldn't lie to you, Heather. I might not always tell you everything—"

"I was about to say you're impossible," she broke in, "but that's not so. You're definitely *possible*. If you don't get killed, *probable*."

"I'm a sure thing—and stop talking about people getting killed. Let's discuss important matters—like sex and what's for dinner."

"I can handle the first topic," the smiling veterinarian told him, "but you'll have to try Mrs. Parrish for the second."

Dunn began to open the malt Scotch.

"I will. Say, where did you ever find that good lady? Cooks like that don't grow on trees."

"One of the security men phoned an employment agency the day I got back. It was sheer luck. She'd just finished another job. When she heard I was in a cast—"

"She came right over," Dunn finished.

"How did you know?"

"What else would such a nice friendly lady like that do?"

"She's that. A little more water in mine, please."

Dunn complied, and they lifted their squat highball glasses in silent toast. It was when she finished her first sip that she noticed the odd gleam in his eyes. He was amused.

"Charlie?"

"It's *okay*."

"You don't think—?"

"I do," he replied with a grin.

Heather James blinked at the idea that her housekeeper had been sent by the Central Intelligence Agency.

"You don't mind?" she demanded indignantly.

"To quote one of your favorite records, 'Fish gotta swim and birds gotta fly.' Facts of life, my love. My ol' buddies gotta do their thing too."

"Aren't *you* going to do anything, Charlie?"

He finished his drink.

"Absolutely. I'm going to eat very well as long as she's here . . . Aah, Mrs. Parrish. What's on the menu?"

"Crab bisque, swordfish and an endive salad," the housekeeper replied from the doorway. "Dessert's a surprise. Take the Scotch with you."

Dunn laughed.

The dinner was excellent, and Dunn complimented the housekeeper at ten after eight when she prepared to leave.

"Could we have the recipe for the apple crumb cobbler?" he appealed.

"Don't give my recipes. Night, doctor."

Dunn began to chuckle as soon as she'd departed. It was quite audible on the tapes when Emily Axt of the CIA's Counterintelligence division listened to them the next morning.

"*That woman's a real pistol.* Those were his very words, Mr. McGhee," she reported. "Our having an agent in the house twelve hours a day doesn't seem to bother him at all."

"Any problems?"

"The microphones in the living room and bedroom are no longer functioning."

"The bedroom's a question of privacy . . . but why the living room?" McGhee wondered aloud.

"Do you think he's disconnected them?"

"Or smashed them. He might even sell them. Mr. Dunn has an unusual sense of humor. From what I can tell, he's also rude and arrogant."

"Have you ever met him?" she asked.

"No, but it shouldn't be long now. Continue the surveillance."

As she walked back towards her office, Emily Axt wondered why McGhee wanted Dunn and Heather James watched. The chief of Counterintelligence was such a logical man, and the most rational thing would be to concentrate on finding the mole. This didn't make any sense at all.

Unless McGhee thought that Heather James had some connection with the mole.

CHAPTER THIRTY-FOUR

January 4 was a chilly gray Saturday. Almost everyone in and near the District of Columbia was resting. Dunn wasn't. He left the house with his video camera at a quarter after ten, drove through Alexandria and over the Woodrow Wilson Bridge to Rose Valley Airport. There he found the small office of Maryland Heliservices where a freckle-faced man named Dallas Gallo was waiting.

He was wearing an aviator's coveralls. Eight $50 bills and fourteen minutes later, Gallo was at the controls of a Bell helicopter with Dunn seated beside him. Following Dunn's instructions, Gallo guided the rotorcraft over to sprawling Andrews Air Force Base—the big complex where military transports and special government planes such as the president's Air Force One landed.

Gallo circled Andrews as Dunn looked down through powerful binoculars. Then the pilot flew over the highway from the airfield into downtown Washington while Dunn taped. This wasn't nearly as exciting as those Vietnam missions on which Gallo had commanded a helicopter gunship, but it paid the rent.

Now Dunn pointed at a large building 2,300 feet below and swung his finger in a circle. Gallo wouldn't fly over that building because it was "restricted" airspace, but he didn't mind piloting the chopper in a loop around it. Dunn had explained that he was scouting locations for a Richard Pryor film—a zany comedy about a black president. For such a movie it made sense to plan sequences that included the White House.

Then Dunn gestured for a wider circle. This time he taped the roofs of buildings in a 700-yard radius around the presidential residence. When he was satisfied, he poked the pilot on the shoulder and pointed back towards the USAF base. They flew a different route back—with Dunn taping all the way. When they reached Andrews, Dunn gave Gallo a thumbs-up gesture of approval. The pilot smiled in appreciation. Six minutes later they were climbing down from the copter onto the runway at little Rose Valley Airport.

"Thanks," Dunn said.

"Ask you something?"

Dunn nodded.

"What kind of guy is Richard Pryor anyway?"

"Never met him," Dunn answered truthfully.

He drove back into Washington. Traffic was light as he rode through the midtown area and turned off onto fashionable Connecticut Avenue Northwest. It was only a few minutes to the bridge over Rock Creek Park. The embassy was just beyond. This was the Kalorama section of the capital, a neighborhood of well-tended lawns and big houses. The tall brick embassy stood out among them.

Dunn circled it slowly twice, eyeing the adjacent homes . . . the walls and fences . . . the guards provided by the federal Executive Protective Service. The embassy didn't look like the nearby mansions, but resembled some of the adjacent high-rise condominiums. He recognized the flag—bright red with a large yellow star and four smaller ones. Dunn knew the bold banner as well as he knew that nation's infantry weapons, rockets and tanks.

He stopped the car and videotaped the street and one side of the embassy. Then he drove on to another vantage point to repeat the process. He didn't stay too long at any spot, for there was the risk that some overachieving security agent might note his car's license plate numbers. Dunn would have to come back to tape again—in a few days—in another vehicle.

He drove to a small Greek restaurant for lunch, and returned to Falls Church at half-past two. The housekeeper had gone.

"I don't like the idea of you being alone," Dunn announced.

"Relax, Charlie. You yourself said that nobody would want to hurt us," Heather James reminded. Then she pulled the Beretta from her bathrobe pocket.

"How's that for speed?"

"*Terrible*. Want to see some videotapes that are just as bad?"

He inserted a cassette in the player, paused

and checked the living room for concealed
listening devices.

"Again? You did that yesterday, Charlie?"

"And I will tomorrow. Dear Mrs. Parrish—or
whatever her name is—could have slipped in
two or three new bugs. All right, my love.
Here we go."

They looked at the new tape for fifty-five
minutes before she spoke.

"You're really hung up on the White House,
aren't you?"

"Every red-blooded American boy is," he
replied, "and why not? I could be president.
I've got great teeth and you dress well."

"You're crazy, Charlie."

"That's no handicap in politics."

Now scenes of the embassy filled the screen.

"I know that building! I know that flag too!
Red China!" she said excitedly.

"PRC," he corrected.

"What?"

"People's Republic of China. That's what
they call themselves."

"I've been in that building, Charlie. Up on
Connecticut Avenue—just across the bridge. I
was there for a reception eight months ago."

The tape rolled on steadily, offering other
views of the embassy.

"Charlie, there's something else I ought to
mention to you," Heather James said suddenly half a minute later.

"I went out for a short walk an hour ago—
just down to the mailbox with a letter to my
dad. I think I saw her—the Oriental woman—
the one who was watching me in the bookstore in Athens."

"Sure it was her?"

"Ninety-five percent sure. She was sitting in a brown Buick, watching this house."

"*Son of a bitch*," Dunn muttered softly.

"Does she work for the Agency—or someone else?"

"I'd bet on *someone else*. Okay, I'll check it out. Maybe I'll have a *talk* with her."

"She might be a friend of Spalding," the veterinarian speculated.

"Don't think he had any. I'll be careful though," Dunn assured.

The screen was suddenly blank. He rewound the cassette to play it all over again. Halfway through, Heather James's wide blue eyes closed and she nodded off into sleep. When he'd completed the second viewing, he turned off the VCR and went to a window at the front of the house. There was no brown Buick in sight.

At 9:10 the next morning, Heather James heard a noise. It was just loud enough to awaken her. For several moments she felt warm and creamy and very serene. It was good to be with a man who loved her and loved well.

Where was he?

He should have been in the bed beside her. He wasn't.

She heard another sound. There was someone downstairs—toward the back of the house. The cast felt heavy and the flesh beneath it itched, but she couldn't think of such things now. Easing herself out of bed carefully, she picked up the .32 from the bedside table. Walking barefoot to minimize the noise, she made her way down the stairs.

A thump from the kitchen told her where the intruder was. Was he armed? She braced herself, pushed the kitchen door open and thrust the gun forward.

"Happy birthday!" Dunn said.

The scent of fresh coffee and bacon filled the room, and she saw the fluffy omelette in her big heavy pan. He was making Sunday breakfast.

"Thanks—but it isn't my birthday, Charlie."

"Of course it is," he contradicted cheerfully. "Eat your breakfast."

When they were finished eating, they settled down with the bulky Sunday newspaper in the living room. With an album of Jean-Pierre Rampal and the Baroque Chamber Ensemble playing Bach pouring pleasure from her record player, they sat side by side on the couch reading—until five after eleven. That was when Dunn suddenly rose to his feet.

"This is Sunday, Charlie. No watching those tapes today."

"Certainly not. I'm running."

He ran a mile and a half that day and two the next. On Wednesday he increased the distance to two and a half. Dunn had done a lot more running during the years in Vermont, and he'd continued it in the weeks before they'd left for London. He was running for fitness, muscle tone, stamina and *concentration*. He was preparing for battle.

Each day he'd run in the morning and spend an hour on a nearby pistol range in the afternoon. He was shooting with a pair of

.22-caliber target guns. He'd fire four clips with his right hand and four with his left. Then he'd repeat it. He had to be absolutely accurate with both.

And he had to be right. He spent a lot of time thinking and rethinking, and he devoted two hours a day to studying the videotapes. The solution was in those pictures. He had to find it soon, for time was running out now.

It was while he was running three miles on Saturday morning that he made his decision. Though he'd gone over the variables more than a hundred times, he knew that it was a calculated risk. He had to make his move. At 10:40 P.M. he did.

"Going out for a bit," he told a surprised Heather James.

She didn't ask any questions. She'd noticed the tension building up within him. Now Dunn was going to do what he had to.

"Don't wait up," he advised.

Before she could answer, he kissed her and walked out into the night.

CHAPTER THIRTY-FIVE

"Don't move," someone ordered.

Martin McGhee was frightened. It wasn't merely the fact that it was 2:00 A.M. and his bedroom was pitch black. It was the cold metal circle pressing between his eyes. It must be a gun, and he'd never had a gun pressed against his head before.

He could hardly believe it. Things like this didn't occur in such expensive little houses on the well-patrolled streets of gracious Georgetown. They certainly didn't happen to the chief of Counterintelligence of the powerful Central Intelligence Agency.

Ten seconds ago McGhee had been sleeping soundly. He never dreamed or struggled with nightmares. Now he was awake and right in the middle of a nightmare. He fought to beat back the wave of terror. He had to be calm. He had to know who held the gun to his head, and why. If it was information they wanted, they'd get none.

"I won't tell you anything," McGhee vowed tensely.

"I'll tell you. I've come to talk to you—not kill you."

"Who are you?"

A penlight blinked on for a few seconds, just long enough for McGhee to recognize the face that the beam had so briefly illuminated.

"Dunn!"

"Charles J.," Dunn replied and recited his CIA serial number.

"You won't get away with this, Dunn."

"I just did. Now relax and listen, will you? This is important."

The muzzle was no longer pressing against McGhee's forehead. His eyes were adjusting to the darkness. He could make out the silhouette of a long-barreled pistol pointing at him.

"You can sit up if you want," Dunn offered, "or smoke. Just don't diddle any alarm buttons. Don't even think about it."

"I don't smoke," McGhee replied righteously and sat up with rigid dignity.

"If this has anything to do with your money, I'm the wrong person. You were supposed to call Barringer back on that days ago," McGhee accused.

"I've been busy. Now let's talk about something a lot more urgent—Victor Spalding."

"Why speak of the dead?"

"You may be a creep, McGhee, but you're too smart to buy that convenient auto crash."

Now the head of Counterintelligence sat up straighter.

"We do have the dental X rays and fingerprints," McGhee reminded. "They might have duplicated the dental work, but not the fingerprints."

"You mean *these* prints?"

The penlight flicked on again. It was aimed at Dunn's right hand.

"What the hell are you saying?" McGhee demanded.

"The prints you got from Tokyo were *mine*—not the corpse's."

"Can you prove that?"

"I've got sworn affidavits from two reputable men who saw me do it," Dunn announced. "One's a doctor at the hospital and the other's the police inspector who handled the case. Those were *my* prints."

Now the room was completely black again.

"Jesus, Mary and Joseph!"

"Maybe," Dunn replied, "but not Victor Spalding. You've been had."

McGhee didn't answer. He was trying to absorb and apply what he'd heard.

"Aren't you going to thank me?" Dunn asked. "I've just done your job. The person on your staff who checked those prints and said they were Spalding's is a liar—and an enemy agent. *That's your mole!*"

"I'll look into it . . . could I see those affidavits?"

Dunn tossed an envelope onto the bed.

"Photocopies. I'm keeping the originals," he said.

"Is there anything else, Mr. Dunn?"

"Spalding. This whole number was to save him for a very special hit . . . here . . . *soon*."

"Who?"

"Wu Fang Teh—he's arriving tomorrow afternoon."

The new prime minister of the People's Republic of China was making his first visit to the United States. On the fifteenth he'd sign an historic "friendship and mutual assistance" treaty at the White House. Columnists and TV sages had been speculating about possible military-aid sections in the agreement.

"How do you know it's Wu?"

"It's part head and part gut. Wu is one of the four most important people alive—and the one that some folks in Moscow might want dead. Moscow runs both Spalding and the mole."

"Is that the head or the gut part?" McGhee asked testily.

"Don't mock either, mister. I nailed your goddamn mole with that head and that gut."

The head of Counterintelligence changed the subject.

"How could Spalding get near him? There'll be very heavy security—both United States and Chinese," McGhee reasoned.

"Heavy security is Spalding's specialty. This is a big target. He'll do it big," Dunn predicted. "I've been thinking about where. Probably some place on the standard VIP tour for top foreign visitors. I've checked a few of them out." He heard McGhee sniff in the darkness.

"Mr. Dunn, this is conjecture. What do you *know?*"

"Spalding's training, style and mind. He's a showboat. I say *the White House.*"

"Ridiculous—he'd never get inside."

"*Outside.* My guess is he'll attack the chopper that's bringing Wu in from Andrews—that he'll try to blast it over the White House.

With the TV cameras rolling, he'll dump the body right at the president's feet."

"That's your *guess*, Mr. Dunn?"

"My *educated* guess. I'm a professor in this field, remember?"

Silence.

Five . . . ten . . . fifteen seconds.

"There isn't much time," Dunn said. "He's landing at Andrews at half-past three. That gives you a fraction more than eleven hours."

"I'll call you in the morning," McGhee declared coolly.

"You know where to reach me. By the way, thanks for Mrs. Parrish. She gives great kitchen."

"That sounds lewd."

"It was meant to," Dunn replied, and slipped out into the night.

As he drove back to Falls Church, he kept wondering whether he'd handled it right. Did McGhee really believe him? Would he act? Well, Dunn had done what he could. It should work. It would—unless Martin McGhee was the mole.

CHAPTER THIRTY-SIX

Three blocks from the White House, the Axelrod Building is twelve stories high and very well maintained. Though it has not been a status address for years and does not compete with the flashy new towers, it is still the respectable home of many small law firms, accounting partnerships, commercial photographers, business newsletters, orthodontists and assorted trade and scholarly associations. There were also two foundations.

One of these was the International Astronomy Foundation, which had moved into a small office on the eleventh floor two months ago. It was one of those low-budget academic outfits with a single aged employee. He was bent, white haired and half-blind if those thick glasses were any clue. Not too strong either, for he'd been out sick for weeks. Dr. Ira Chamberlain was probably a retired professor, everyone on the building staff agreed.

At 2:05 P.M. on January 13, Dr. Chamberlain entered the lobby of the Axelrod Building. As usual, he carried his cane in one hand and the worn black leather briefcase in the other.

Glad to see the old man back, the uniformed elevator starter held the door for him.

"Thank yuh," Chamberlain acknowledged in that Florida accent.

"You're welcome, sir."

Some fifty seconds later, Chamberlain shuffled into Room 1107 and locked the door behind him. He picked up the clump of astronomy journals and other scientific magazines that the mailman had shoved through the slot and heaped them atop the bookcase that already held at least sixty issues of similar publications.

The office was sparsely furnished. There was a coat rack, two filing cabinets, a tired-looking pine desk and three wooden chairs. There was a manual typewriter—at least a decade old—on a wheeled metal stand. There was a large globe on a small table near the window, and a three-feet-by-four-feet framed chart of the heavens on one wall.

Dr. Chamberlain hung his coat on the rack, unlocked the closet and took out a tripod some four feet high. He placed it near the window. Then he returned to the closet for the telescope. He was standing straighter now as he began to unscrew the barrel. By the time he was finished, he wasn't the bent old professor anymore and the telescope looked different too.

Connecting it to another piece that he removed from the closet, the man who wasn't Dr. Ira Chamberlain now held a weapon familiar to U.S. infantrymen. It was a light rocket launcher—standard issue and stolen from a military depot—that fired a heat-seeking antiaircraft missile. Spalding had chosen this U.S. Army weapon quite deliberately. It would add to the embarrassment of the American government when it was discovered whose hardware had killed the prime minister.

And they wouldn't even come searching for him.

Who would hunt a dead man?

Spalding opened his briefcase, took out the special radio and turned it on to listen to the traffic controller in the Andrews Air Force Base tower. The Chinese jet transport was actually two minutes ahead of schedule—830 miles west of Washington.

Estimated time of arrival: 3:28 P.M.

That meant the chopper would be over the White House helicopter pad at five or six minutes to four.

And then there'd be no Wu Fang Teh or Dr. Ira Chamberlain either—just Victor Spalding, the wealthiest and most successful assassin on this earth.

It was time to clean up the office. He'd brought two cloths for just this purpose. Spalding went to work rubbing and polishing every surface that might hold a fingerprint. There must be no trace that Victor Spalding had been here. He took special care with the rocket launcher.

2:57—the Chinese Pilot was speaking to Andrews again.

The large jet must have been slowed down so it would roll down the Andrews runway precisely on schedule.

ETA now 3:30 P.M. as specified.

Spalding heard it all—the traffic controller's instructions to the Chinese pilot who spoke quite good English . . . and then the tower-operator's orders for the take-off of the helicopter.

At a quarter to four, Spalding mounted the rocket launcher on the tripod near the window. Though it worked as a shoulder-fired weapon, he felt it would be even more accurate on a tripod. Once it was set up, he took one of the long thin missiles from the locked trunk in the closet and loaded the rocket into the launcher. Then he took a pair of $630 binoculars from a desk drawer and began to sweep the skies near the White House.

Nothing yet.

He moved a chair so he could sit behind the launcher, which was only inches from the window. There it was—a distant dot in the D.C. afternoon. It was moving in at about one hundred miles an hour—much too slow and too low for a fixed-wing jet. It had to be the chopper.

The hour he'd planned for was at hand.

"King of Death!" Spalding boasted aloud as he raised the window. A blast of thirty-nine-degree air rushed in, but that did not deflect him. In three or four minutes Victor Spalding would change history.

He moved the tripod forward to the open window, settled onto the chair behind the weapon and raised the binoculars again confidently.

The helicopter was much closer. It was about three-quarters of a mile away. That put it within range, but Spalding would wait until the craft flew a bit nearer. He probably only had one shot. It had to be his best.

What was that?

Another helicopter . . . and another . . . and more. Three . . . four . . . five . . . six.

Six choppers? What was going on?

He studied them carefully, and recognized the shapes. Three were standard passenger "birds" used for VIPs. The others were military—combat machines. No doubt about it. They were gunships loaded with rapid-fire twenty-millimeter cannon, twin-mounted .50-caliber machine guns and rockets.

What the hell were they doing over downtown D.C.?

More important, in which chopper was the Chink?

Spalding switched on the scanner to search for the helicopters' radio frequency. As the choppers moved closer, the device did its work.

"Hard Ball One to Hard Ball Two. Hard Ball One to Hard Ball Two. You see anything?"

"Negative . . . Negative . . . I don't think—"

"There he is! Hard Ball Three to Leader. The son of a bitch is off to the left . . . that gray building . . . one floor from the top . . . See him? . . . Sun's hitting his weapon!"

Now another voice sounded in the background.

"Get him! Get him!"

It was that fucking Dunn.

"Hard Ball Leader to all street teams. Home Run! We are preparing to attack. Gray office building west of Eagle's Nest. I'm going in!"

It was hopeless. Two of the gunships stayed with the three passenger-craft. Five "birds"—their engines would confuse the heat-seeking missile. And one of the attack choppers was boring directly toward the Axelrod Building.

How had Dunn known he was alive?

How had he figured out the plan?

No time for those questions now. The gunship was only 500 yards away—closing fast. In ten seconds those .50s would open fire. Police units were undoubtedly racing towards the building at top speed. Yes, there were the sirens.

Victor Spalding jumped up and turned towards the door.

Then he ran for his life.

CHAPTER THIRTY-SEVEN

"The president was *very pleased*. Said our performance was *gratifying* and *outstanding*," Hartley told Barringer and McGhee the next morning.

"Called me *himself*—not ten minutes ago," the exultant Director of Central Intelligence continued. McGhee automatically looked at his calendar-digital wristwatch. January 14 . . . 9:58.

"This ought to help us with the budget," Barringer thought aloud.

"Exactly what he said. Told me, 'Bill, I hear you've been having some money problems on the Hill. Well, that's done. You've got my word, Bill.' *Great*, isn't it?"

McGhee and Barringer—who had lived through the eras of at least three presidents who routinely lied and broke their firmest commitments—nodded in solemn approval. Now the DCI pointed an ebony finger at Barringer.

"Your Designated Hitter really did it. You were right about that man," Hartley complimented.

"Thanks, but it was *that man* who was right, general."

"Fair enough. There's plenty of credit to share around."

"And cash," Barringer said. "He's earned his fee—all of it—ten times over."

"You think he's earned it all?" Hartley asked McGhee slyly.

"Give him his money and let him go back to Vermont," the Counterintelligence chief replied.

"Spalding's still on the loose," the DCI reminded.

"Not for long, general. Every cop in the country's looking for him, and the FBI has half its entire strength covering airports and harbors," McGhee reported.

The general could not entirely suppress a smile at the mention of the Federal Bureau of Investigation. Hartley was a fine soldier, but also an excellent bureaucrat. Internal security—which included stopping assassins—was an FBI responsibility. The embarrassment of a rival agency was not wholly distressing.

"We'll pay Dunn," Hartley announced.

"I'll get the paperwork moving," Barringer said and left immediately.

"Now how about your mole?" the DCI asked.

"Definite progress. I think I know who it is," McGhee answered.

"Who is he?"

McGhee shook his head from side to side.

"*She*. A woman in . . . ah . . . the Counterintelligence group. A highly trained computer specialist—and obviously one of the top KGB people."

Hartley nodded at the laudatory description of the mole. By building her up, McGhee was following Rule One for survival: protect your image and your ass.

"She had the computer override number, general. Emily Axt could get into anything. Of course, we're not sure she is Emily Axt. They might have switched identities ten or thirteen years ago when the genuine Mrs. Axt took two trips to Vienna."

"Find out, will you?" the DCI suggested sarcastically.

"You can bet on it. We've got plenty of work there."

"It's your turn," Hartley joked. "Dunn's finished his. Hope he's relaxing with a good cigar right now."

Charles Dunn was not smoking. He was shooting. He'd run his three miles earlier in the morning, and now he was at the range. He fired twice as many rounds as usual with each hand. Then he began shooting both pistols simultaneously. The manager of the range watched with interest and admiration. He'd never seen Dunn do that before.

CHAPTER THIRTY-EIGHT

The morning of January 15 was crisp and clear. By 9:10 Dunn had run and showered and finished breakfast. He was putting the dishes in the sink when the doorbell rang.

"I'll get it," he called out as he drew one of the P-15 semiautomatics. He walked to a window at the front of the house. There was a gray van parked at the curb nearby, and an Hispanic male standing at the entrance to Heather James's home. Though the man was four inches too short to be Spalding, Dunn released the safety catch on his gun before opening the door.

"Dr. H. James?"

"That's my name," Dunn lied easily. "What's yours?"

"Delivery from Ajax," the messenger replied and thrust forward a slim tan envelope. Since it was too thin to be a letter bomb, Dunn reached out to take it.

"You gotta sign first," the messenger objected.

"Who says so?"

"For Chrissakes, it's the company rule. *Here*,"

the man said grumpily and shoved forward a receipt pad with a cheap ballpoint pen. Dunn scrawled a forged signature, and the courier departed. Dunn glanced down at the pen still in his hand and smiled. Like the gray van the man was entering, it bore no name or identifying mark.

"Who was that?" Heather James asked moments later.

"He didn't say."

Dunn gave her the envelope. She opened it and stared.

"Charlie, it's a check for ten thousand dollars!"

"Good ol' Ajax."

"I never heard of them. You know who they are?"

Dunn nodded and lit a cigar.

"Folks who owe you ten thousand. Glad to see they're paying promptly," he told her and blew a smoke ring.

"The only people who owe ... Charlie, is this from Mr. Barringer? Is *he* connected with Ajax Research Limited?"

"Yes to both. What do you care so long as the check's good?"

"Is it?" she asked mischievously.

"Sure."

"Then I'll deposit it right now. I was going to ask you to drive me to the bank for some money anyway. If you're not busy—"

"Free as a bird till my eleven o'clock shooting appointment," Dunn told her.

They were halfway to her bank when she asked the question.

"What's going on, Charlie?"

Before he could answer, she spoke again.

"Spalding's on the run and nobody wants to hurt us, so why the gun when you go to the front door? Life is peaceful and we're going to Barbados in three days, so why continue the shooting drills? What is it, Charlie?"

"Spalding—he has *another* plan to hit the Chinese prime minister."

"Spalding's probably one thousand miles from here."

Dunn shook his head.

"No, he isn't. He's very close. I can almost *smell* him."

Heather James wondered what to say. Was he right, or was this some primitive obsession?

"You stopped him, Charlie," she said. "You've won."

"I know he's got a backup plan," Dunn continued grimly. "That's standard drill. If something goes wrong, be ready for a second strike. It has to be very different. Surprise is the key. Surprise and imagination."

"Let go of it," she appealed. "Tell the police and let them do it."

"I did that. Told the cops and McGhee, but they thought I was being paranoid. They were polite. They said they'd beef up security, but they didn't really believe me."

She'd never heard such urgency in his voice.

"Spalding will go for it, you know," Dunn predicted. "He's got to. For the money, for his reputation in the trade—and for his sick head. He has to show me. He's *very* crazy. *Shit*, I guess I sound crazy too."

"You're not crazy, Charlie—but you're not

God either. You can't be everywhere, and you can't know everything."

"That's the problem. He could attack at any of six or seven places. I've been thinking about them since the cops broke into that office. Where will he strike?"

"Not at the Virginia People's Bank, Charlie. That's it on the next block."

Dunn remained in the car while she went in to deposit the check. The two questions kept racing through his mind as if on a tape loop. Where would Spalding attack? How?

Something different.

Totally different.

From *below* this time.

A bomb or a mine—radio controlled. Spalding had probably put it in place weeks ago. That was his backup plan if the heat-seeking missile failed.

Where?

The prime minister had already paid his ceremonial visits to Arlington and the Lincoln Memorial, and this morning's news broadcasts had reported his opening the exhibit of ancient Chinese scrolls at the Freer Gallery. This was his last day in Washington. Spalding would attack sometime in the next six or seven hours.

Where was the goddamn bomb?

Frustrated and impatient, Dunn flicked on the radio. He heard the last thirty seconds of a Kenny Rogers ballad, and then an idiotic commercial for a new laxative. That was just ending as she emerged from the bank. She opened the car door—and the network news poured from the dashboard speaker.

"Fast, wasn't it? One of the officers took care of me. Felt sorry for the poor lady in the cast," she explained.

Dunn started the car and began the trip back to the house.

"I've got half of it—I think," he said. "It'll be a bomb."

She nodded in acceptance. He couldn't be stopped.

"What's the other half, Charlie?"

"*Where.* If I get *where* then I know *when.*"

"The Israeli cabinet will meet again tomorrow," the CBS newsman announced briskly. "In Washington, preparations are proceeding for today's signing of the treaty. Prime Minister Wu Fang Teh is due at the White House in twenty-five minutes, and the historic document is to be signed before an audience of top congressional leaders some fifteen minutes later."

"That's it! I've got him!"

"What is it, Charlie?"

"Has to be. Spalding will blast him from the one place they'll never expect him to go— back to the Axelrod Building. Clear view of the White House. I've got the son of a bitch!"

If he could get there through the mid-morning traffic in time. Dunn swerved the car into a gas station, jumped out and began ramming coins into a pay phone.

"Mr. McGhee's office."

"This is Dunn. It's urgent. Priority Red."

"Mr. McGhee's not in. His assistant is here. Would you want to speak to her?"

"Fast."

Ten seconds later he heard a cool unfamiliar voice.

"Mrs. Axt. Can I help you, Mr. Dunn?"

"It's Spalding. He's in the Axelrod Building—getting ready to set off a radio-controlled bomb. Get some cops. I'm on my way."

Dunn sprinted back to the car. Every minute counted now. He drove swiftly and expertly, hoping that no well-meaning policeman would stop him. It was a race. He could not afford to be delayed by anyone or anything.

10:12 . . . he had seventeen minutes before the prime minister's limo rolled up to the White House. The car would be bulletproof, but that wouldn't help. Spalding would use a massive charge—enough to smash a tank.

Traffic grew heavier as they neared Washington. Dunn fought grimly, swerved in and out and cut ahead of two startled and irate motorists to get onto the bridge. Other drivers blew their horns and cursed, but he ignored their fury. He swung his car into the wrong lane, barely avoided a head-on collision and pressed ahead.

Maybe the police would be there by now.

They should be—but he couldn't risk it.

10:21 . . . eight minutes.

Traffic was much worse as they roared off the bridge. Every damn yard was a struggle. Dunn battled on until he was trapped in a tangle of cars just four blocks from the building. The life-and-death seconds were ticking away.

He couldn't wait.

"Take the wheel," he snapped, and jumped out of the car. Sucking in his breath, he sprinted towards the building where Spalding had to be. Zigzagging between startled pedestrians and vehicles, Dunn ran as fast as he could. As he entered the Axelrod Building, he caught a glimpse of the lobby clock.

It was 10:27.

Two minutes.

There wasn't a policeman in sight.

Was Spalding really here?

In the foundation office or on the roof?

If Dunn guessed wrong, the prime minister was doomed.

CHAPTER THIRTY-NINE

On the roof of the Axelrod Building, a man in the blue uniform of the District of Columbia police looked out towards the White House. Despite the matching coat and cap from which straight black hair emerged, he felt the chill.

Still, this was better than the sewer where he'd spent an hour and a half last night. It had taken him that long to remove the plastic charge from where he'd hidden it weeks earlier and to place it under the manhole cover in front of the White House. Knowing that the Secret Service would check such possible danger spots the day before the damn Chink arrived, Victor Spalding had waited until *after* Wu Fang Teh paid his first visit to the president's home before putting the bomb in place.

Spalding looked at his watch.

One minute.

Now they'd see who was "Garbage" and who was the best.

The radio-control device sat on the ledge just eight inches away. Spalding raised his binoculars, peered down Pennsylvania Avenue and saw the motorcade approaching.

Ten cycle cops first ... then three cars filled with U.S. security agents and two more crammed with the prime minister's own bodyguards. Then four vehicles carrying Chinese diplomatic officials—and the stretch Cadillac limousine that was the target. More official cars followed, but they didn't count. Spalding had watched the motorcade at the Freer Gallery the night before. He knew which car must be destroyed.

It was a matter of seconds now. Spalding felt the cool thrill of anticipation he knew so well. No, this was better than anything he'd experienced. This would be his greatest success. He was smiling as his hand moved to the radio-control unit. In a dozen seconds he'd make history.

At that moment, Dunn stepped out onto the roof with a P-15 in each hand. Both guns thundered at once—blasting the transmitter into electronic scrap. Spalding dropped the binoculars and spun, his right hand thrusting for the police .38 in his regulation holster.

"Don't do it!" Dunn yelled.

He was coiled in the shooter's crouch, aiming a pair of 9-millimeter French semiautomatics at Spalding's face. If he squeezed those triggers, most of Spalding's head would rain down on the street below. Glaring hatred, Spalding froze.

"Get 'em up, Victor! High!"

Spalding complied.

"Take it easy, Victor. I want to talk to you. I've been trying to talk to you for weeks."

"Fuck you."

"Pay attention, will you? This is important."

Spalding cursed him again.

"All right. I'll get straight to the point," Dunn announced and shot him through each upraised palm. Spalding screamed and screamed in agony. He took a step towards Dunn in rage.

"Stop," Dunn ordered.

With blood pouring from his maimed hands and moaning in animal hurt, Spalding froze.

"Now that I've got your attention, I'll make it short. You've got to stop the killing, Victor. You have plenty of money, so that should be no problem. I'm suggesting a mid-life career change would be good for your health. *Tomorrow*." Spalding was gasping and grunting in agony.

"It'll be a year before you'll be able to tie your shoelaces—if you find a great surgeon. Maybe more. Use that time to start a new business," Dunn urged. "A pizza parlor in Bangkok or a whorehouse in Manila. Stay out of the Western Hemisphere. That's an order. The Western Hemisphere is *mine*."

Then Dunn thought about Heather James and Makumba.

"And *Africa* too," he added. "If I find you there, you're dog meat. Don't think twice about it, Victor. We've just established who's *the* goddamn best, haven't we?"

Spalding was rocking back and forth in pain.

"You'd better see a doctor, Victor, and you'd better move fast. Cops should be here any minute."

Somehow Victor Spalding managed to make it to the elevator. He pressed the button with his elbow. His hands seemed to be on fire. Dunn would pay for this. No matter how long it took to recover, he'd come back and kill Charlie Dunn. If he couldn't, he'd hire someone to butcher Dunn—and the blonde woman too. They'd be hacked to pieces.

In the street below, Heather James found there was no place for her to park. So she simply turned off the motor and climbed out—wincing as her shoulder throbbed. Then she saw Spalding. He was wearing a police uniform and a black wig over his blond curls, but it was him. His face was twisted in anger.

Suddenly the Oriental woman stepped into view. It was the woman from Athens. She was carrying a bouquet of flowers. Spalding saw her too and his smashed hand moved in desperation for the holstered police weapon.

The Oriental woman pointed the paper-wrapped bouquet at Spalding, and it exploded. The sawed-off shotgun inside hurled two shells into him at a range of five yards. Blood spurted from his throat and his whole face turned into pulp. Then he reeled, fell and died.

People were screaming and the sounds of sirens were growing louder. None of this deflected the Oriental woman. She took out the ugly little shotgun, reloaded both barrels and pointed the weapon at the corpse—just in case. That was when Dunn emerged from the building.

"It's *her*, Charlie," Heather James blurted.

"I know," he replied calmly. "It's time you met. Heather James, this is my friend Teresa Kamiya. She was with the Agency too. She's a private investigator now. By the way, she's *not* Chinese. Her grandparents came here from Tokyo about fifty years ago."

"I don't understand," the puzzled veterinarian announced.

"Charlie hired me as his backup, doctor. I was to cover his flanks so nobody'd ambush him from behind. I didn't mean to frighten you . . . I didn't intend to burn Victor either. But he recognized me and went for his piece."

"You acted in self-defense, Terry," Dunn said firmly.

Now Heather James looked up into her lover's eyes.

"Is it over yet, Charlie?" she asked intensely. "Is it really over?"

Dunn nodded. Tears began to course down her cheeks, and she was still weeping softly when the police arrived.

CHAPTER FORTY

At 10:30 on the morning of January 18, a chauffeur-driven Cadillac stopped in front of the Smithsonian Institution's modern National Air and Space Museum at Seventh Street and Independence Avenue Southwest. Three pieces of new baggage were in the trunk.

"Five minutes," Dunn told the uniformed chauffeur.

"Yes, sir."

The driver slid from behind the wheel and opened the street-side door of the big car so Dunn, Heather James and Teresa Kamiya could step out gracefully. When they entered the building, Dunn stopped to look up in respect and patriotic pleasure at the first U.S. space capsule and the amazing little single-engine "Spirit of St. Louis"—the very plane in which Lindbergh had made the first non-stop solo flight across the Atlantic.

"May 1927," Dunn recalled. "Lot of guts, huh?"

"Look who's talking," the woman in the cast replied lovingly. She stopped smiling when she saw Barringer, three other men and a thin brown-haired woman approaching. One of the men gripped a black plastic attaché case.

"Good morning, Howard," Dunn greeted.

"Morning. This is a strange place to do business, Charlie," the Deputy Director for Operations complained.

"It's preposterous," McGhee chimed in curtly.

Then McGhee and Barringer saw Teresa Kamiya. They recognized her and the green-paper-wrapped bouquet she held.

"That wasn't necessary," Barringer protested.

"What?" Dunn tested.

"*Is* there a shotgun in that package?"

"Do you really want to find out, Howard?"

McGhee looked coolly amused.

"Come, come, we're playing on the same side," he said. "Excuse my manners. Dr. James . . . Mr. Dunn . . . Miss Kamiya, this is my assistant, Emily Axt."

Then McGhee coughed twice and glanced down.

He didn't want Dunn to see whatever was in his eyes.

"I had only a minor role," Emily Axt said modestly as she shook Dunn's hand, "and I still don't know why the police didn't get there sooner. However, it all worked out in the end, didn't it?"

"It isn't ended until I get all my money. That's exactly thirty-one thousand nine hundred and five in expenses and the final two hundred thousand of the fee."

He turned to the veterinarian.

"Five thousand dollars of that's for the whales," he announced.

"*Thank* you, Charlie," she accepted with a glowing smile.

Now Dunn faced the Deputy Director of Operations.

"It's money time, Howard."

Barringer gestured, and the two security agents stepped forward with the case. In an instant the bouquet was pointed at the gray-suited man who held it.

"Does she have to do that?" Barringer fretted.

"Don't you like flowers?" Dunn replied and took the heavy case.

"This place is full of tourists, Charlie. Those *flowers* could hurt somebody."

"Gardenias never hurt anyone."

Then McGhee announced that he and his people had to leave.

"Enjoy Barbados," he said as he prepared to depart.

He couldn't resist telling them that he knew.

"We're going on to Africa after that," Dunn said. "I wonder if you'd do me a favor."

"I'll do it," Barringer volunteered suddenly.

"There's a man named Melendez in jail in Athens. I'd—*we'd*—feel better if he stayed inside for two or three months."

"He will," Barringer promised and McGhee, Emily Axt and the security agents left moments later.

"It's *her*—isn't it?" Dunn asked.

"I don't know what you're talking about," Barringer answered.

"McGhee brought her to make her think he trusts her," Dunn told Heather James softly. "Now he screws her three ways from Sunday—feeding her phony information for as long as Moscow buys it. Then—if she's lucky—they'll trade her for someone."

"If she isn't?"

"Is it still auto accidents, Howard?" Dunn asked confidentially, "or are we into strokes this year?"

Barringer elected to ignore the question.

"In case you're interested," he declared stiffly, "we've just heard that the Sovs sent Sid Lamb back to London last week. Willoughby asked us to thank you."

"Anything else hot and dirty?"

"Maybe. There's a report the head of the KGB had a major heart attack and has already been replaced."

"Heart attacks were *always* good. Well, you can worry about what this one means," Dunn announced cheerfully. "I'm out."

"You really did an exceptional job, Charlie. The DCI was very impressed. He asked me to tell you that the President was too."

It took Dunn five seconds to decode the message.

"Nice try, Howard, but no cigar."

"I don't think you understand."

"Not a chance," Dunn replied.

"I'm talking about the national interest, Charlie. It's getting rough out there again. Both the men you trained are gone, and the agency may need your talents any day now."

"He's offering my old job back," Dunn translated.

Heather James took her lover's arm.

"We don't do that kind of work anymore," she said firmly.

Barringer pretended that he hadn't heard her.

"About the money, Charlie, I think we can get it up to forty."

"She's right," Dunn told him. "No more killing—*ever*. In case you're interested, I enjoyed stopping this hit more than I ever did doing them."

Heather James held up her undamaged arm and wiggled her wristwatch—signaling her impatience.

Barringer reacted immediately.

"*Great* idea, Charlie," he approved enthusiastically. "We never had an antiassassination expert. A brand new approach—Congress will love it."

"This is a con job," the buxom blonde warned.

"Don't interrupt. Now that's a very difficult assignment," Barringer said, "and it might well pay more than forty. I'd bet forty-four or forty-five, Charlie. We'd have to fudge some unvouchered funds, but who'd say no?"

"Charlie," Heather James appealed.

"I asked you not to interrupt," Barringer reminded.

"*Interrupt?* Who the hell do you think you're talking to? You work for me. I'm a taxpayer, and a very angry one. I've been lied to, shot at, spied on and bombed. I've got a broken collarbone and a very low opinion of civil servants who put microphones in the bedrooms of decent citizens."

"She has a *fierce* temper," Dunn said solemnly.

"I'm sorry, doctor," Barringer replied and turned his attention to Dunn again.

"You'd be saving lives, Charlie. That's a noble calling. It's almost like preventive medicine," he argued.

"I'll talk it over with my veterinarian."

"Think of it from a financial point of view," Barringer pressed. "That money won't last forever. You might have a family to support. Besides, you'd get bored doing *nothing*."

The blonde-haired woman said something that the CIA executive didn't quite hear. Dunn smiled.

"I see a sort of detached-duty deal," Barringer continued. "Live anywhere you want—and we'll call if and when we need you."

"Suppose *we* call if or when *we* need *you*?" Dunn replied.

Now Heather James spoke again in a tongue that Barringer did not recognize.

"That's Noro, Howard," Dunn explained. "The language of Dr. James's blood brothers. Don't you speak Noro?"

The CIA executive shook his head.

"It's not too hard. Dr.James has been giving me lessons. Good-bye, Howard."

"Wait a minute. What did she say?"

"The first time or the second?"

"Both."

"The first—if you don't mind a rough translation—referred to your mother."

Barringer gritted his teeth.

"And the second time she said 'Let's go.'"

Then Dr. Heather James hooked her right hand around the left arm of Charles Jefferson Dunn—and they went.